For every reader who has supported me and made my dreams come true. I am forever grateful,
Sadie x

FIERCE BETRAYAL

LA RUTHLESS: BOOK 3

SADIE KINCAID

RED HOUSE PRESS LTD

LA RUTHLESS

Fierce Betrayal is a Dark Mafia, dad's best friend, age gap romance that deals with mature themes which may be triggering for some. Trigger warnings include discussion of past serious sexual abuse/ assault.

It is Book 3 in the LA Ruthless Series and can be enjoyed as a standalone. However, if you'd prefer a little background to Jax and Lucia first, you can read the Fierce King/ Queen duet first.

Alejandro and Alana Montoya are hotter than hell in the first two books of the LA Ruthless series. Available on Amazon and FREE in Kindle Unlimited

Click here to read Fierce King now or visit Amazon

PROLOGUE
LUCIA

I lick the salt from my hand and down the shot of tequila before Kyle shoves a lemon wedge into my mouth.

"Ugh!" I groan as the sour juice runs over my tongue. This must be my fourth one and it still tastes as awful as the first.

"It's good, right?" he shouts, flashing his eyebrows at me.

"No," I shout back to be heard over the loud music. "Nothing about that tasted good."

He laughs and takes the glass from my hand. "You'll get used to it, chica." Then he winks at me and drags me back onto the dance-floor to join his two friends.

The heavy bass of the music feels like it's vibrating through my body as I dance. Kyle is just a friend, at least he was until tonight, but something about dancing with him in this club is making me see him differently. He keeps staring at me with those dark brown eyes. Occasionally his hands stray to my hips and dangerously close to my ass. I'm kind of surprised that I don't completely dislike it. I've never seen him that way before. But maybe it's the music? Or maybe it's the tequila?

"More shots?" Bailey, Kyle's roommate, mouths, miming the action of throwing back a drink.

"Sure," Kyle replies before his two friends disappear through the crowd and back to the bar, leaving the pair of us alone.

I take my cell out of my purse and message my friend, Jordan. She was supposed to come with us tonight, but she has three kids and her ex-husband had to work unexpectedly.

I understand her struggle.

I'm a single mom too. That's kind of how we bonded, although Jordan is ten years older than me. I don't go out often, but my parents are watching my son tonight.

I type out a text message to her.

Lucia: *I wish you were here. This place is awesome.*

I go to put my cell back in my purse but it vibrates in my hand.

Big Bad JD: *Where the hell are you, Lucia?*

I stare at the name on the screen. Shit! How the hell did I manage to text Jackson Decker instead of Jordan? And how do I get my stupid ass out of this?

"Everything okay?" Kyle shouts in my ear.

I look up at him and smile. Aw, he is cute. How did I never notice that before tonight?

"Yeah," I say looking back down at my phone. What the hell am I so worried about? This is what college kids do, right? I'm a grown-ass woman. Yeah, I may be twenty and technically not supposed to drink in clubs, but Jackson is not my father—he only works for him.

Still, I lie my ass off anyway.

Lucia: *I'm at home. Safely tucked up in bed.*

Big Bad JD: *No you're not.*

I type back furiously. Is he spying on me?

Lucia: *How do you know that?*

Big Bad JD: *You just told me.*

Oh, damn! Yeah I did.

Big Bad JD: *Where are you?*

Lucia: *Out!*

I go to put my cell away again when it starts vibrating like crazy in my hand. I glance back at the screen to see his name and face lighting it up, signaling he is calling now.

"Who is Big Bad JD?" Kyle laughs as he looks at the screen with me.

"A pain in my ass," I shout back, with a dramatic eye roll thrown in for good measure. "I gotta take this. Be back in two secs."

"I'll be right here, chica," Kyle smiles.

I step into a quieter part of the club and answer the call. "Hey, Jax."

"Where are you, Lucia?"

"In some club," I reply. I look up to see Kyle making his way over to me with another shot of tequila in his hand.

"Have you been drinking?"

"Only one or two," I lie again as Kyle hands me a drink. He pulls me close to him, his hand skating over my waist and making me giggle.

"Lucia."

"Or maybe more," I admit. "I kind of lost count. The guys have been buying me shots."

"Shots? What guys?" he snarls. "What's the name of the club?"

"I'm not sure," I admit as I look around.

"Lucia!"

"Hang on," I sigh, covering the mouthpiece. "What's this place called?" I ask Kyle, who is now standing behind me, pressing his body into mine as he tries to get me to dance with him.

"Deemon," he replies in my ear.

I take my hand from the phone. "Kyle says it's called Deemon."

"Jesus fucking Christ, Lucia. What the hell are you doing in that dive bar?" Jax snaps. "Stay right where you are."

I groan loudly down the phone, but he hasn't finished speaking.

"And tell Kyle if he lays a fucking finger on you, I will tear off his arm and shove it up his ass."

The line goes dead and I put my cell into my purse before turning back to Kyle. Should I tell him my father's right hand man is on his way here right now to drag me out of this club?

"Okay?" Kyle grins at me.

My head swims slightly and I blink in the dim light.

"You okay, chica?" he asks again, handing me another lemon wedge to go with my tequila shot.

"What? Yes." I smile before I down it in one. "Let's go dance."

"I love this song," I shout as the first bars of *Señorita* by Shawn Mendes and Camila Cabello play loudly over the last song.

"Hey! Me too." Kyle grins at me as he puts his arms around my waist. I stare into his eyes as our hips sway to the music. "You are so fucking hot when you dance, chica," he whispers in my ear.

"You think?" I giggle.

He doesn't have the chance to respond because he is gone — dragged backwards by the collar of his polo shirt until I am left staring up at the giant wall of muscle and fury that is Jackson Decker.

"What the hell?" I slur but he turns his attention to Kyle.

"You think it's okay to get underage girls drunk?" he snarls as he brings his face close to Kyle's.

"She's twenty," Kyle stammers in his defense.

"Last time I checked that was still underage, asshole." Jackson snarls as he grabs Kyle by the throat.

"Jax," I shout, taking a hold of his forearm and making him turn his anger-filled gaze back to me. "Please don't do this. These are my friends."

"Friends do not get you drunk so they can feel you up, Lucia," he snarls.

A few seconds later, three bouncers are surrounding us too. I swallow hard as I wonder what the hell is going to happen next. Jax could take the lot of them out if he chose to. And then what? More bouncers?

I feel sick as I picture a mass brawl in this club and me never being able to show my face on campus again, but one of the bouncers speaks to Jax.

"Everything okay here, Mr. Decker?" he asks.

"No. She is drunk and she is underage," he snarls. "Do you even check ID in this place?"

They don't. Not very well anyway. It's why this club is so popular with college kids. "We're sorry. It won't happen again."

To my relief, Jax releases Kyle from his grip, but not without a warning first. "You ever touch her again and I will cut off your hands. You got me?"

Kyle nods furiously while I sway on the spot.

"I feel sick," I shout.

Jax turns to me and then he scoops me up into his arms and strides out of the club. If I didn't feel so woozy, I think I would die of embarrassment. I suppose there is plenty of time for that tomorrow.

As soon as we are out in the fresh air, my head starts to spin. "Jax," I groan as I cling onto his neck.

"I got you, Luce. I'll take you home," he says softly, all the anger gone from his voice now.

"I'm sorry," I whisper as he places me in the front seat of his truck and fastens my seatbelt.

When he climbs in and starts the engine, I lean back and close my eyes. "Thank you for not killing Kyle," I mumble sarcastically.

He grunts in response.

"He was just my friend, Jax. And even if he was more..." I trail off. It's hard enough being Alejandro Montoya's daughter without having Jax threatening every guy who takes an interest in me. Not that many do. I think the fact that my father is the head of the Spanish Mafia kind of puts most of them off.

"Guys who like you shouldn't have to get you drunk to make you like them back, Lucia."

"He didn't do that," I protest.

"No? You said he's your friend, right?"

"Yeah."

"You ever let him put his hands on your ass when you're not drunk?" he snarls and I have no response for that, because I have never let him do anything like that before tonight. Kyle's not my type really. He's too clean-cut and he doesn't have any tattoos, or stubble on his jaw.

I open my eyes and look across at Jax. His knuckles are white as he grips the steering wheel. His forearms are huge, with dark tattoos winding around them, merging together and snaking all the way up to his shoulders. My gaze travels up to his neck where some of his ink peeks out of the collar of his t-shirt and curls around the thick column of his throat. They can't be seen when he wears a dress shirt and I know he likes it that way, because sometimes he wants to look clean-cut too.

But he's not. He's dangerous. He is fire and fury, and burning. The most lethal man I know. And I have been in love with him for three long years.

"I'm sorry, Jax," I mumble sleepily as my eyes roll in my head and I have to close them again. "Thank you for rescuing me."

"Any time."

"I love you," I mumble.

Crap! Did I just say that out loud? Well, maybe he didn't hear me anyway.

"Get some sleep, Angel," he growls.

Did he just call me Angel? Or did I imagine it?

CHAPTER 1
TWELVE MONTHS LATER

LUCIA

I step out of the elevator and into the hallway. There is only one room on this floor of the hotel—the presidential suite. The two armed guards who always stand sentry at the door smile at me as I approach.

"Buenos días, Ms. Montoya," they say in unison.

"Buenos días, guys. Is he in?"

They nod.

"Is he alone?"

"Yes," they reply.

I heave a sigh of relief. I'm not sure how he's going to take the news of my decision, but one thing I do know is that he will deal with it a whole lot better than my mom.

I open the door and step into the expansive and luxurious hotel suite. His office is in the corner and the door is open. I cross the room, my sneakers not making a sound on the plush carpet, until I'm standing in the doorway. As I expected he's sitting at his desk, his brow furrowed as he stares at his computer. Dressed in one of his impeccably tailored suits, his biceps bulge out of the fabric as he rests his hands under his chin and frowns at something on the screen.

Alejandro Montoya.

The King of LA.

My father.

He is an imposing sight and I wonder how many people have stood in this doorway full of fear and terror as they wait for the attention of the man who fills the entire room with his presence. I shift from one foot to the other and the movement must catch his eye because he looks up, his frown transforming into a smile.

"Buenos días, *mija*," he says, pushing back his chair and standing up.

"Buenos días, Papi." I smile back as he walks toward me and pulls me into a hug.

"This is a nice surprise, but I thought you were checking out that new place today?"

"I just came from there now. I don't think it's for me," I say with a shrug.

He scowls at me. "What? It's perfect for you."

"No, Papi. It's perfect for you. It's too big for me and Matthias. I'd feel lonely in a place so big."

"But..." he starts but then he presses his lips together and draws in a deep breath through his nose. The two of us have been arguing over where I am going to live for months now.

I love my apartment by the beach. It's the perfect size and location for me and my four-year-old son, Matthias, but if my father had his way I would be living in a huge gated mansion, much like the one he arranged for me to see today. I have agreed to look at some places to keep him happy, but deep down he knows this is a fight he won't win. I love that he accepts my independence, because I know how hard it is for him to let me go.

"Fine," he eventually says with a shake of his head.

"Thank you, Papi," I reply as I give him a soft kiss on his cheek.

"So, why I am being blessed with a visit from you this morning? You're still coming for dinner tonight, aren't you? Your mama is making her famous bacon cheeseburgers and if you deprive her of yours and her grandson's company, neither of us will hear the end of it."

I can't help but laugh at the look on his face when he talks about my mom. He might be the King of LA and have the toughest and most ruthless of men quaking in terror at the mere mention of his name, but it is my mom who makes us both tremble with fear. She can bring my father to his knees with a simple look. She is the kindest, but fiercest woman I have ever known.

Alana Montoya isn't my biological mother, of course. That would be a physical impossibility given that she's not quite thirty yet. Alejandro Montoya isn't my biological father either. They adopted me when I was seventeen and every day since then they have loved me as much as if I was their own flesh and blood. I couldn't ask for better, or more loving, parents.

"I wanted to talk to you about something," I say.

He frowns again. "Then make yourself comfortable." He indicates the chair opposite his desk before returning to his seat.

I wait until he's settled before I speak because I'm pretty sure he'll want to be sitting down for this. He stares at me, his dark brown eyes full of concern and trepidation.

"I've finished college and you and mom agreed that I could do what I wanted to as long as I got my degree."

"I remember."

"Well, I've given this a lot of thought and I want to join the family business."

"Well, your mama will be pleased to have you on board," he says with a flash of his eyebrows, because he knows that is not what I mean.

My mom took over the running of the women's and children's shelter she worked at two years earlier and since then she has gone on to set up her own charitable organization to support abuse victims across the whole of the Unites States. She does this all while raising my two younger brothers and being an amazing mom to me and grandma to Matthias.

She is a superwoman and I admire her and her work greatly, but that's not the kind of business that excites me.

"You know that's not the family business I'm talking about, Papi."

He sucks in a breath and leans back in his chair, his fingers steepled under his chin. "Lucia," he warns with a shake of his head.

"What, Papi? I'm not cut out for charity work, you know that. You also know this is the life I was born for. It's in my blood and I can't change that. I wish that I could."

"This world is dangerous."

"I know that," I remind him. I watched the man I believed was my biological father and my two older brothers slaughtered when I was fourteen years old. "Is it really any less dangerous working in one of Mom's shelters?"

He stares at me for a few moments. I love our relationship. Despite only being in my life for the past four years, he is my father in every sense of the word. He understands me in a way that my mom doesn't, and even though I know it's hard for him, he treats me like an adult and lets me make my own decisions. He jokes that it is the only way to prevent his hair turning gray, but I also know that it is because he recognizes that the same animal he has inside him — one that will never be tamed — lives in me too.

He arches one eyebrow at me. "She will be heartbroken."

"I know, but this is my decision and you both said that you would respect my choices. I'm twenty-one now. I'm not a child anymore. I don't need your protection any longer."

"Lucia! You are my daughter, and you will always have my

protection, whether you want it or not," he replies sharply, causing me to sit back in my seat.

"I know." I swallow, conscious of not pushing him too far. He may treat like me an adult but he is still an overprotective father. "But you know there is a role for me here. I can be an asset to you and to the Montoya Corporation."

"I know that," he sighs, running a hand through his hair. "It would be much easier if that weren't true."

"So, you will speak to Mom?"

"Oh, no," he chuckles and shakes his head. "You're such a grown up, you can speak to your mama tonight at dinner."

I groan loudly, like a petulant teenager.

"But," he adds, "I will be there and I will help you smooth things over."

"Thank you, Papi." I smile at him.

"Did you purposely choose to tell her this news the night before we go to London?" he asks, narrowing his eyes at me. He knows me far too well.

I shrug. "Well, I figure a week-long vacation in London with you will be the perfect way for her to come to terms with my decision."

He laughs as he shakes his head. "You truly are my daughter, chica."

Pride swells in my chest at that statement. Both my biological father and the man who had raised me as his own until I was fourteen were cold-hearted and cruel men. Some might say that is true of the man sitting before me, but he has shown me nothing but love, compassion and patience and I am proud to be his daughter.

I am about to reply with a snappy comeback when he looks behind me and smiles.

"Hey, amigo," he says. My heart beats faster in my chest and my stomach flutters in excitement. I know who just walked into the room before I even turn around.

I turn in my seat anyway to seat to see Jackson Decker, or Jax as he is more commonly known, stroll into the room. He is my father's best friend, his most trusted soldier and his brother in all but blood. He is the smartest man I know. He could have done anything he wanted to with his life, but he has worked for my father since he was sixteen years old, and the two of them would be lost without each other.

Jax also fills a suit like no one I have ever met before. He is six feet four inches of muscle and tattoos, and I know this because I study him every single chance I get. I first developed a crush on him when I was sixteen and he bought me pizza. But now, well it's a full blown obsession. He is way off limits for many reasons, but that doesn't stop me fantasizing about what it would be like to have those huge hands of his running over my skin. I clench my thighs together as dirty thoughts of him make warmth spread through my core.

"Hey." He nods a greeting to my father before he turns to me. "Good morning, Lucia," he says in his soft Southern drawl that makes my insides turn to melted chocolate.

"Hey, Jax." I snap out of my daydream and plaster a polite smile on my face as I watch him walk past, trying not to stare at his fine ass in front of my father.

He stops a few feet away from me, leaning against the nearby cupboard, stuffing his hands into his pockets until the material of his trousers is stretched taut across his thick thighs. I have to stop myself from licking my lips and drag my eyes away from his whole groin area, remembering that my very protective and violent father is also in the room.

"Everything okay?" Jax asks with a frown as the room falls silent.

"Lucia has decided she's like to join the business," my father replies with a flash of his eyebrows.

"Oh, wow." Jax grins at us both. "Does Alana know yet?"

My father chuckles softly.

"Not yet. I'm telling her later at dinner," I reply.

"Hey, it's your funeral, kid," he says and I feel a pang of disappointment. What had I hoped for? That he would give me a hug and tell me he can't wait to spend more time with me? But then he winks at me and I almost melt into a puddle.

"You're still coming to dinner, right?" my father asks him.

"Well I sure wouldn't miss it now." He flashes me one of his incredible smiles before he takes a bottle of water from the side and opens it up.

The room is quiet again and there is a nervous energy crackling through it that I can't quite figure out. Or perhaps I am imagining it and it's all coming from me because I feel all kinds of things I shouldn't whenever I am around Jax.

I need to break the tension before I say something completely inappropriate. "I'd better go. I have to go and pick up some things from my place," I say as I push myself up from my chair.

"You and Matthias are going to stay over tonight, right?" my father asks.

"Sure. Then the boys and I can wave you off before we trash the place." I grin at him.

"Don't even joke about things like that in front of your mama later, Lucia," he warns me. "Do you have any idea how hard I had to work to persuade her to leave the twins for a week to go to London?"

"Hmm. I can imagine." I laugh. My twin brothers are almost two years old and my parents had thought they may never have biological children of their own. We were all overjoyed when they eventually conceived after fertility treatment. Due to some complications when the twins were born, they—and me of course—are to be their only children. My mom hates to leave them even for one night, but my father's cousin is getting married in England and she has begged them both to attend the wedding, so he has finally convinced my mom that I can be trusted to look after my little brothers for a week.

I love my apartment near the beach, but I can't deny I'm looking forward to spending a week in my parents' beautiful house in the Hills. The place is so huge, it should come with its own zip code. Of course I could live there permanently if I chose to, but I love my freedom and my independence too much. It's stifling enough being the daughter of the King of LA without living with him too.

"I just dropped my car at the shop. It needs new tires. Do you think someone could give me a ride?" I ask hopefully.

"Of course," my father replies.

"How about you, Jax?" I ask with a smile and a subtle flutter of my eyelashes.

Jax clears his throat and looks at my father. "As long as you don't need me for anything, amigo?"

My father shakes his head. "No. In fact I was going to ask you if you could have a word with Anton and his team. They're at the club. You could drop Lucia on the way?"

"Perfect," I say, jumping up from my seat a little too quickly and revealing my eagerness to be alone with Jax. But what the hell. This is just a little bit of fun, right? There could never be anything between him and me, but that doesn't mean I don't enjoy flirting with him outrageously every chance I get.

"Can I have quick word before you go?" my father asks. His question is directed at Jax and the tone of his voice also lets me know I'm excused.

"You know I'm going to have to be party to these conversations soon, right?" I flash my eyebrows at him.

"Yes, but you don't work here until you have spoken to your mama and she agrees to it."

"Fine," I say with a dramatic sigh. "I'll see you later."

"Hey," he snaps as he stands from his chair and holds his arms wide.

I walk over and give him a hug. "Bye, Papi." Then I turn to Jax. "I'll wait for you in the hall."

CHAPTER 2

LUCIA

I lean back in the soft leather seat of Jax's truck and hum along to the radio while he concentrates on the road. I glance at his thick thighs and his huge hands and try to stop myself thinking about how good he looks beneath that suit. I've seen him almost naked plenty of times at my parents' house when he's been in the pool and the sight of him in those wet swim shorts gives me a lady-boner every single time.

"So, you're coming to dinner tonight then?" I ask.

"Of course," he says with a smile. "Why wouldn't I be?"

"Because it's Friday night. I assumed you'd have a hot date?" I say with a shrug.

He arches an eyebrow at me. "I do, but not until after dinner."

I hide the sting of jealousy behind a smile and a head tilt. "Oh, that kind of date?"

"What other kind of date is there?" He chuckles softly.

"You're such a player, Decker. Do these poor unsuspecting women know they won't even get breakfast in the morning?"

"Hey! I'm a good Southern gentleman. I always provide breakfast."

"Yeah? To go." I shake my head at him, feigning my indignation, but the truth is I'd much prefer he had casual hookups than a stable girlfriend. I would hate to have to play nice with whoever he dated seriously—and I would have to do that. He's so much a part of our family and our life that I wouldn't be able to avoid her. Of course, the thought that he might fall in love with someone and ditch us completely, or move halfway across the country, is even more depressing. He's from Dallas originally, and he still visits there a couple of times a year.

"What about you? Anyone serious around?" he asks.

I lean back in my seat and close my eyes. "I'm sure you'd know if there was, Jax."

"Well, you're pretty good at covering your tracks when you want to, Lucia. Can you say Brad?"

"Ugh," I groan. "How do you know about him?"

"It doesn't matter how I know. Why didn't you tell me about him?"

"Because, Jax, I don't want to tell you about every single guy I meet and have you vet them before I can go on a date. That's why," I snap.

"Luce, you know that's not what this is."

"Isn't it?" I fold my arms across my chest.

"Your father worries about you. I worry about you too."

That makes my heart swell a little in my chest, but I know he only means it in an uncle kind of way. Him and my dad are so bloody overprotective. I get that our family has enemies, but that shouldn't mean I don't get to have a life. "Well, I can take care of myself," I snap.

"So, Brad?" he presses.

"He was a complete jackass," I say with a sigh.

He turns to me, a scowl darkening his handsome features. "Why? What did he do?" he snarls.

"Nothing worth beheading him for," I say with a roll of my eyes. "He was just a player too. That's all."

"Did you and him—?"

"Jax!"

"Sorry," he mumbles. "You need me to pay him a visit?"

"No! Definitely not." That would be the worst thing ever—having my father's hired muscle hang Brad up by his balls because he blew me off to go on a date with a Lakers' girl instead is the last thing I want. I didn't even like him all that much anyway, but he asked me out every single day for a month and I finally agreed. I suppose it was all about the chase for him.

I didn't date much at all through college—I didn't have the time between caring for Matthias and my studies—but I spent two freaking hours getting ready to go out with that jackass only to have him dump me five minutes before he was due to pick me up. He claimed he had diarrhea. It was only the next day his social feeds were filled with pictures of him and the aforementioned Lakers' girl. Asshole!

"So there's nobody?" he asks again.

"No, Jax," I snap at him. It's unnecessary, but I can't help it. "We're not all lucky enough to be able to hook up with complete strangers every night of the week."

"Lucia."

"What?"

"Hooking up with randoms. That's not for you."

"You're a hypocrite. You know that?" I snarl.

"And you're fucking exhausting," he rolls his eyes. "We've been in the car less than ten minutes and you're already giving me attitude."

"I'm not." I pout, aware that I'm completely proving his point.

"I hope you're not going to be this much of a spoiled brat once you start working for Montoya Inc."

I turn and glare at him, my mouth open as I'm about to give him a snarky comeback, but he's grinning. He knows I hate it when he calls me a spoiled brat. I'm not one and he knows that too.

"You're an asshole." I say instead with a grin.

"An asshole and a hypocrite?" he chuckles softly.

"Yup!"

"Good to know."

We're both quiet for a few moments before he speaks again. "I didn't mean that you couldn't hook up with randoms," he says softly. "Just that I know it's not your style, is all."

"Yeah, well, hooking up with anyone looks attractive right now," I sigh deeply. He's right that I'm not usually into casual hookups, but I haven't even dated anyone for months. I see other people my age out in clubs and meeting people, and I wonder if I'm missing out on something.

"You'll meet the right guy one day," he offers.

I swallow hard and resist the urge to tell him that I already have met him, but he is completely off limits and will only ever see me at his best friend's daughter. "Yeah," I say instead.

We stop at a traffic signal and he reaches over and cups my chin, making electricity crackle up my spine. "Hey."

I turn and face him again.

"You will, Lucia, because you're…" his dark eyes search mine. I try to look away because I feel like he can read my mind, but he holds me with the intensity of his gaze.

"I'm what?" I whisper.

"You're… you."

"I'm me? Wow! That's some deep shit, Jax." I arch an eyebrow at him.

The traffic moves again and he turns back to the road. "Stop cussing. And I hope you're not going to be this annoying when we're working together."

"You and me will be working together?" I blink at him because the idea of that is both terrifying and exciting.

"Yeah. Your dad asked me to show you the ropes for a few weeks."

"You mean babysit me?" I say with a roll of my eyes.

"No. I don't do babysitting. You should think yourself lucky. I don't usually take rookies under my wing."

"So why am I getting special treatment then?"

"Like it or not, you're the boss's daughter. You want to work with us, you got to learn the business, and who better to learn from than the best?" He winks at me and warmth floods my center.

"You're so modest." I flutter my eyelashes at him.

"You're a real smartass today, aren't you?" he grins. "But boss's daughter or not, any of that attitude when we're working together and I will think nothing of whooping your ass."

"Hmm, we'll see." I smile as I settle back in my seat again and close my eyes.

Images of Jax putting me over his knee and spanking me are now swimming around my head and they are not even the slightest bit unpleasant.

CHAPTER 3

LUCIA

I park my car on the driveway of my parents' huge mansion and climb out before helping Matthias out of his seat. He looks up at me, his huge brown eyes shining and I ruffle his thick dark hair. This kid is my whole world. Thankfully he looks nothing like his father, Blake.

Blake Fielding was a friend of my older brother, Luca. I hated Luca, and most of his friends were assholes just like him, but Blake had always been kind of sweet. So, at the age of fourteen, when I had to flee my home after watching the man I thought was my father, and my two older brothers murdered, I turned to him for help.

I soon learned he was an even bigger asshole than my brothers. He was six years older than me but that didn't stop him from taking advantage of me in every way. He took every single cent I had.

Of course, he pretended to be all concerned and caring at first and he was even smart enough to wait until I was sixteen before he had sex with me. I even believed that I loved him, that was until the day I found out I was pregnant and came home from my shift at the diner early to find him screwing one of the other waitresses, all while he was telling her how stupid and naïve I was and how my name was the only thing that had any value to him.

Back in Chicago, I was a Ramos, and that name once had some meaning there, before Miguel Ramos upset some very bad people, anyway. At the time, I had no clue why Blake had thought the Ramos name could be any use to him, but now I wonder if he had discovered that Miguel wasn't my biological father and I was actually a Montoya.

I jumped on the first bus I saw, which happened to be headed to LA, and fate, or something else, brought me to the shelter where my mom worked. The rest is history.

"Are we having Nana's burgers, Momma?" Matthias snaps me from my thoughts of his father.

"I sure hope so," I say with a grin as I take hold of his hand. My mom makes the best bacon cheeseburgers ever.

The door is opened before we reach it by my parents' house-keeper, Magda, who ushers us inside. She presses a piece of candy into Matthias' hand and he squirrels it away in his pocket as though I won't see. It's a ritual the two of them have and it makes me smile every time. Magda is a woman of few words and she can come across as stern, but she actually has a heart of gold and is one of the kindest women I've ever known. She says that having Matthias and my twin brothers around makes her feel young again and she spoils all three of them.

"The boys are with your papa in the garden," she says to him as she cups his chin in her hand. "They have been waiting for you all day."

"Can I go play, Momma?" he asks me.

"Of course, munchkin. I'll be right out," I say and watch as he scampers off down the hallway.

"My father is home?" I ask.

Magda nods. "Jackson is here too."

I wonder why she says that with a smile on her face and then I remember that Magda sees and knows all.

"And Mom?"

"In the kitchen fussing over dinner," she says with a roll of her eyes. "As if I cannot be trusted to make some burgers."

I laugh because Magda and my mom have a wonderful relationship. My mom doesn't speak to her own parents for many reasons, and Magda has taken on something of a maternal figure in her life. She has worked for the Montoya family since my father was a child and she is much a part of the family as Jax is.

"I'll go find her. Are you joining us for dinner?"

"Not tonight." She shakes her head. "I'm going to watch a movie with Jacob."

"Oh?" I waggle my eyebrows at her. Jacob works here too. He operates the gate and sometimes drives my father.

"It's nothing like that," she admonishes me, but I see the twinkle in her eye. "We simply need a break before you move back home for a week."

I open my mouth in feigned indignation and she walks away, chuckling to herself.

I walk down the hallway to the kitchen to find my mom. She is drying her hands on a towel when I walk into the room, having just finished prepping dinner.

"Hey, sweetheart," she says with a huge smile as she crosses the floor and wraps me in a warm hug.

I lean into her and feel the weight of guilt overwhelming me because I am about to break her heart. I wrap my arms around her and hold onto her a little longer than usual. She always smells so beautiful and she gives the best hugs ever. She is without a doubt the best person I know and I should be honored to work by her side in her organization. I know that's what she wants and what she's hoping for, particularly as I once needed one of those women's shelters myself, but that life just doesn't feel right to me. I am a Montoya through and through.

"Is everything okay, sweetheart?" she asks as I hold her tight.

"Sure. I'm going to miss you is all," I say.

She pulls back from me and brushes my hair back from my face. "I'm going to miss you too. Are you sure you'll be okay with the boys?"

"Yes, Mom," I resist the urge to roll my eyes. "We're all going to be fine. Besides Magda and Jacob are here too."

"I know. I've just never been away from you all for so long before."

"You have a whole week with Papi in London ahead of you," I remind her.

She blushes and I can't help but smile. My parents still act like love-struck teenagers around each other and it is both embarrassing and wonderful. "Not to mention a fabulous wedding to attend."

"Yes, there is that," she replies with a smile. "And I'm looking forward to meeting your father's cousin, Lauren."

"There's my two favorite girls," my father's voice booms across the kitchen as he walks into the room with Jax close behind him.

"Where are the boys?" I ask.

"Hugo is teaching them the fine art of wrestling," he replies.

"Alex!" my mom admonishes him. Hugo is another pseudo family member. He is my mom's and the twins' bodyguard and my little brothers adore him. He also teaches my mom and me some Krav Maga and self-defense once a week, and he practically lives in my parents' pool house.

"What?" My father shrugs as he slips an arm around her waist. "You are never too young to learn how to pin an opponent."

She shakes her head in exasperation but then she stares up

at him adoringly until he kisses her. I look across at Jax who rolls his eyes at me.

"Lucia," my father says when they finally remember that there are other people in the room. "Did you have something you wanted to discuss?"

I swallow hard. I was at least going to wait until after dinner until everyone was too full of food and maybe a few glasses of wine to argue, but I suppose the sooner I do this, the sooner my mom can come to terms with it.

"Yes, I do." I sit on one of the stools at the kitchen island.

"What is it, sweetheart?" my mom asks.

My father winks at me and it is all the encouragement I need. "I want to work with Papi."

"What?" she looks between him and me, blinking in shock.

"I appreciate you offering me a position in the charity and I love you for it, Mom, but I want to work for Montoya Inc."

She licks her lips and we all wait with bated breath for her to speak. "You mean like managing the hotel or something?"

I look at my father and then at Jax, but neither of them are meeting my eyes.

"No. Like with Papi and Jax," I reply.

"No," she shakes her head before I've even finished speaking. "You can't."

"It's what I want, Mom."

"But, Lucia, you just finished college. You have your degree. You're so smart. You don't have to work with me in the charity, you can do anything you want to."

"I know that. That's why I want to work with Papi."

"Alejandro." She glares at him and he knows he's in trouble because she only gives him his full name when he is. "Did you know about this?"

"Yes, but Lucia only told me earlier today," he replies.

"Surely you told her that it is out of the question?" she snaps.

He sighs deeply as he wraps her in his arms. She tries to pull away but he holds her in place. "She is a grown woman, Alana. As her parents we have to let her make her own decisions. Just because we don't agree with them, it doesn't make them wrong."

"Even if those decisions might get her killed."

"Alana!" he warns and I realize this discussion no longer involves me. Only he has the power to refuse me and she expects him to use it.

"How the hell can you even consider this? It's madness."

"Do you think that Lucia shouldn't take over the Montoya family business one day? Is she any less deserving than our sons?"

Wow! He went straight for jugular, using the fact that I'm adopted and that she's a huge feminist in one fell swoop.

"No." She pulls back from him but she glares up at him, all five feet four inches of her full of anger. "How dare you suggest that's what this is about?"

"Then what is it? Because you know I want to hand over my legacy to my children. This is what I do, Alana. If Lucia wants to be a part of it, then I won't stop her. The fact that she doesn't want to be a spoiled rich kid who lives off her parents makes me proud of her."

"A spoiled rich kid like me? Is that it?"

"I never said that," he growls and the tension in the room becomes so thick I could cut it with a knife. My mom was never a spoiled rich kid, but my father believed that she was when he married her. It's why he calls her princess. It started as an insult but became a term of affection.

I look at Jax hoping that he has some magical way to deal with what's going on here but he shakes his head at me, as if to tell me to stay out of it. He knows my parents better than anyone. But I feel awful. I have started a huge fight between them the night before they leave for their first vacation in two years.

"Daddy." I hear one of the twins shouting from outside the room.

He turns to the door momentarily and then he looks at me. "Lucia, can you see to your brother, please?" he snarls before he turns back to my mom who continues to glare at him.

"Sure." I swallow, relieved to have an excuse to get out of the room. My parents rarely argue, but when they do it's epic. Why the hell did I do this tonight?

"I'll come help you," Jax mumbles and the two of us walk out of the room and into the hallway.

"Luch-ee," my little brother Dario says with a huge smile when he sees me.

"Hey, kiddo," I scoop him into my arms. "What's up?"

"Tomás said I can't whistle," he pouts and I can't help but smile at him.

"And can you whistle?" I ask him.

He shakes his head. "No."

Jax laughs too and he ruffles Dario's hair. "Go tell Tomás that I'll teach you both to whistle as soon as you're old enough."

"Okay," he grins and then clambers down out of my arms before running off down the hallway back to his brother.

"I hope you know what you're letting yourself in for," Jax smiles at me.

"A whole week with the three of them." I shake my head. "I feel exhausted just thinking about it."

"I feel exhausted for you."

"You are the twins' godfather though, and you are Matthias' second favorite person after his Papa, so I think that means you're contractually obliged to help me out this week," I remind him.

He arches an eyebrow at me. "Is that so?"

"It most definitely is." I feel the heat flush unexpectedly over my cheeks. Being in his company never used to be this awkward. "You think they're okay?" I look back toward the kitchen where we left my parents arguing.

"Well, I haven't heard a gunshot or anything breaking yet so that's a good sign, right?" he laughs.

"Don't, Jax," I shake my head. "I feel so bad for causing this."

He wraps an arm around my shoulder and gives me a quick squeeze before dropping it back to his side. "There's no need to, Lucia. Your mom is just worried about you."

"I know. What if I spoil their vacation though?"

Jax laughs out loud as we head out to the garden to the kids. "Are you kidding me?" he checks his watch. "Those two will be make-up fucking already."

"Jax," I nudge him in the ribs. "They're my parents."

"Yeah, I know. You've lived in the same house as them so you know I speak the truth."

"Ugh," I groan. "I do and it's gross."

"People in their thirties still fuck, you know?" He grins at me and my pulse starts to thrum against my skin. "A lot!"

Then he walks into the garden and scoops the nearest shrieking toddler into his arms and I stare after him wishing he would give me a practical demonstration.

B y the time dinner is served almost an hour later, we are all ravenous with hunger and my parents are no longer glaring at each other, making me wonder if Jax was right earlier. I shudder at the thought. It has nothing to do with their age though, simply the fact that they are my parents.

As my mom places the bowl of salad onto the dining table, she takes hold of my arm and pulls me to one side. "I will be just as angry when the boys decide to work for your father too. But they're still so young. I thought I had more time with you, that's all," she says as her eyes fill with tears.

"Mom," I say as she makes me want to cry now too. "You will always be my best friend," I whisper. Because that is how we started out and how we will always be. I was almost seventeen when I first met her. Pregnant and scared and alone, and she was the person who rescued me, convincing my father to take me in when I had nowhere else to go. I owe her everything.

"And you will always be my favorite daughter," she says with a smile. "I love you, sweetheart."

"Love you too, Mom."

CHAPTER 4

JAX

Alejandro left for his vacation two days ago and it's kind of strange being in his house when he's on the other side of the world. He's been on vacation before but he's always been a short plane trip away. Not that the house is any quieter without him around—his sons have more energy than any kids I have ever known. I honestly don't know how Lucia is coping with the three of them on her own this week. She could have help from the house staff if she wanted it, but I know that she is far too independent to ask. She seems to have a burning desire to prove to everyone that she is capable of handling things on her own.

I promised Alejandro and Alana that I would look in on her and the kids while they were away and so here I am, with Jell-O on my t-shirt and peanut butter on my jeans, surrounded by plastic dinosaurs and action figures.

"I'm just going to put the twins down and then I'll come back for Matthias. Okay?" Lucia pops her head inside the den, with one of her twin brothers in her arms and the other clinging to her leg.

"Yeah," I smile at the sight. "You need a hand there?"

"No." She blows a strand of hair from her eyes. "I got it." She nods to her son. "Can you just watch the munchkin for me?"

"Sure. The T-Rex is about to save Iron Man from certain death over here," I say with a wink.

"Thank you," she mouths and then disappears out of the door.

Matthias looks up at me and smiles, a plastic Iron Man figure in one hand and a Venom one in the other. "You save him, Jax," he giggles.

I pick up my T-Rex and swoop him through the air, catching Iron Man in the dinosaur's mouth and plonking them both on the sofa, which Matthias has deemed is the safety of Avengers HQ.

"Safe!" Matthias declares triumphantly, tossing Venom into our makeshift Lego volcano and throwing himself onto me.

"Hey," I laugh as I catch him. "You have way too much energy for this time of night."

He settles on my lap, his head against my chest. "Momma said I could stay up late to play with you," he says. "The twins try to ruin my Avengers game." He sighs like this is the most terrible problem in the entire world. I suppose when you're four, it is.

"I know, little buddy. But they're a bit younger than you, aren't they?" I ruffle his hair. "You're a big boy and you have to teach them to play nicely."

Matthias and the twins love to play together, but the two year age gap is stark when it comes to any imagination play and Tomás and Dario haven't quite grasped the concept yet.

"Are you their daddy, Jax?" he looks up at me, his eyes shining.

"No, buddy. Your papa is their daddy, isn't he?"

"But momma said you're their Gob-father."

Damn, this kid is too cute. He is so bright too. He retains

every bit of information he's given and tosses it back at you at a later date when you're least expecting it.

"Their Godfather," I correct him. "It means I get to look out for them too, especially when your papa and nana aren't around."

"Oh?" he frowns, deep in thought. "Are you my Godfather too?"

"No, buddy."

"Why not? You look after me sometimes." He frowns and I wince. How the fuck do I explain this?

"Well, yeah, but your Uncle Philippe is your Godfather."

"Why can't you be?"

"Because your mom asked your uncle to be."

"Why didn't she ask you?" he looks at me, all wide-eyed and innocent. How do I tell him that I hoped she'd ask me and was a little hurt when she didn't?

"She chose your Uncle Philippe because he loves you very much."

"I want you to be my Godfather, too," he declares as he presses his cheek against my chest.

I look down at his dark hair and wrap an arm around him. I don't even know how to argue with that.

"Momma says my daddy is in heaven," he says matter-of-factly and I shake my head.

Do kids ever stop talking? I don't argue and tell him that I'm sure that his father has his very own place in hell.

"But maybe I'll get another one some day? My momma got a new daddy. And so did my friend Luna. Her momma found her a new daddy and they got a puppy too."

"She did, huh?"

"I don't want a puppy though. I'm scared of dogs," he insists.

"You are?" I look down at him. I've never known this kid afraid of anything. He is fearless like his mom.

"Yeah. A big one stole my ice cream in the park. Momma chased him away and the man told Momma he'd buy me a new ice cream."

"Well, that was kind of him after his dog stole yours."

"Uh-huh. And then he told Momma she was pretty and he asked if he could buy her some ice cream too," he goes on and suddenly I am much more interested in who this jackass in the park was.

"And what did your mom say?"

"She told me not to eat too much ice cream before dinner," he yawns as he snuggles against me.

"No, I mean..." I stop talking, aware that I'm trying to shake down a four-year-old boy for information on his mom's dating habits. I'm only looking out for her, though, aren't I? Yeah, right, Jax.

"You two look cozy," Lucia's voice startles me.

"You were quick," I say as I turn to her.

"Yep." She arches an eyebrow at me. "Those two wear themselves out so much they go out like a light as soon as they have a bath and are tucked up in bed." She crouches down to Matthias. "Your turn, munchkin."

He reaches up his arms and she takes him from my lap. "Night, Jax," he mumbles sleepily.

"Night, buddy."

"I won't be long," she smiles at me and I nod. I'll be right here waiting for her even though I know I should leave.

CHAPTER 5

LUCIA

I close the door to Matthias' room and tiptoe along the hallway past my little brother's bedroom too. The three of them are fast asleep at last—whilst I adore them all, I am looking forward to some peace and quiet.

A thrill of pleasure skitters along my spine as I remember that Jax is downstairs too. I can't help but smile to myself at the thought of spending some time alone with him. I wonder if I can persuade him to stay for dinner. I certainly hope so. Even if he wasn't so good to look at, he still makes the best company. He cracks me up like no one ever has before and he is such a great listener. He catches me unawares and I often forget that he is my father's best friend. I have been guilty of pouring my broken heart out to him a few times in the past and as far as I know he has kept my secrets. It's one of the many reasons why I love him so much.

I have had the biggest crush on him forever, but as I've gotten older, it's turned into something much more, at least on my part. I find myself thinking about him often, wondering what he's doing and who he's with. The thought of unexpectedly bumping into him makes me feel giddy and nervous and I look forward to any time spent in his company.

I sense a shift in him too, or perhaps I want to see one so much that I am imagining it. Not that he is ever inappropriate, but sometimes I think I catch him watching me. Then whenever I look up, he looks away. He checks up on me often for my father, I know that much, and I enjoy keeping the pair of them on their toes. I smile as I recall the times I have led them to believe I have a far more interesting dating and love life than I actually do.

As I walk down the staircase, I hear the sound of the television in the den and smile. That's a good sign that Jax is sticking around for a while. If he wasn't, he'd be hovering around the hallway waiting for me to come downstairs so he could leave.

I walk into the den and he smiles when he sees me, that slow sexy one that makes my insides turn to jelly.

He flashes one eyebrow at me. "The last little monster finally asleep?"

"Yes," I say with an exaggerated sigh as I flop down onto the sofa next to him.

"I assumed you'd be hungry. I ordered us some pizza."

"Oh, you're a mind reader," I giggle "I would sell one of my kidneys for a huge slice of pepperoni right now."

"Steady on, wildcat. No need for that. It will be here in ten minutes," he laughs.

An hour later, Jax and I are sitting on the floor surrounded by the remnants of two large pizzas. I rub a hand over my stomach and groan loudly. "You shouldn't have let me eat so much."

He laughs and shakes his head. "Are you kidding me? One

thing I have learned in all of my years on this earth is to never come between a hungry woman and her food."

"Well, you do study the opposite sex extensively." I arch an eyebrow at him.

He narrows his eyes at me. "I do?"

"From what I've seen, Jackson Decker, you must have screwed your way through the entire state by now?"

"Lucia," he warns me but there is a mischievous twinkle in his eye.

"Anyone special right now?" I ask before I take a sip of the soda beside me.

"They are all special to me." He winks and my internal organs turn to molten lava.

I roll my eyes to disguise the fact that I want to jump his bones. "Such a smooth talker."

"How about you? Anyone special?"

"You tell me, Mr. Decker." I grin at him, my head tilted as I challenge him to answer. I know that he vets every single man I have ever dated, had sex with, or shown any modicum of interest in. I became aware of this fact in my second trimester of college and ever since then, I have taken great delight in dropping various names into conversations to send Jax chasing false leads and dead end trails.

"Well, not Jordan."

"Nope." I smile. Jordan was in my economics class at UCLA. I did enjoy talking to my papi about how smart and fun *Jordan* was to hang out with. I did neglect to mention she is a single mom of three kids who still likes to hook up with her ex-husband occasionally; I might have let him assume that she was a college frat boy.

"Not Dolly-douche-face either?"

I almost snort soda from my nose. "You mean Dolos?"

"Dolos. Douche-face. All the same to me. Who calls their kid Dolos anyway?" he frowns.

"It's not his real name. It's his gamer name. Dolos was a Greek god."

"Yeah. But of all the amazing Greek gods there are, why the hell would you call yourself after the god of trickery and manipulation?"

I blink at him. He knows Greek mythology too? Of course he does. Jax is the smartest man I've ever met. Could he be any more perfect? He stares at me and I realize I haven't answered his question. "Well it kinds of fits his gamer persona. And isn't most people's online presence all about deception and trickery?"

"You like him?" He narrows his eyes at me.

"Not like that. He's smart though and fun to hang out with," I shrug. Dolos is a huge gamer and has zero interest in me that way. In fact, if a woman isn't pixelated, then he doesn't even notice her. "Which Greek god would you be? Zeus I suppose?"

He winks. "No. Heracles, obviously."

"Ah, of course." I smile at him.

"And you're definitely not dating Archer?" Jax fakes a scowl when he says his name.

"Nope. He would be more interested in you than me."

"Yeah, I kinda got that." He chuckles softly and I wish I could have been a fly on the wall during that particular interaction. Archer Henderson is one of my best friends from college, and he is fun and smart and sexy as hell, but he is only interested in guys.

"You should be flattered. Archer is hot." I grin at him. "And he usually only goes for other young hot guys too."

Jax is taking a swig of his Coke and he almost spits it back out of his mouth as he laughs. "You saying I'm not young and hot?"

"Hmm." I bite on my lip as I consider him. "I mean for an old dude, I guess you could say you're handsome."

"Handsome?" He shakes his head. "I'll have you know, I am in my prime, Lucia Montoya."

Damn right you are! "Well, that's certainly open to debate," I say instead and he laughs softly before taking another drink and leaning back against the sofa.

"You remember the very first time I met you, you bought me pizza?"

"I do," he replies with a nod. "I remember when you came into the hallway and gave me the stink eye. You looked me up and down like I was a vacuum salesman."

I laugh out loud at that. "I did not."

"You did," he laughs too. "I thought you were a spoiled brat. Standing there with your hand on your hip while you decided whether I was worth your time."

"Well, lucky for you, I decided that you were, isn't it?" I pull a face at him.

"Hmm. When I came here looking for Alejandro, I didn't expect to find some pregnant kid here instead."

For some reason the way he says that makes emotion well up from my chest and into my throat.

"Shit, Luce," he says with a frown. "I didn't mean anything by that."

I shrug. "It's fine. I was just a pregnant kid." I shrug.

"You were never *just* anything. I'm an asshole though."

"You're not." I shake my head. "It just hurts to think about who I was back then, you know?"

He stares at me but he doesn't speak, allowing me to go on talking without feeling the need to interrupt or make me feel better.

"I was so messed up. I can hardly believe it was just four years ago. Sometimes if feels like it was yesterday and sometimes it feels like it was another lifetime and she was a different person. Does that sound crazy?"

"Not at all."

"I worry that I'll wake up one day and it will all go away. Like it won't have really happened or I don't really deserve it. I mean what happened to me is kind of a fairytale, right? Having Alejandro and Alana adopt me. So, why me?" I feel a tear running down my cheek and wipe it away quickly. I hate crying.

Jax shuffles across the hardwood floor until he is sitting close to me. "You went through enough shit to last four lifetimes before you wound up here, Luce. You deserve nothing but happiness. And they adopted you because you were an amazing kid." He bumps his shoulder against mine.

I turn and look at him. "Thanks."

He stares into my eyes. "You're still pretty amazing now," he whispers and something passes between us that makes the wet heat pool between my thighs. Surely I am imagining this and he's not looking at me like that? I have wanted this for so long, I'm seeing things that aren't really there.

Electricity crackles between us as I stare back at him and for a heart-stopping moment, I think he's going to kiss me. His head dips forward, so close that I smell his incredible cologne. His breath skitters over my cheek and I hold mine in anticipation.

"Momma!" An ear splitting screech fills the room and my heart starts again as though I've been hit with a defibrillator. "Momma!"

"Matthias." I jump to my feet and race out of the room with Jax close on my heels. One of my father's armed guards is standing in the hallway with his weapon drawn and an anxious look on his face. There is always at least one of them in this house, but they have developed the unique skill of being able to live in the shadows, so much so, that I often forget they are there.

I recognize this one though because he has been assigned to protect me many times before.

"It's okay, Enrico. He has nightmares sometimes," I say as I place a hand on his arm and he holsters his weapon before I run up the stairs to my son, taking them two at a time.

As I run into Matthias' room, he continues to shout and scream, his body twisted in the covers as he thrashes on the bed. I sit beside him and pull him into my arms. His body is damp with sweat.

"Momma," he whimpers.

"I know, munchkin. I'm right here," I soothe as I stroke his hair.

Jax looks at us both, his face full of concern.

"He has night terrors sometimes," I whisper. "Although he hasn't had any for a while."

"Oh," Jax frowns, "poor kid."

"He'll be fine. He doesn't even remember them in the morning. Could you fetch me some clean pajamas? They're in the dresser."

"Sure." Jax nods and walks across the room to the dresser while I start to peel Matthias' damp clothes from his body. He is completely relaxed now, while still sleepy and he smiles at Jax as he walks back toward us.

"I chose the dinosaur ones," Jax says.

"Cool." Matthias smiles sleepily as he looks up at the man standing in front of him. He adores Jax. They talk about dinosaurs and superheroes and boy stuff that I have no interest in. Matthias spends a lot of time with my father and they have a beautiful relationship. He is so close in age to my little brothers that I never worry about him not having enough male influences in his life, but seeing him with Jax makes me feel guilty that his father isn't around.

Jax would be an amazing dad. Despite who he is and the role

he plays in my father's organization, he has endless patience when it comes to the people he cares about. I suppose I am fortunate that my son and I are some of the few lucky people to be in that particular club, and I should be thankful for that. So why does it feel like it's no longer enough? Why can't I stop wanting more from him?

"Can you check on the twins for me?" I ask. There isn't a sound coming from next door and my little brothers could sleep through an earthquake, but Matthias' screams were pretty loud.

"Sure," he says as he ruffles Matthias' hair. "Night, buddy."

My son yawns. "Night, Jax."

I watch Jax walk out of the room and turn my attention back to my little boy. He looks up at me, his dark brown eyes wide and full of innocence and my heart almost bursts with a rush of pure love for him. His father, Blake, might have been a Grade A asshole, but I am thankful that he gave me the most precious thing in the world.

I walk back into the den and Jax is on his feet pacing the hardwood floor, a signal that he is waiting to leave. "Is he okay?" he asks.

"Yes. He's sound asleep again now."

"Good." He nods. He fidgets as he stands there staring at me and then he stuffs the pockets of his jeans.

"Were the twins okay?" I ask.

"Fine. Still sound asleep too."

"Thank you for your help."

"Any time. You know that," he replies, his voice suddenly thick with emotion.

"Are you going somewhere?"

"No. Yes," he stammers. "I need to leave, but I didn't want to just take off without saying goodbye."

"Oh, okay." I try to hide my disappointment but I obviously don't do a very good job.

"Don't look at me like that, Lucia," he sighs.

"Like what?"

"Like I just told you your puppy has died or something."

"I don't have a puppy."

"You know what I mean." He grabs his coat from the back of the sofa and shrugs it on.

"Thank you for the pizza. How much do I owe you?" I ask, unable to keep the sarcasm from my voice. But I'm not a kid anymore. He doesn't have to buy me pizza. I can afford my own.

He rolls his eyes and walks toward me. "I'm sorry about before. I should never have let that happen."

"Nothing happened, Jax. Did it?"

"No," he whispers as he looks down at me with those goddamn twinkly dark eyes. "But I..."

"You what?" I fold my arms over my chest as I glare at him.

"I like spending time with you, Lucia, but I don't want to give you the wrong idea."

I can't help but scowl at him. I hate when he treats me like a child. "And what idea would that be?"

He runs a hand through his thick hair and his Adam's apple bobs in his throat as he swallows hard. He looks so uncomfortable and it makes me wonder what the hell happened earlier. Was it me who leaned in to him for a kiss, because it sure as hell felt like it was the other way around. "I would never betray your father."

"Nobody is asking you to."

He nods. "Night, Lucia," he growls before turning on his heel and walking out of the room.

A few seconds later, I hear the front door closing behind him and my heart sinks in my chest. I look around the huge den and have never felt so lonely.

The sound of my phone vibrating on the coffee table distracts me. I always keep it on silent and I groan inwardly as I see the notification from the social media app. I don't do a lot of social media. My parents have drummed the need to be careful of revealing too much information about myself online, given who our family are and the enemies we have because of that. But I am on one app. I use a fake name, *Chica21* and an avatar as my profile pic and there's nothing personal about me on there. I use it to watch videos of cute dogs, follow my friend Archer's band and find parenting hacks mostly, but there is this one douchebag who continues to message me on there.

I have blocked his account at least a dozen times, but he just makes a new one and finds me again. It's become like a game to him now. At first it was just those stupid messages fishing for a conversation or a quick hookup. But they seem to be getting more sinister, like I'm really annoying him that I don't want to engage with him. As though I have the time to chat to random strangers on the internet.

I swipe the app open and read the message request from user10987636565—I mean couldn't he try and be a little more original?

It's me, chica. You can't get rid of me that easily.

I delete the request without responding. Douchebag!

Maybe I should mention it to Jax and see if there is a way to permanently block the guy, but I know he'll tell me to delete my account. And it's not like this guy actually knows anything about me—he's just annoying.

I toss my cell onto the sofa and sigh before walking to the bookshelves and picking up my mom's kindle. I open it up and browse through her latest downloads.

TL Swan's new release. Nice!

And my mom's already read it. Naughty!

I suppose book-boyfriends are the best kind, right?

CHAPTER 6

JAX

I floor the accelerator of my truck as I turn out of the driveway of my best friend's house. In all the times I've been there, I have never left the place so quickly, yet been so desperate to stay.

"Fuck," I snarl, slamming my hands against the wheel. What the fuck am I playing at here? I know how dangerous it is to be in her company alone, but I do it to myself anyway. Torturing myself with the whisper of a promise of something I can never have. Of all the women in LA, why is it Lucia Montoya who seems to occupy my every waking thought?

Is it because she's so unattainable? I don't think so though. I have never been into the chase. I'm more of a cards on the table and let's do this kind of guy. So what the fuck is it? Why can I not get this fucking woman out of my head? Not only is she Alejandro's daughter—and he would cut off my balls for even thinking about her that way—but she is way too young for me.

I know she has a crush on me. She's had one for years, but I always told myself it was harmless because I would never act on it in a million years. So when did our relationship become something more than what it was? When did I start looking forward to seeing her and wondering what she was doing? When did I start imagining what it would be like to have those beautiful red lips wrapped around my cock and to hold her incredible ass in the palm of my hands? Not to mention the thought of actually fucking her makes me feel like I'm going to blow my load like a horny teenage boy.

My cock throbs in my jeans and I groan out loud, glancing down at my groin. "This is all your fault," I mutter.

As soon as I figure I've put enough distance between Lucia and my overactive cock, I slow down. I blew off a date with a Victoria's Secret model to spend the evening with Lucia and the boys tonight. She only comes to LA a couple of times a year and we always hook up, and it is always fun, so why the hell didn't I stick to the script and go out with her?

I don't do relationships. I do casual sex and fuck buddy arrangements, and they have served me well ever since I started dating. In my line of work, it's better not to get too attached anyway, so why does it feel like it's no longer enough?

I think about Lucia again. The way her long dark hair falls over her shoulders. The way she smiles at me when she thinks no one else is looking. The way she laughs. Her firm tits and that juicy round ass. *Argh. Fucking stop it, Jax!*

She's had a rough start in life. When she first met Alana, Alejandro had me look into her. Of course, back then we had no idea she was actually a Montoya—Lucia didn't even know herself. But what I uncovered was that she had been neglected and abused her whole life. Her mom killed herself when Lucia was just eight and after that she was left to the mercy of the man she believed was her father and her psychotic older brothers. I never uncovered the extent of what happened in her home growing up but I can use my imagination and I don't like where it takes me.

Lucia Montoya is a woman of stark contrasts. Both the

toughest, and yet in some ways, the most fragile woman I know. To the outside world, she is Alejandro's daughter. And being the King's daughter is not an easy crown to wear, but she does it well. With humility, class and plenty of sass. She is feisty and independent. She is intelligent, quick-witted and has the kind of smart mouth that makes me want to put her over my knee and spank her ass. Hard.

That is what everyone else sees. But to the few people who are blessed to know her, she is also kind, funny and sweet. She would do anything to help a friend in trouble. She's an amazing mom to Matthias. She has the richest parents in LA, but she lives a modest lifestyle and is grateful for every cent and every single thing she gets. She could kick back and take some time off now that she's finished college, but she refuses to let someone else pay her way now that she is able to.

She might not be Alejandro and Alana's biological daughter, but she manages to embody the finest qualities in each of them. She's a wildcat. Never backs down from a fight. Always has to have the last word. But, I see every part of her, even the ones that she tries her best to hide. The part that craves approval and affection. The woman who never quite feels good enough no matter how much evidence to the contrary. The woman who would make stupid choices for a chance at true love.

Isn't that why I can't stop thinking about her? Because I know all there is to know about her. I know her flaws but all I see are strengths.

CHAPTER 7

LUCIA

It has been four days since I last saw Jax. He has called me every day my parents are away to check if I needed anything and each time I've told him that I don't. I could have invited him over for dinner but my pride wouldn't let me. If he wanted to see me so badly, he would just drop by like he usually does instead of calling to ask permission first.

I've been so busy with the boys this week that I haven't too much time to think about him at all, but during the evenings when the boys are in bed and the staff have retired to their own quarters, I have thought about him too much, wondering what he was doing and who he was doing it with. Even if it wasn't for my huge crush on him, he's like my best friend. I confide in him way more than I do anyone else.

As I watch the boys play in the den my cell starts to ring. Jax's name flashes on the screen.

"Hi," I answer.

"Hey, Luce. How are things?"

"Fine."

"Those little devils worn you out yet?"

"Not yet. But they're trying their best," I say with a sigh.

"Well, your folks will be back tonight and you can have a well-earned break."

"I can't wait," I lean back in my chair and smile. It's so good to hear his voice. I wish that it wasn't, though.

"I just called to make sure you're all okay and you didn't need anything."

"We're all good. Thanks, Jax."

There is a few seconds awkward silence before he speaks again. "You got any plans for the day?"

"I'm taking the boys to the park to let them burn off some energy."

"You need some help?" he asks and I hate the thought that he is only asking out of some sense of duty.

"No, I'll be okay. Hugo is coming with me." Hugo has been great with the boys this week; I don't know what I'd have done without him.

"Oh. Okay." Does he sound hurt or am I imagining it?

"I'll see you tomorrow at work though?" I offer. That is a place where I feel on a more equal footing with him. A place where we can focus on the job and not how awkward it is to be in each other's company lately.

"Yeah," I hear the change in his voice. "I'll pick you up at ten. We have some contracts to sort out downtown."

"Great. Sounds like fun." I can barely hide the happiness in my voice and I mentally chastise myself.

He laughs softly and the sound warms me from the inside. "See you tomorrow, Luce."

I t's almost eight p.m. by the time my parents get home. I stand on the driveway with Matthias and my twin brothers as their car pulls through the huge gates.

"Mommy! Daddy!" the twins squeal and jump up and down

in excitement.

"Papa! Nana!" Matthias shouts too, joining in with them. I can barely keep the smile from my face either. I have missed them so much.

When the car pulls to a stop, the boys run to it and my father climbs out first, somehow managing to scoop all three of them into his arms at the same time before smothering them with kisses. One by one they all clamber over to my mom too and she hugs them tightly. Once the boys have allowed my parents to move, I walk over to them.

"Hey, sweetheart." My mom is the first to pull me into her arms. We spoke on video call twice a day while they were away, but she still hugs me like she hasn't seen me in months.

"Hi, Mom." I hug her back. "Did you enjoy your trip?"

She pulls back from me, her eyes shining with happiness. "Yes. London was fabulous. The wedding was amazing. I told your dad we must go back with you and the boys some time soon."

"Sounds like a plan." I smile at her.

"Hey, kiddo." My father comes up behind us and plants a kiss on my head. "Everything okay here while we were away?"

"Of course."

He winks at me. "You ready for your first day tomorrow?"

"Yes," I reply, feeling flutters of excitement in my stomach—and they're not just about starting my new job.

"Can we at least get into the house before you two start talking about work?" my mom chides us good-naturedly.

He arches an eyebrow at her. "Says the woman who took a conference call in the middle of the night while we were in London."

"That was a funding emergency." She nudges him in the ribs and he smiles at her. I hope that one day I find someone who looks at me the way he does her.

CHAPTER 8

JAX

I look up at Lucia's apartment as I park my truck. I'm a little early but I'll wait out here rather than going up to get her. I haven't seen her since the night at her parents' house when I almost fucking kissed her. God, I'm such an asshole.

I spoke to Alejandro last night and this morning to catch him up on what he's missed and both times I considered suggesting that he show Lucia the ropes himself. Both times I backed out and now as I sit here waiting for her, I can't help but wonder why.

I tell myself it's because he'd want to know what prompted my change of heart and I wouldn't have an answer for him—at least not one that wouldn't end in him crushing my nuts in a vise —but the real reason is I'm looking forward to seeing her, working with her and just spending time with her.

She's not like any other twenty-one-year-old woman I know, not that I know many on a personal level. She's way smarter than almost anyone else I've ever met. She's more mature than most of the guys I work with who are decades older than her. I suppose it comes from having to look after herself from so young and also becoming a mom at seventeen.

Her apartment is in a nice building. It's a short walk to the beach and there's a park nearby where she likes to take Matthias. It's close to his kindergarten too. I know Alejandro would have bought her an apartment on the beach if she'd chosen one, but she was more than happy with this. It's not that it's lacking by any means, but the fact that she chose something much more modest than what he was offering makes me proud of her, whether I have any right to be or not. I like to tease her that she's a spoiled brat, but we both know it couldn't be further from the truth.

I stare at the door to her building and wonder if I should at least call and tell her I'm early but then the door opens and she steps outside.

I close my eyes and suck in a breath. This is going to be the longest day of my fucking life. When I open them again, my cock twitches in my pants as if to remind me that yes, she is dressed like that. Not that there's inherently wrong with how she's dressed. It's a pencil skirt and a white blouse. I mean, if she was going to work in an office somewhere, it would be the perfect outfit. And what else is she supposed to wear? A suit like her father and me?

She walks toward the truck and the sight of her hips swaying in that damn skintight skirt makes me feel like I'm about to have a heart attack. What is it about her wearing a pencil skirt that makes me think of bending her over a desk and fucking her brains out?

Stop it, Jax.

"Hey, Jax," she says with a smile as she opens the door of the truck and steps inside. "I wasn't sure what to wear today. My dad said businesslike. Is this okay?"

I look at her, my eyes fixed on her face for fear of losing my shit if they drop any lower. "You look fine," I manage to say with a smile.

"Good."

"I'm so glad I'm with you today," she says, her eyes shining as she stares at me.

"You are?" I frown.

"I mean, because ... it's my first day ... and I'm..." She stumbles over her words as her cheeks flush pink and that image of her bent over a desk pops back into my brain. What the fuck is wrong with me?

"I guess I'm a little nervous," she says, brushing the hair back from her eyes, "and so I'm glad that you're with me." Her cheeks turn even pinker and I realize I am not improving her situation by simply sitting here and staring at her instead of putting her at ease. "I mean, because ... it's you. Fuck." She shakes her head. "Am I babbling?"

I finally find my voice "It's natural to be nervous, Lucia, but there's nothing to worry about. We have a straightforward day ahead." I wink at her.

"Yeah." She lets out a long breath. "I don't know why I got so flustered." She laughs as she fans herself with her hand.

Maybe it was because I was staring at you like I wanted to throw you in the back seat and eat you? "It's hot out," I say instead. *Smooth, Jax.*

"Sure is," she agrees as she sits back in her seat. "Thank God for air con."

"Hmm," I mumble as I start the engine and pull away from the curbside.

"You speak to my dad yet?" she asks.

"Yeah, caught up with him last night and saw him this morning. He and your mom seemed like they had a good trip."

"Yeah. I'm so glad they're back though. Watching those three kids on my own was exhausting."

A pang of guilt stabs me in the chest. "I'm sorry. I should have come around more."

"No you shouldn't." She shakes her head. "You were busy taking care of business stuff. I was fine. They're just a lot together, is all."

"I'm sorry, Luce," I say.

"I told you it's fine."

"Yeah," I nod. I wasn't apologizing for that, but I also don't want to open that can of worms again.

"Everything is fine," she adds as she looks at me, telling me that she's thinking of it too. "Now where are we headed?"

"Downtown. We need to negotiate some new transport contracts."

"Sounds fun." She smiles at me.

I have a feeling she would think anything sounds fun—she's so excited to be starting work. I've chosen some of the more straightforward aspects of our business for our first week. I'm not sure Alejandro would appreciate me introducing his daughter to the darker side of what we do on her first day.

An hour later, we pull into the haulage yard and I kill the engine. I gave Lucia all of the information she needed to know about this contract on the drive here.

"How do you feel about handling the negotiations?" I ask as we climb out of my truck.

"Me? You think I'm ready?"

"Sure. And I'm right here if you need me."

"Then yes," She beams at me and I can't help but smile back.

We walk into Mason Michaelson's office. Three of his goons are in there with him but they sit around on sofas. There is no reason to think they'll be needed today. Still, having these assholes around Lucia makes me twitchy. I see their gazes roam over her body and settle on her ass as she walks past. I glare at them and they avert their eyes.

"Jackson." Mason stands when he sees me and holds out his hand.

"Mason." I shake his hand and place my other on the small of Lucia's back. "This is Lucia. She'll be handling your contracts from now on."

"Lucia." Mason smiles and I watch for his reaction to her. If there is even a hint of disrespect or disdain for her then he will regret it, but he's a professional businessman and he knows exactly who she is. "It's a pleasure to meet you."

He offers us a seat and we take it. Then I watch with a mixture of awe and pride as Lucia hammers out a new contract with him. She certainly has her father's negotiation skills and it makes me so fucking proud to see her in action.

Mason mops his brow when they finally settle on a price and I smile to myself knowing the usually cool and collected businessman is hot under the collar.

"It was a pleasure to meet you, Mason," she says as she stands.

"The pleasure was all mine, Lucia," he replies with a smile. "I look forward to working with you in the future."

Did he just fucking wink at her? No. I mean I was looking at her so I wasn't giving him my full attention. Surely he didn't, though? Not right in front of me.

She doesn't give any indication of being uncomfortable so I give him the benefit of the doubt. I mean the guy is old enough to be her father and the irony of that is not lost on me.

We say our goodbyes to Mason and start to walk out of his office. One of his asshole goons is standing by the door. He must be new because I don't recognize him and I never forget a face.

"Excuse us," Lucia says politely as we approach and he doesn't move. I resist the urge to move him out of the way myself, but this is her show today.

He steps out of the way, looking her up and down as he does. "I hope we're going to be seeing a whole lot more of you around here." He licks his lips. If that wasn't bad enough he reaches out and brushes his fingertips through a strand of her hair.

I am just about to rip his arm out of its socket when she acts first. Grabbing him by his balls, she squeezes so hard that he squeals like a piglet. "You ever touch me again and I will roast these on a skewer and feed them to you after. Understand?" she hisses.

He nods his understanding as his face turns purple.

"Good." She smiles at him before she releases his nuts and I laugh as the two of us walk out of the door. As soon as we're outside, she sucks in a deep breath and reaches out for me, grabbing my forearm and squeezing.

"Are you okay?" I frown at her as she gasps for air.

She shakes her head. I put an arm around her waist and walk her to the truck. I want to help her but I don't want any of Mason's assholes to see her having some kind of panic attack. She just put on an epic show of power in there and I would hate for them to see her vulnerable.

"I'm going to get us in the truck and out of here. Okay? Just keep breathing, Angel."

She nods as she walks with me, clinging onto my arm. As soon as I get her into the truck, I climb in after her and get us out of there. When we're a few hundred yards down the road I pull over. Her breathing is less labored now and I feel relief wash over me.

"Luce?" I say and she turns to me.

"I'm sorry." She wipes a stray tear from her cheek.

"What happened?"

"My brother, Luca," she shudders. "He used to look at me like that. I don't know—it took me back to a place I didn't like." She shakes her head like she doesn't want to talk about it any longer. "I'm sorry if I overreacted."

I act on instinct, pulling her into my arms and giving her a quick hug before she sits back again. "You didn't overreact, Luce. You were right to show that asshole he can't put his hands on you. I would have if you hadn't."

"Thank you for letting me deal with it."

"You were a fucking legend in there."

"You think so?" She smiles at me. Fuck, she is so desperate for approval it makes me want to kill every person who ever hurt her and made her believe she was worthless. Luckily for them, the ones who did the most damage are already dead.

"Yes."

"Thanks, Jax," she says and then I don't know if it's the emotion of the day but she flings her arms around my neck and hugs me. I hug her back, feeling like a complete deviant because she feels so fucking good in my arms that I never want to let her go.

F ortunately, the rest of the day is much more uneventful and I drop Lucia off at her parents' house after our final meeting, where Matthias is waiting for her.

"Are you not coming in?" she asks.

"No. Your dad is still at the hotel and I need to catch up with him," I lie. Well, it's not a complete lie. I am going to meet with him, but I have something else to take care of first.

"Okay. Thank you for today," she whispers. "I'm sorry I freaked out on you this morning."

"You were a pro. I'm proud of you." I smile at her.

"Thanks. Please don't tell my dad I screwed up on my first day."

"Hey. You didn't screw up. Some asshole put his hands on you and you dealt with him. What happened after is between you and me. I just told you I'm proud of you and I wouldn't lie to you, Luce."

"I know." She nods but her eyes brim with tears. "I hate thinking about him, Jax," she says as she looks down at her hands, and I assume she is talking about her brother, Luca. "I do my best not to, but when I do..."

Before I know it, I pull her into my arms and brush her hair back from her face. "It's okay," I say in her ear.

She melts into me and I bury my face in her hair, inhaling the familiar scent of the shampoo she always uses.

"I'm sorry. We shouldn't..." She pulls back and wipes her face with her hands.

I frown at her. "Shouldn't what?"

"Nothing. I..." She shakes her head. "Thanks, Jax. I'll see you tomorrow."

"If you're upset, I can stay a while longer."

"No. I'm fine. I'll be fine. You should go take care of whatever it is you need to do." She places her hand on the door handle.

"Yeah. Bye, Luce."

"Bye."

I watch her climb out of my truck and walk up the driveway to the front door of her parents' house and wish there was some way I could make her see just how incredible she really is.

I take off my jacket before climbing out of my truck. The sun is setting but the yard is still open. Walking to Mason's office, I'm pleased to see he and his goons are still in there. They are sitting around his desk with serious looks on their faces, as though they're discussing business.

"Jackson?" Mason looks up in surprise when I stroll inside without knocking. "Is everything okay?"

"Not really."

He stands and buttons his jacket. "What can I do for you?"

"Absolutely nothing," I reply without making eye contact.

Instead I look at the asshole sitting in front of his desk who is just about to take another swig of his beer. "But you can." I glare at him.

"What?" He frowns at me but Mason sits back down in his chair, realizing why I'm here. The asshole with the beer doesn't though as he stares at me with his mouth hanging open.

I don't wait for any further response from any of them as I grab him by his hair and slam his face down onto his boss's desk.

Mason doesn't flinch but his employee howls in pain while the other two guys scramble from their chairs. I don't know if they're planning on taking me on or they're just getting out of the way, but right now I don't care. I will deal with every one of them if I have to, but not until I've done what I came here to do.

"What the fuck, man?" the asshole squeals as I lift his head back up.

I lean close to his face. "You are never to go anywhere near her ever again. You understand me?"

He blinks at me in confusion as blood pours from his nose, and it only angers me more that he doesn't know what I'm talking about. I grab hold of his busted nose and twist it and the sound of cartilage and bone snapping makes him scream. One of the men standing behind me retches. Mason doesn't flinch, though. He has worked with me and Alejandro long enough to know how we operate.

I lean my face closer to the jackass who touched Lucia earlier and reminded her of her brother. "Lucia Montoya," I growl at him as I pull his head back by his hair.

Realization dawns on his face and he whimpers, opening his mouth but coughing on the blood running down his throat before he can speak.

"When she has a meeting with your boss in future, you will be nowhere near here. If you should ever find yourself unexpectedly in her presence, then you should get yourself as far away from her as you possibly can as quickly as humanly possible," I snarl as anger pulses through me.

He nods his understanding.

"And should so much as your breath ever touch her again, I will chop off all of your extremities before I bury you alive. You got that?"

"Yes," he sputters.

I push his head back, releasing him from my grip. "Make sure that she never lays eyes on him again, Mason," I bark as I turn to the door.

"Of course, Jackson," he replies.

CHAPTER 9

LUCIA

I lie back on the sun lounger in my parents' garden, keeping an eye on Matthias and the twins as they play in the pool with Hugo. All of the boys can swim and Hugo would die before he ever let anything happen to any of them, so I should be able to relax, but I can't. I replay the events of the day over and over in my head. How much that asshole reminded me of my oldest brother. The way that he looked at me made me feel like I was thirteen again, fighting off Luca's wandering hands. Trying to fade into the background so that he wouldn't notice me. Wedging a chair under my door each night to prevent him from getting into my room.

A shudder runs the length of my spine as I recall his hands on my skin. The smell of his foul breath. A tear runs down my cheek and I swat it away. He is dead. He can't hurt me anymore and he doesn't deserve another second of my time.

The night my two brothers and the man I believed was my father were murdered was one of the worst nights of my life, but it also signaled the start of a new one for me. My freedom.

After my biological mom died when I was eight, my life had

been a living hell in that house. I never understood why the man I believed was my dad hated me so much that he left me to the mercy of my animal older brothers.

It was only once I came to LA and met Alana that Alejandro discovered my real father was actually his uncle, Carlos Montoya. He was a psychopath, too. He kidnapped me and my mom in some crazy takeover attempt. I was pregnant with Matthias at the time and I remember being so terrified that we were all going to die in the filthy basement where he was keeping us prisoner.

My mom was so fierce and protective and the way she handled the whole thing makes me so proud of her, but it was my father and Jax who rescued us. That was the first time Jax ever hugged me and I think it was the moment when I fell in love with him. I always expected it to fade. I mean what girl wouldn't fall in love with the handsome man who rescued her from a psychopath? But instead of fading, my feelings have only grown stronger over time.

Thoughts of Jax make me happy and sad at the same time. It was so good to work with him today. He has so much confidence in me that it makes me want to make him proud. We were having such a great day until I went and ruined it. And then he hugged me and I felt all kinds of things I shouldn't feel about him. Making everything awkward between us again. Why can't I just accept that it will never happen between us?

"You okay, sweetheart?" my mom says as she takes a seat beside me and hands me a glass of fresh lemonade.

"Yes," I lie.

"How was your first day?"

"Great." Only a half-lie this time.

"Your father will be home soon. I'm sure he can't wait to hear all about it. Are you going to stay for dinner?"

"Yes, please," I say with a smile. It will be nice to have some company. "Do you mind if Matthias and I sleep over?"

"Of course not. You sure everything is okay?"

I take her hand in mine and squeeze. "Yes, Mom."

"Hmm." She sips her lemonade and I know she doesn't believe me, but she also knows me well enough to know that I will only talk when I want to.

"You must have missed going out with your friends while you had the three boys last week?" she says.

"No, Mom," I sigh.

"I'm not prying," she laughs. "But you're twenty-one, Lucia. You need to go out and see people other than your father and me. When was the last time you went dancing?"

"I can't remember," I say with a frown.

"Then your father and I will have Matthias this Friday while you go out with your friends."

I turn and smile at her. "Actually, Mom, that's a great idea. Thank you." I lean over and kiss her cheek. What better way to get over Jackson Decker than to go out and have some fun?

I take my cell from my pocket and type out a text to my friend, Archer.

Lucia: *You fancy coming to The Blue Flame with me Friday night?*

He texts back immediately.

Archer: *VIP treatment??*

Lucia: *Of course*

The Blue Flame is the hottest club in LA, and it also belongs to my father.

Archer: *Then hell yes*

Lucia: *Great*

Archer: *I'll come to your place at 8 for pre-cock cocktails?*

I laugh to myself and my mom smiles at me. I forgot how much fun Archer is.

Lucia: *It's a date x*

Archer: *Love you x*

I put my cell on the table beside me.

"Well?" My mom asks because she just can't help herself.

"I'm going out with Archer Friday night. To Papi's club."

"Ooh, Archer." She grins at me. "Is he the drummer with the blond hair and twinkly eyes?"

"Yes, Mom," I laugh. "Don't let Papi hear you talking about some dude like that. You know he has a jealous streak."

"Archer's gay. He won't mind."

"Papi once told me your ass had the power to turn gay men straight," I remind her.

She laughs so loudly that Hugo and the boys look over at us.

"I remember that. When he was going on and on about my bikini that day at the beach."

"Yes." I laugh too. "So I don't think he will appreciate you getting all swoony over Archer's twinkly eyes."

"He does have a possessive streak," she chuckles as she wipes a tear from her eye.

"It's kind of cute the way you two are so into each other," I say with a sigh.

"Hmm." She looks into the distance with a dreamy expression on her face.

"Mom," I snap. "Are you thinking dirty things about Papi right now?" I pull a face to make my disgust obvious.

"No." She frowns at me.

I shake my head and lean back. "Liar." I shake my head and lean back.

"Don't call your mother a liar, Lucia," she pretends to chastise me.

"What if there are no guys like that out there for me, Mom? What if I never find anyone who looks at me the way Papi looks at you?" I sigh.

She reaches over and squeezes my hand in hers. "For you, my beautiful daughter, there is a whole world of love and opportunity. I promise you." Then she lifts my hand to her lips and kisses it softly.

CHAPTER 10

LUCIA

I sing along to the radio as I drive. Jax sits in the passenger seat chuckling to himself every time I can't hit the high note. It's Friday afternoon and we have finished our last meeting for the week. I know he doesn't usually work office hours but he's tried to have a little structure for my first week, before he allows me anywhere near the real business of my father's organization—where all of the fun stuff happens.

I'm driving today because he declared he needs a day off from being my chauffeur, which is fine by me. I love driving. It gives me a sense of freedom.

My phone rings and Archer's face flashes up on the screen of my dash. My finger hovers over the button. I'm not sure I want to take this call with Jax listening in.

"You not going to answer that?" he asks.

I roll my eyes and press the button to answer.

"Hey, Lu," Archer's smooth, deep voice fills the car.

"Hey," I reply.

"You still on for tonight? We need to get my favorite chick a big fat—"

"Archer!" I interrupt him before he finishes that sentence. "You're on speaker and my dad's friend is in the car."

"Your dad's friend?" he purrs. "Not Mr. Decker by any chance?"

"Yes," I reply.

"Well, hello, handsome. Remember me?" Archer immediately camps it up and Jax rolls his eyes.

"Hello, Mr. Henderson," he replies, his voice as smooth as chocolate.

"Yes, we're still on for tonight. My place at eight," I say.

"Fabulous. I'll see you later. Kisses." He blows a kiss down the phone and hangs up.

"Your dad's friend?" Jax asks with an arch of one eyebrow.

I frown at him. "You are my dad's friend."

"Right," he mumbles.

"What else did you want me to say?" I ask as I glance between him and the road. What's his deal? He is the one who is always reminding me that my father is his best friend.

"Nothing." He shakes his head and stares out of the window.

I sigh inwardly. I feel like I can't win with him sometimes. "If I'd said you were my friend then he would have gone and finished that sentence, and neither of us wanted that."

"About you going out to chase dick tonight?" he snaps.

"Exactly."

He stares out of the window and the tension in the car becomes unbearable.

"Are you mad at me for something?" I eventually ask.

"Not at all, Lucia," he replies with a fake smile.

I shake my head and go back to focusing on the road. Asshole!

.   .   .

Archer lies on my bed, his muscular arms behind his head as he watches me try on every dress in my closet.

He has dismissed almost every single one. *Too frumpy. Too flowery. Too frilly. Too old. Too pink.*

"Argh. I have nothing," I groan as I take off the green halter that even I hate. I have no idea why I allow it to take up space in my tiny closet.

"Yes you do. That hot little black number you tried on a half hour ago." He flashes his eyebrows at me before taking a sip of his Cosmopolitan.

I shake my head. "It's too revealing." I shake my head.

"Lucia Montoya!" He stands and places his drink on my nightstand before picking up the tiny black dress and handing it to me. "You have a rocking body. You are twenty-one years old. We're going to the hottest freaking night club in California. Show a little skin, baby."

I take it from his hands. The fabric is so thin it's almost sheer. I haven't worn this dress in over a year. Not since the night I got drunk on tequila and Jax had to come rescue me from a dive bar.

I hold it up against my body. "I'll have to wear a G-string," I sigh. "They're so freaking uncomfortable."

"Oh for the love of God!" he snaps.

"You walk around with a wedgie all night then. See how you like it," I challenge him.

"Girl, if it would get me the dick that dress is going to get you, I would. Now put the fucking dress on."

"Okay." I relent and go to my underwear drawer to find a G-string.

"If you are ever going to get over Jackson Decker, then you need to get under someone else. And fast," he reminds me.

"I know," I sigh. He is the only person who knows about my

Jax obsession and the poor guy has had to listen to me talk about him for the past hour and a half.

He wraps his arms around me. "He is a damn fool not to want you, baby girl."

I lean back against his hard chest. "Thank you, sweetie."

Then he slaps my ass. "You're welcome. Now get dressed so I can go act all rich and important in your daddy's club."

P utting my empty glass onto the bar and with a wave to Archer, who winks at me to signal he is more than happy to remain chatting to the muscular blond at the bar, I follow the guy I've been chatting to for the past five minutes to the dance-floor. His name is Chase. He works in security and he has sandy brown hair, blue eyes and tattoos all over his forearms. He might be just my type.

We worm our way through the crowd until we find ourselves a space. It's so packed in here, we are already pressed up against each other before we even start dancing. But that is fine with me. Archer is right. I need to get me some action and forget all about Jax. And Chase is hot, right? I mean he's not Jax-hot, but he's got that tall and mysterious thing going on. I bet he has some hard abs under that shirt of his, too.

I lick my lips as I look up at him and he is staring back at me with pure undisguised lust in his eyes.

I can do this. Right?

He slides his warm hands around my waist and pulls me closer to him. The heat from his body seeps through the flimsy fabric of my dress and I lean into him and wrap my arms around his neck. This feels nice. I have forgotten the pleasure of two bodies molded together. The closeness. The heat. We are ultimately primal creatures after all, craving connection, no matter how fleeting. Our hips sway in time to the music and when he rocks his groin against mine, I feel his erection through his jeans.

He dips his head low and his breath dances over my neck, sending a shiver skittering up my spine. I lean my head back to give him easier access when I feel my cell vibrate in my purse which is sandwiched between us.

I contemplate not answering it, but it could be my mom about Matthias.

Taking it out of my purse, I glance at the screen. It's a text from Jax.

Big Bad JD: *Lose the asshole.*

I roll my eyes and open my purse to put it back inside and the cell vibrates in my hand.

Big Bad JD: *Now!*

I glance around the club. Damn Jackson Decker. He must be in here somewhere. Of course he is. It's Friday night and he's looking for some action too, but who the hell does he think he is, telling me who I can dance with?

I put the cell back in my purse and Chase smiles at me. "Everything okay?" he mouths.

"Yeah," I smile as I edge closer to him again. He places his hands on my hips as we move to the music and I'm not entirely unhappy when they slide to my ass. I think Chase and I are going to get along just fine.

As our bodies press together again, my cell starts vibrating like crazy. We both glance down at my purse which is nestled between our bodies. "Sorry," I mouth as I take it out again. If this is Jackson, I'm going to block his damn number.

Big Bad JD: *Don't make me come over there*

I type out a quick reply.

Lucia: *I'm just dancing.*

Big Bad JD: *That is not dancing*

Lucia: *You're worse than my father*

Big Bad JD: *If he puts his hands on your ass one more time...*
Lucia: *You'll what, Jax?*
Big Bad JD: *Don't fucking test me, Lucia!*

I frown at the screen. Don't test him? Seriously? What the hell is his problem? He's made it abundantly clear that he has zero interest in me. I click on his contact details and press block. I smile at my own genius. That will teach him. I'll unblock him again tomorrow of course, but for tonight, I need a breather from him.

I need a breather from being me.

"Is everything okay?" Chase shouts over the music.

"It is now." I smile at him and wrap my arms around his neck.

He smiles back and puts his hands on my hips again. A few seconds later *Señorita* comes on. "I love this song!" I shriek and Chase laughs as he grinds his hips against me and bends his face close to mine. A few seconds later, his hands slide onto my ass again. I look into his eyes and they are still dark with lust. Maybe I can do this random one night thing after all?

It's the expression on Chase's face that tells me something is drastically wrong. He goes from smiling to looking like he is about to pass out in a matter of seconds. I feel heat at my back as another hard body is pressed against mine and I am suddenly sandwiched between two men.

"If you want to have the use of those hands in the future, I suggest you take them off her ass right now," Jax growls loudly over the music.

Chase does as Jax says without even an ounce of resistance and while I know that the man behind me is kind of terrifying, it still it annoys me that Chase would give me up so easily. For all he knows, I might be about to get kidnapped, or carried off by some serial killer. Chase skulks off into the shadows and I spin on my heel and come face to face with an incredibly angry Jackson Decker towering over me.

"What the hell is your problem?" I push him in the chest but he remains in the same position, like a wall of rage.

"I warned you," he snarls.

"You're an asshole," I snarl back and then I turn around and make my way through the crowd, marching out of the club with Jax hot on my heels.

"Lucia," he calls after me.

"Leave me the hell alone," I shout as I keep walking straight out of the club and into the cool night air.

"That guy was an asshole," he snarls as he reaches me. "He had his hands all over your ass in the middle of the fucking club."

"We were dancing, Jax. That's what people do when they dance."

He grabs me by the elbow, stopping me in my tracks and turning me to face him. "That was way more than dancing."

"Well, maybe I wanted to do more than dance, Jackson," I hiss at him as I start walking again. I am so over him treating me like a child. "Even my father wouldn't have embarrassed me like you just did in there."

He takes deep breaths, his nostrils flaring as he tries to keep his temper in check. It's not often Jax loses his cool, but when he does—well, we just saw the outcome of his last little temper tantrum. "That's because your father doesn't look at you the way I do," he growls.

I frown at him. "And how exactly is that, Jackson?" I use his full name again, because he and I are no longer friends as far as I'm concerned.

"God help me, Lucia," he hisses through gritted teeth. "You drive me fucking crazy. Now get in the fucking truck."

I glance behind me to see that we've somehow walked to his

truck and I hadn't even noticed. His truck isn't some old pick up. It's a Hennessey Goliath with a custom interior, dark tinted windows and sleek black lines. The perfect fit for a cowboy in LA. "I can find my own way home," I snap.

"Who said I'm taking you home?" he snarls as he opens the door wide.

Something in the tone of his voice makes my internal organs turn to molten lava. I roll my eyes and climb inside, scooting over to the passenger seat until he climbs in beside me and locks the doors.

He turns in his seat and stares at me. "What were you really doing with that jackass, Lucia?" he asks, his tone softer now.

"I was dancing," I whisper. I don't have to explain myself to him, but I can't help being open with him. I always have been. I feel like he can see into my soul.

He narrows his eyes at me. "You would really have gone home with him?"

"Yes," I admit.

"Jesus!" he hisses as he shakes his head.

"What?" I snap. "I'm a grown woman, Jax. If I choose to have sex with a dude I meet in a club, then that's my business. It's what people do. You do it often enough."

He rubs a hand over the stubble across his jaw. "You don't though. Trawling clubs for action isn't usually your style."

Damn, I hate that he knows me so well. "Yeah. Well the guy I'd really like to go home with doesn't even know I exist." Crap! Did I just say that out loud?

"He doesn't?" Jax frowns at me.

I swallow hard as my heart starts pounding in my ears. "Well, he does. But he doesn't see me that way."

Jax's eyes drop to my thighs. They are almost completely exposed thanks to my mini dress which has only hitched up higher now I'm sitting in this truck. He runs his tongue over his lip and I swear my ovaries just exploded.

"You said my father doesn't look at me the way you do, Jax. How do you look at me?" I ask. I am tired of this back and forth between us. Me trying to forget about him and find someone more attainable, and him being so damn sexy and attentive that he pulls me back in.

"Fuck," he groans.

"Jax, please? Why are you doing this to me? You don't want me, so why are you bothered what guy I go home with?"

"You think I don't want you?" he growls and his words vibrate through my body and make a beeline straight to my groin.

"You made that pretty clear," I snap and then I turn to open the door and climb out of his truck, but he lunges forward, his hand covering mine as he stops me.

"Lucia," he says, his breath dusting over my hair and making goosebumps prickle along my forearms. I turn my head and he is leaning over me, his body just inches from mine in the confines of the truck.

"What Jax?" I breathe.

"I'm going to burn in hell for this," he growls.

"For what?" I whisper as the air crackles between us.

He doesn't speak. Instead he seals his lips over mine. I gasp and when I do he takes the opportunity to slide his tongue into my mouth as his hands fist in my hair.

Oh, sweet Jesus! I have never been kissed like this before. Wet heat pools in my core as he literally tongue-fucks my mouth. I wrap my arms around his neck and pull him closer to me. He shifts his weight slightly, his hands sliding over my hips as he turns me on the seat and lifts me until he can settle between my thighs. He rocks his hips against me until I feel his cock, hard and thick and encased in his jeans, pressing against my pussy through my panties which are now embarrassingly damp.

His hands slide beneath my dress, skating up my outer thighs and making every nerve in my body tingle with hot, sweet anticipation. He reaches higher, until his fingers hook into the waistband of my G-string.

I wrench my lips from his and gasp out loud as my heart beats wildly in my chest. Damn! We're really going to do this? Right here in his truck?

"Jax," I breathe.

"Is this okay?" he growls.

"Yes," I gasp. I mean it's way more than okay.

He leans back, pulling my panties over my hips and all the way down my legs. When he's removed them, he stuffs them into his pocket before he leans over me again. I reach for his belt and tug at the leather, desperate to touch him too, but he grabs my hands and stops me, pinning them against the window behind my head as he positions himself between my thighs. "Not yet, Angel." He grins at me.

"Jax," I hiss as he rubs the seam of his jeans against my clit.

"Fuck! I can smell you, Lucia," he growls. "You're soaking through my jeans, Angel. Tell me who you're dripping wet for? Me or that creep you were just dancing with?"

I blush at his words. "You," I pant before he kisses me softly.

Then he pushes himself back again and drops his head between my thighs and runs his tongue the length of my pussy. My hips almost shoot off the seat as a hot spike of pleasure rockets through my body but he is too quick for me. He keeps my wrists pinned with his left hand while he uses the other to push one of my legs over the back of the seat. Then he switches his grip, holding my wrists with his right hand so he can press his palm against the inside of my other thigh, flattening it against the seat until I am completely spread open for him.

Holding me in place, he nuzzles my clit with his nose while he laps at my opening.

"You taste even sweeter than I imagined you would," he groans as he brings me to the edge of an orgasm quickly.

He releases my wrists and wraps his hands around the backs of my thighs so he can pull me closer. I plant my hands on the window behind me, hoping that the dark tint will obscure us from view, as wet heat surges through my core. I have never felt anything like this before. My head spins as warm pleasure sizzles and dances through my legs and stomach before converging in that one sweet spot where he has his mouth.

"Jax," I whimper.

"I'm so fucking desperate to be inside you, Luce," he murmurs as he pushes two of his thick fingers deep into my pussy and my whimpers turn to loud, unrestrained moans. My walls clench around him as spots flicker behind my eyelids. When he swirls the tip of his tongue over my clit, I shout his name as my climax crashes over me like a full scale tsunami.

My thighs tremble. My head swims. I gasp for breath as he pushes himself up onto his forearms and looks down at me with pure fire in his eyes. The thought of what might happen next makes my heart begin to race and my blood thunder in my ears. His face is glistening with my arousal and he licks his lips, making me blush.

He reaches down and brushes a strand of hair from my face. "I have waited so fucking long to do that."

"Really?" I breathe out as the waves of my orgasm keep on pulsing through my body.

"Don't pretend you didn't feel this between us, Angel. Isn't this what you were hoping for when you were grinding yourself all over that jackass in the club? That I'd carry you out of there and fuck you instead?"

"I thought..." I swallow. Of course I felt it, but I assumed it was all me. I feel so out of my depth here. This is everything I've ever wanted, but I can't let him know that. Jax is all about the casual hook up and if he knew just how much being with him like this meant to me, he'd drive me straight home. "I didn't even know you were there tonight. And in case you haven't noticed, you haven't fucked me." I narrow my eyes at him.

His eyes twinkle in delight. "My little wildcat," he says with a grin. "But I am going to fuck you, Luce." He reaches over to the glove compartment and pulls out a condom before he turns back to me. "If I'm going to hell, I might as well go all out, right?"

"Yes." I nod my agreement. I have never wanted anything more in my life.

His eyes darken. His Adam's apple bobs in his throat as he swallows and the air in the truck is thick with heat and desire.

"How about you climb onto the back seat so I can fuck you properly?" he growls. I push myself up and do as he asks, shifting through the gap in the seats until I'm sitting on the bench.

Jax follows me, squeezing his huge frame through the space until he's kneeling on the floor in front of me.

He unzips his fly and pulls his cock free and I swallow. Jesus! He is huge. I mean, I'm no virgin, I've got a kid, but I've had sex with like four guys in my life and none of them were hung like him.

He must see the look of surprise in my eyes because his brow furrows in concern. "You okay, Luce?"

I bite my lip. How do I say this and not give him an ego the size of Texas? "You're pretty big," I whisper.

He gives me one of his slow, sexy smiles before he tears open the condom and rolls it down over his thick shaft. "I won't hurt you, Angel. Promise," he whispers as he leans over me again, the tip of his cock nudging at my entrance. "Besides, you're soaking wet. I think you can take all of me like a good girl."

Damn! The rush of heat almost winds me. Why is that so hot? I blush again and he smiles at me. He makes me feel so nervous and inexperienced.

He gets up onto the seat, grabbing my hips and pulling me toward him until he's kneeling between my thighs. "You're dripping all over the seat of my truck," he growls as he looks down at my pussy. Then he leans over me and starts to trail soft kisses along my throat. His stubble gently tickles my skin and I squirm but he holds me in place with the weight of his body.

"You want me to fuck you, Lucia?" he whispers in my ear and I feel another rush of wet heat between my thighs.

"Yes," I pant. "Please, Jax?"

"On one condition," he growls.

"What?" I whisper as he edges the tip inside of me.

"After I fuck you in my truck, you come home with me and let me fuck you in my bed. Just give me one night with you."

That's not a condition, that's like a dream come true. "Yes," I gasp and he edges in further, stretching me wide open. I hiss at the burning sensation and he kisses me softly. "Relax, Angel. Let me all the way inside. I want to feel your tight little pussy squeezing my cock when I make you come again."

I groan as I wrap my legs tighter around him, pulling him in deeper even as it burns.

"Fuck, Lucia," he hisses. "You're so fucking tight."

"I want all of you, Jax," I plead. "Please?"

"Soon," he growls as he edges deeper inside. "I should take you to my bed right now and take more time with you, but I am fucking desperate to be inside you."

"I want you right now," I pant.

"You have any idea how hard it's been trying to keep my hands off you," he growls as he thrusts deeper and I moan loudly.

A group of club-goers walk past the truck and hover nearby, talking and laughing and I clamp my hand over my mouth.

Jax removes it and narrows his eyes at me. "When you come for me, I want to hear every single sound you make. You got that?"

"Yes."

With a final roll of his hips, he drives all the way inside me, and I cry out in pleasure and pain. But it is a delicious pain and I want more of it. "Fuck me, Jax," I beg him.

"Fuck," he hisses as he starts to drive into me so hard that my head bumps against the door of the truck, but I don't care. This is everything I have ever wanted. My walls clench around him as he buries his head against my neck, wrapping me in his huge arms as he nails me to the seat. It's full of passion and longing. Raw and primal. But I have never felt so wanted and desired as I do being banged in the back seat of Jackson's truck with people all around us, separated only by a dark pane of glass.

"Your pussy," he growls in my ear, but I don't hear the rest of his sentence, if indeed he even finishes it, because I come hard, and loudly. Crying out his name as he drives into me further while he grinds out his own release.

When he is done, he lifts his head and stares at me as we both pant for breath. "You," he pants and swallows hard. "You're gonna be my fucking undoing, Luce."

CHAPTER 11

JAX

I have never driven home so fast in my life. Lucia sits next to me on the front seat, her hair messed up because I've just fucked her in my truck, her cum dripping out of her because her panties are still in my pocket. My cock is already hard again because all I can think about is how hot and wet and tight her cunt is and how as soon as I get her home, I'm going to be buried deep inside it again.

I suppose being fixated on the fact that her bare pussy is only a few feet away from me is a good thing, because it means I can't give too much attention to how wrong this is. I tell myself that I've done it now, so it doesn't matter whether I fuck her once tonight or half a dozen times. It's still just a one off. Never to be repeated.

All I know is I would rather battle Lucifer himself and his legion of demons than not take her to my bed right now.

I glance across at her. She sits biting on her lip and fuck me if she isn't the most beautiful thing I've ever seen.

"You okay?" I place my hand on her thigh.

She turns to me and smiles. "Better than okay."

"Fuck, Angel," I growl as I slide my hand between her legs,

my fingertips tracing over her soft, supple skin. She spreads them wider for me, allowing me access to her pussy without me even needing to tell her what I want. My hand runs higher until I can run a finger through her soaking wet folds.

"Jax." My name catches on the breath in her throat and she grips my forearm, pulling me closer.

"You want my fingers inside you?" I hiss.

"Yes," she gasps as I dip one into her hot pussy.

I am so fucking tempted to pull this truck over and finger fuck her until she screams my name again, but it won't be enough. I need her naked and in my bed. If I only get one night, I am going to savor every single inch of her.

I pull my hand away and she groans.

"Soon, Lucia. I've got you all night long and if I don't stop touching your pussy in here, I'm going to crash this fucking truck."

"Okay," she purrs but she grabs hold of my hand, pulls my finger to her lips and sucks it clean. Her soft, wet tongue swirling over it makes my cock throb as I imagine how good her mouth would feel sucking me off.

Fuck! Me! I draw in a shaky breath as I turn my eyes back to the road. "If you don't stop doing that, Angel, I'm going to pull over and make you suck something else," I growl.

She giggles, catching my finger between her teeth before releasing it and I rest my hand on her thigh again. "Did you like tasting yourself on me?"

"Yes," she puts her hand over mine and I turn mine palm side up, lacing my fingers through hers.

"Good. Because you'll be tasting yourself on my cock later."

"Jax," she purrs my name as she blushes and I think I might fucking die if I don't get inside her again soon.

. . .

B y the time I get her into my house, I can barely keep my hands off her. Picking her up, I wrap her legs around my waist and carry her straight to my bedroom, throwing her down onto the bed. I pull off all of my clothes and she does the same with hers. I'd prefer to peel them off her myself, but as long as the outcome is her being naked I suppose I don't mind.

I crawl over her and she wraps her arms around my neck, staring up at me with her huge brown eyes, full of innocence and trust.

I am going straight to hell.

Her hand slides between us and she grips my hard cock in her hand. "I want to taste you," she purrs and any lingering doubts I had just vanished.

I roll onto my back, pulling her with me until she's straddling me. Damn, her tits are fucking incredible. I don't have much time to look at them though because she bends her head low and starts to trail feather soft kisses over my chest and stomach. I hold her head, my hands fisting in her hair as those soft lips dance over my skin.

She's teasing me. I'll allow it because this is one time. Just tonight and then we can pretend this never happened.

"Jax. You taste to so good," she swirls her tongue over my abs and I groan. I need her lower. Like now.

"Suck my cock, Angel. Then you'll see how good I taste," I growl.

She chuckles softly. "You're so impatient."

"Fuck, Lucia. If you don't wrap those lips around my cock right now you won't be coming for the rest of the night. Then we'll see who needs a lesson in patience."

She looks up at me as my hands stay in her hair. I could guide her to where I want her, but I'd rather she made her own way. Her eyes stay fixed on mine as she moves lower and presses the flat of her tongue against the base of my shaft, then she licks the length of me before sucking my cock into her mouth.

"That's it, Angel. Take it all like a good girl."

She groans loudly, the sound muffled by me filling her mouth. She gags slightly but she doesn't stop, licking and sucking as she keeps taking me deeper and deeper.

I can tell she's inexperienced, but she more than makes up for it in her eagerness to please me. If I had more time, I would teach her how to open her throat to take me all the way down, but I don't, so for now I lie back and enjoy the feel of her hot mouth as she sucks me greedily. It's such a fucking turn on to see how much she enjoys sucking on my dick.

"You feel how hard you make me?" I growl as I hold her thick hair back from her face so I can see every single fucking move she makes.

When she looks up at me again, her huge brown eyes wet from gagging on my cock, it makes my balls draw up into my stomach.

"I'm going to come, Luce," I groan, giving her the option of stopping. I'd rather she didn't, but I'd be happy enough to come all over those perfect tits of hers instead. She doesn't stop. She swallows my load as I pump into her throat, sucking and licking every last drop I can give her.

When there's nothing left I let my hands fall from her hair.

"Fuck," I hiss.

She crawls up the bed to me, licking her lips.

"Was that okay?" she whispers, seeking my approval.

"It was fucking perfect," I smile at her.

"Thank you," she blushes. "I haven't done it much before."

I reach up and brush her hair back from her face. "You are fucking perfect, Angel."

She looks down at me and there is something in her face that makes me feel guilty and happy at the same time. I roll her onto her back. Now it's my turn to taste her, and I will take my fucking time because she is the sweetest thing I have ever eaten in my life.

"How many times you think I can make you come tonight?" I arch an eyebrow at her.

"I have no idea," she giggles. "You've already done it more than anyone else ever has."

I frown at her. "What?"

She covers her eyes in embarrassment and I pull her hand away. "But you have come before, right?"

"Of course. By myself," she whispers.

"No one else has ever made you?"

"No." She shakes her head.

What? I have no idea how that is even possible because I have never made a woman come so easily as I have her tonight. "You're serious?"

"Yes. Why? That's okay, isn't it? It's not like it's a big deal?"

Yes it's a big deal that I'm the only man who's ever made you come, Lucia! "No," I lie to her instead.

"So how many times have you made a woman come before in one night?" she whispers.

"I can't remember," I tell her honestly. "I've never wanted to count before." I bend my head and suck her hard nipple into my mouth. I want to bite down on it. I want to mark her as mine, even if she's only mine for a little while. I slide my hand between her thighs.

"You're soaking wet for me," I growl as I press kisses over her stomach.

"Jax," she moans softly as

I slide two fingers inside her and her walls squeeze me, pulling me in further.

I curl the tips, pressing deep inside and her legs shudder when I find that perfect spot. "That's my good girl. Come for me, baby," I growl and for the first time in her entire life, Lucia Montoya does exactly what I tell her to when I tell her.

"God, Jax," she cries out and I fucking love the sound of my name on her lips when she loses control. Knowing she has never moaned another man's like that makes me hard as fucking iron.

"That's one, Luce," I chuckle, "and I haven't even got my mouth on you yet."

CHAPTER 12

LUCIA

.

Holy sweet mother of Jesus! Jackson Decker is some kind of magician with his tongue. He has made me come three times tonight already, twice in his truck and once in his bed not even ten minutes ago, but here I am, pulling at his hair and riding his face to my fourth. I spread my legs wider as I pull him closer.

"Oh! Jax," I hiss out a breath as I rock my hips against his mouth. He holds me steady with his powerful hands clamped around the back of my thighs while his face is buried in my pussy, maintaining total control while I am on the edge of complete oblivion.

I have made myself come plenty of times before, but it's been nothing like this. Nothing like the feeling of losing complete control and falling off the edge of a cliff. Every nerve ending in my body is screaming for release. Stars flicker behind my eyelids as my orgasm crests a wave.

Shit! I'm going to pass out.

"Good girl," he mumbles as he sucks my clit harder.

No, I'm going to die. My soul is about to leave this earthly plain, but damn I will go out with a smile on my face.

. . .

I wake up and blink in the dark room. For a horrible second I forget where I am, but then I see the huge tattooed arm draped over me and a jolt of warm, wet pleasure shoots through me. I'm in Jax's house. In Jax's bed. With Jax Decker. And he is everything I dreamed he'd be and more.

I stretch my arms and legs, trying not to disturb him. Glancing at the clock, I see it's only five a.m. and we didn't go asleep until after two. Every muscle in my body aches in a delicious way and my pussy throbs, making me smile.

"It's early, Angel. Go back to sleep," he mumbles in my ear.

"Do you call all women, Angel, in case you forget their name?"

"No, Lucia." He nips my shoulder blade in warning. "Only you."

I shift my weight until I'm lying on my back with his huge arm over my stomach now.

"Jax?" I whisper. "I think you've broken me." I stifle a giggle.

"What? Why?" his eyes flicker open as he frowns at me.

"I don't think I'll ever be able to make myself come again. Well not like you did."

"I'm sure you'll manage it."

"Hmm, Maybe. Can you remind me what you did though? With your fingers?"

"No, Lucia," he growls and I feel a pang of disappointment, but I suppose he's tired after our epic session. "Because if you want me to make you come again, or fuck you, then I want you to ask me to. Like a grown up."

"You're an ass," I pout.

"Hmm." He pulls me tighter to him.

I lie there for a few seconds as my pussy gently thrums with growing need. "Jax?"

"What?"

"Would you please make me come?" My words sound loud in the quiet room but there is something both exhilarating and empowering about asking for what I want.

The growl rumbles through his chest. "It would be my pleasure. Do you have any preference for how I make you come?"

"With your fingers first," I whisper.

"First?" he breathes as he nuzzles my neck while his hand slides over my stomach and between my thighs. "And then?"

I suck in a breath. I am so out of my comfort zone here, but his hand feels so good as it slides over my pussy and he starts to circle my clit.

"Tell me what you want, Luce," he growls.

"And then I want you to fuck me," I breathe, blushing as I say the words even after everything we've done tonight.

"Fuck! You're so damn sexy when you tell me what you want. And you are also fucking insatiable," he groans as his fingers gently rub my clit.

He maintains a slow steady rhythm that makes every part of my body tingle with electricity. I rock my hips against his hand, desperate for more friction but he refuses me. And I remember that I'm supposed to ask.

"Jax," I groan as my body pulses with need.

"Hmm?"

"I need more."

"More?" he whispers against my neck.

"I want your fingers inside me," I hiss as even saying the words makes the wet heat flood my pussy.

He slides his fingers lower before pushing two of them deep inside me and making me gasp out loud. How can he make me feel so good with only two fingers? "Like that, baby?" he breathes in my ear as he drives them in and out of me.

"Yes. Exactly like that."

I close my eyes and concentrate on the pleasure flooding my senses. His hard body pressed against mine. The warmth of his breath on my neck. His forearm flexing against my stomach as he works my pussy like no one ever has before.

"Your tight little cunt is so greedy for me, Luce," he growls as he edges deeper and presses against a spot that I've only ever reached with a vibrator before. "The next time you touch yourself, will you pretend that it's me inside you?"

I groan loudly. I always thought about him anyway, and now how the hell will I ever have sex again and not think about this night. When he presses against my clit with the pad of his thumb I lose all sense of time, space and reason.

"God, Jax!" I scream as my orgasm crashes over me.

"Fuck, Luce," he groans. "The way you squeeze me like that when you come makes me so fucking hard." Then his fingers are gone and I lie trembling and panting for breath while he gets a condom from the nightstand. As soon as he's put it on, he rolls on top of me, spreading my thighs wider apart with his knees.

"Now it's my turn to tell you what I want," he growls as he drives his cock into me, pinning me flat to the mattress. "I want to make you come again on my cock, Angel. I want to fuck you so hard that you'll remember what I feel like inside you forever. Whenever you're fucked again you'll think of me and the way I claimed you and know that no one will ever make you come as hard as I'm about to, and I want my name on your lips when you do."

I look up at him as a rush of wet heat surges between my thighs.

How am I supposed to give this up now that I've had a taste of him? How can I sit back and watch him date his endless stream of women when I know that this is what they get when he brings them home for the night? Is it so selfish to want it all for myself. To want him for myself?

I wrap my arms around his neck and pull him closer. If this is all I get then I need to make the most of it, don't I?

CHAPTER 13

JAX

I pour a coffee and look out of the window at the ocean view but it's a poor substitute for what I'd see if I went back to bed. Leaving Lucia alone to wake up in a strange bed is a shitty thing to do, but it's kinder than what would have happened if I'd stayed there with her. I close my eyes and my cock twitches as I remember waking with her perfect round ass nestled against me. How easy it would have been to slide myself inside her hot, wet pussy.

"Fuck!" I mumble. I should go back in there right now and do exactly that, but that would be unfair to her. And that would turn one night into this morning too, and maybe the afternoon, and that cannot happen.

Because one night can be explained away, can't it? Forgiven even? A mistake. A momentary lapse in judgement. Even if I did spend almost the entirety of said night buried inside her. Even if I said far too much about claiming her and wanting her to feel me inside her forever. That was an asshole move, even if it is true, because being with her felt right and made sense in a way that nothing ever has before her, and nothing might again.

The sound of soft footsteps padding over the wooden floor

breaks my train of thought and I turn around to see her walking into the room. That mini dress looks even better on her this morning, with her freshly fucked hair and her beautiful face devoid of any make up. She looks innocent and sinful in equal measure and it turns the twitch in my cock into a throb.

She looks down at the floor, the wildcat in her completely subdued as she heads into the kitchen.

"You want some coffee?" I offer.

"Please," she whispers, still refusing to make eye contact with me and I recognize that look on her face. She is full of regret and guilt. That's good though, right? It's what I feel too. I should let her feel that, because then she would realize that this thing between us can never happen again.

I walk toward her and she looks up at me, her huge brown eyes wide and full of something so much more—anxiety and shame and something else I can't put my finger on. She is questioning her own worth when she should be questioning mine. I am the only one at fault here.

And that's when I realize I can't do this to her. Before she met Alana and Alejandro, she had a horrible childhood full of abuse and neglect. Everyone who was ever supposed to protect her let her down and I know how the scars of our past can leave a mark. As much as she is fearless and independent and tough, she is also vulnerable and full of self doubt.

I reach out and run my hand over her arm. Her skin is soft and warm and the memory of trailing my lips and tongue over every part of her burns a fresh imprint into my brain.

"Lucia," I say and her name almost gets caught in my throat. "Last night was..."

She blinks at me, her eyes searching my face for what? Approval? Validation? And isn't that what I get off on? I should tell her it was a mistake, but I can't. "Incredible," I finish and right there is the moment I have just fucked up her life, because that smile, it's one I never want another man to see. It's mine!

"You're incredible. But you and me can never happen," I say with a heavy sigh.

"Because of my father?" she whispers.

"Yes," I admit but as much as that is true, it's not the only reason. "And because I'm way too old for you, Lucia."

"You're only thirty-seven," she frowns at me.

"Yeah, and you're only twenty-one, Angel. You have your whole life ahead of you."

She crosses her arms over her chest and I bite back a smile because it is good to see the feistiness in her again. "You say that like you're some decrepit old man, Jax. You still have your whole life too."

My hand runs up her arm and her nipples harden beneath the flimsy fabric of her dress so I drop it to my side before my cock starts to take over the show. "But I have lived so much more than you have. I have done—"

"You mean you've screwed around?" she snaps.

"That's not what I meant, but yes, there is that." I narrow my eyes at her. "Can we not just see last night for what it was?"

"And what was that?"

There she is again, searching my face for some validation. This time I can't give it to her. "A night of amazing sex between two consenting adults?" Fuck! Could I have worded that any fucking worse than I just did?

"You're an asshole, Jax," she says. A tear runs down her cheek and she wipes it away with her hand, then turns on her heel and walks out of the room.

My instincts tell me to run after her and wrap her in my arms. My cock tells me to carry her back to bed and put that smart mouth of hers to better use.

I do neither, thinking with my head, which is after all what I do ninety-nine percent of the time. So why didn't I last night? Why didn't I let her go home with that guy from the club? Maybe he could offer her something I can't? But something about seeing his hands on her, the way she looked at him, it overpowered every single rational thought in my brain.

CHAPTER 14

LUCIA

As soon as the text alert flashes up on my cell phone, I walk through Jax's huge open plan living area and toward the door. I've been hiding out on his deck while he got a shower and dressed. I wish it was as easy for me to wash away what we did last night. Why did I even for one second consider that I meant any more to him than any of the dozens of women he brings home on a regular basis? Why was I naïve enough to think that I could be just like him and pretend that sex isn't a big deal for me?

I've never been able to separate emotions from sex. I wish that I could. It's why I've never done the whole casual hook up thing before. Why I had to prove that theory with Jax of all people I don't know, but it was complete lunacy on my part. As if I didn't already spend enough time thinking about the guy and now I know that he is some kind of sex wizard too. He did things to my body and made me feel things that I didn't even know were possible. What if I never have sex like that again for the rest of my life?

"Where are you going, Luce?" Jax's voice cuts across the

room. *Does he want me to stay?* "I can take you home." *No, of course he doesn't. Don't be ridiculous, Lucia!*

"Archer is waiting outside for me," I say, trying to sound cool and calm while my stomach is churning and my heart is breaking.

"Oh? Right," he runs a hand through his hair and I look away from him so he doesn't see the hurt on my face and realize who I really am—just some naïve little girl with a huge crush on him.

"Bye, Jax."

"Bye, Luce."

A few moments later, I climb into Archer's car and he wraps an arm around me and gives me a quick kiss on my forehead. "I'm sorry, baby girl," he says.

"Thank you," I say as I fasten up my seatbelt. "Can we get out of here?"

"Course," he replies and pulls the car away from the curbside. "I saw you leave with him last night and I was so freaking psyched for you, Lu. Was it awful?"

"No." I shake my head. "I almost wish it was, then I could forget about it."

"Oh no. Was it good?" He looks at me with huge puppy dog eyes.

"It was incredible, Archer."

He puts an arm around me. "Let's go for waffles and you can tell me everything."

I lean back in the booth, pushing my waffle around my plate with my silverware as Archer sits beside me. I've given him most, but not all of the glorious details of last night and he sat and listened completely enraptured throughout.

He spears a piece of my uneaten waffle onto his fork and

stuffs it into his mouth. "I have never seen you not eat your waffles before," he mumbles.

"I'm not that hungry."

"Shit! This is bad." He flashes his eyebrows at me.

"Asshole." I smile at him.

"Come on, Lu. Let's look on the bright side here?"

"And what's that?"

"You finally fucked Jackson Decker." He grins wickedly at me and I throw a bunched up napkin at him.

He stares at me, swallowing down the remainder of his food before he speaks again. "I have to ask though, Lu…"

"What?"

"I mean, he just exudes big dick energy." He pops an eyebrow at me and I can't help but laugh.

"Well, yeah."

"I knew it. How big?" he whispers.

"Huge! I mean like oh my God how is that even gonna fit, huge."

"Fuck," he giggles. "I could tell. And he was still that good? I mean some guys with huge dicks think that's all they need and have no freaking clue what to do with it. It can be such a let down." He sighs dramatically.

"Oh he knew exactly what to do with it." I grin wickedly. Maybe Archer is right and I need to start thinking of the positives of this situation. I did just have the most incredible, mind-blowing night of my life. "And every other part of his anatomy too," I add.

"Fuck! Me!" Archer hisses. "The holy trifecta?"

"Yup!" That is Archer's definition of a guy who is good with his hands, mouth and his cock.

"Oh, baby girl." He makes a sad face and wraps his arms around me.

"I know." I fake a wail as I lean against his hard chest.

"You sure he never left the door open for more fun? Like you work together, right? Maybe some more action in his truck?"

"We work together for my father." I remind him.

"Oh, shit, yeah." He rubs a hand over his jaw. "But he said it was incredible too, right?"

"Yeah," I nod.

"Then I think all hope is not lost, Lu."

"Don't, Archer," I groan. "Don't encourage me to think this might be more than it was. One night he said."

"Hmm? But you know what you have to do Monday when you go to work with him for the day?" He waggles his eyebrows at me.

"What?" I frown.

"Wear the sexiest outfit you own. If last night was really as amazing as you're telling me, Lu, then he'll be thinking about it just as much as you are."

"You think?"

"I know," he says full of confidence and certainty.

"Hmm," I take a sip of my milkshake. "Anyway. Tell me about the blond guy. Did you go home with him?"

He rolls his eyes and pulls a face and I laugh as I listen to Archer's disastrous hookup and it is the absolute best thing to distract me from my own.

CHAPTER 15

LUCIA

I stand on the steps of my apartment building, chewing my lip and fidgeting like a nervous teenager about to go on her first date. I have been half-expecting a call from my father to tell me I won't be working with Jax this week, or perhaps a text from Jax himself telling me the same, but I've had neither, so I'm standing here waiting for him—a ball of excitement, anxiety and raging hormones.

As soon as I dropped Matthias off at kindergarten this morning, I rushed back home and tried on every single outfit that I own. I want to look professional, obviously, but I also want to look hot enough that Jax can't look at me without remembering what we did Friday night.

The memory causes a rush of wet heat between my thighs that almost floors me. I grab onto the handrail beside me for balance. How am I supposed to work with him all day and not stare at those lips, those hands, and remember the things they can do my body? Oh fuck! This is going to be torture. Perhaps I'm the one who should have called my father and told him I couldn't work with Jax anymore.

As I'm considering the viability of that option, Jax's distinctive Hennessey Goliath pulls up at the curb. His window is rolled down and his tattooed forearm rests on the door because he has the sleeves of his dress shirt rolled up. I mean why are rolled up shirt sleeves so freaking hot?

"Good morning," he says with a slow, sexy smile. I can't see his eyes because he's wearing his aviators, but he appears his usual calm and collected self and it annoys the hell out of me. Does he have no nerves at all? Did what we did mean nothing to him?

I plaster on the biggest, fakest smile I can muster. "Morning, cowboy." I flutter my eyelashes and walk to the other side of the truck, making sure that I give my ass an extra wiggle as I do. Cowboy though? What the hell, Lucia? Since when do you call him cowboy? God, I want to die.

With a racing heart and trembling hands, I open the passenger door and climb inside.

"I thought we could do something a little more interesting today," he says as soon as I have my seatbelt on.

"Oh, what's that?"

"You're going to learn how to fight." He arches an eyebrow at me.

"I can fight," I insist. "Hugo taught me."

"I'm not talking about self-defense. I mean, real dirty, no holds barred fighting," he replies with a chuckle.

"I'm not exactly dressed for fighting, Jax," I look down at my pencil skirt and shirt.

"Don't worry. Toni will have some clothes at the gym for you."

"Toni?" I frown at him.

"Well, I'm sure as hell not fighting you, Lucia," he laughs again. "Toni is an MMA champ and she knows every dirty trick in the book, too. A few one-on-one sessions with her and you'll be able to take down any asshole anywhere."

"Does that include you?" I ask with a sarcastic smile.

"Even me," he replies, ignoring the barb.

He turns up the radio and we don't speak for the remainder of the drive to the gym. I stare out of the window, wondering if I made a huge mistake two nights earlier. How can Jax just sit there and pretend like nothing happened between us? I know he said it was a one night only deal, but how does he just turn his feelings on and off like that? What we did had to have meant something to him, right? I mean it was incredible.

I glance at him and he remains focused on the road ahead. There is nothing in his demeanor to suggest that anything at all has changed between us. But what the hell did I expect? This is Jackson Decker. Women are expendable to him. That was just his regular Friday night, while for me it was the best night of my life.

I blink back the tears and take a deep breath. I will not think about him or that night for one more second of my life. He is a complete and utter jackass and he is not worth even the tiniest sliver of my heart.

B y the time we pull up at the gym I've managed to convince myself that I can do this. I can have sex with someone and then pretend that it meant nothing. I have to learn to be a woman in a man's world, right?

I climb out of the car and follow Jax down an alleyway until we reach a brown nondescript door. It certainly doesn't look like any gym I've ever been in before. He opens it and steps inside, beckoning me to follow him. As soon as we're inside the room the smell of leather, sweat and disinfectant hits me. I look around the windowless space which has a huge boxing ring in the center and various punch bags and equipment dotted around the side.

"Decker!" a voice calls out from nearby and I look around to see a guy with the biggest muscles I have ever seen walking toward us. He is only wearing shorts, revealing a torso absolutely covered in ink—I don't think he has a spare inch of skin that isn't tattooed. It covers his rippling abs as well as his chest and shoulders.

"Benji," Jax replies. "It's good to see you, man."

"Good to see you, buddy," Benji replies and I recognize the same Southern accent that Jax sometimes has, although living in LA for the past twenty years has changed his slightly.

"This is Lucia," Jax says and smiles at me.

"Ah, Lucia," Benji extends his hand and I take it. It's huge and it dwarfs mine as he shakes it gently. "You look just like your father." He narrows his eyes at me, no doubt wondering how that is possible.

"I get that a lot," I say with a smile. Although he is my adopted father, he's actually my biological cousin. Our fathers were brothers and we do actually look alike.

"Where is she?" Jax asks, looking behind Benji.

"Protein shake," Benji flashes his eyebrows and Jax laughs softly but a few seconds later a tall blonde woman, with the most incredibly toned stomach I have ever seen in my life walks out from the back room.

"Hey, handsome," she says to Jax as she reaches us and then wraps her arms around him.

"Hey," he replies and at least he has the good grace to appear slightly awkward as he stands there hugging her.

"And this must be Lucia," she says when she finally lets him go. She turns to me and smiles and I notice her eyes are the most beautiful shade of blue I have ever seen. She is absolutely stunning.

"Yes. Lucia, this is Toni," Jax replies while I stand there staring at her, wondering if he's had sex with her too.

She smiles at me. "Jax has told me all about you. I can't wait to teach you some moves."

I want to like her. I really do. I mean it's not her fault she's beautiful and tough and that Jax is looking at her like that, is it? "Can't wait," I say with a forced smile.

"If you head into the back, there are some things for to change into. They're all new, don't worry," she says with a wink.

"Thanks," I force another smile before I leave the three of them talking like old friends. When I walk into the changing room, there is a pair of sweatpants, a sports bra and some sneakers waiting for me. They are pink and grey, two of my favorite colors and I wonder if that's coincidence or they were chosen specifically. No! That would require Jax to actually know that and for him to tell her my favorite colors. Why do I assume that he thinks about me as much as I think about him?

When I'm changed, I go back out into the gym to find Toni in the ring and Jax and Benji sitting on the bench beside it.

"Come on up," Toni signals to me.

I look to Jax. So, he's just going to sit there and watch his MMA champion girlfriend beat the crap out of me, is that it? He nods his head to the ring, indicating I should do as she says. I roll my eyes and climb in.

"Jax says you know a little boxing and Krav Maga?" Toni asks.

I shrug. "A little."

"Let's see what you got then, princess." She arches an eyebrow at me and I'm filled with a burning desire to punch her in the face.

She edges closer to me, her guard up as she bounces on her toes. I stand there staring at her. I'm about to get my ass kicked here. And for what? So Jax can teach me a lesson? Put me in my place and remind me that this is the kind of woman he usually fucks?

"I don't want to do this," I say, turning around and walking to the ropes.

Jax is up off his seat. "Lucia!" he growls quietly. "Toni and Benji have given up their entire day to do this."

"I don't care. I never asked them to," I hiss.

"You want to work with me and your father?" He narrows his eyes at me. "Then you need to learn to take care of yourself. Now stop acting like a spoiled brat and get your ass back over there."

I glare at him. I hate it when he calls me a spoiled brat. I hate him. I hate Toni and her perfect everything. I want to go home.

But I stand straight and roll my shoulders back. I am Lucia fucking Montoya. I am my father's daughter and I will never back down from a fight.

I turn back to Toni and raise my guard. "Let's see what you got, bitch."

She laughs and flashes her eyebrows at me.

"There's my little wildcat," Jax says as he takes a seat.

"Don't worry, I won't mark that pretty face." Toni winks at me.

I edge toward her, trying to remember everything that Hugo taught me. Keep my guard up. Get a feel for your opponent. Toni strikes first, catching me with a light tap to the side of my head. I shake it off and move forward. When her lightning fast left arm darts out again, I manage to duck it, but she catches me with a right instead.

"Come on, princess, show me what you're really made of," Toni taunts me. "Jax doesn't usually bring me such weak-ass opponents."

Bitch! I lunge for her but she dodges me easily and laughs while she does it.

"Hmm. Pushed a button there, have I?" she says quietly.

"Fuck you!" I hiss.

"Oh, there we go. Use that anger, princess. Come on, hit me."

I go for her again, managing to graze her this time but making no real impact.

She hits me again, this time it stings a little and I snarl at her.

"Come on, princess, you know you want to hit me," she snarls. "Stop all of this dancing around."

I aim a half-hearted punch at her head but she dodges it, grabs my arm and twists me around, wrapping her free arm around my neck until I'm completely subdued.

"You think that people will fight you nicely because of your daddy, princess?" she whispers in my ear. "They won't—in fact they'll make it hurt even more because of who he is." She twists my arm even more and I wince in pain. "They won't play nice, so why are you?"

She pushes me away and I stumble to the floor.

"Get up," she snarls at me. "Get the fuck up and fight me, princess."

"No," I shake my head. I've had enough. I don't have to do this. "I'm done."

"Done?" she laughs. "You haven't even started."

I push myself up and glare at her and she walks toward me. She glances at Jax before she turns back to me. "Is this about him? Don't think you're special, sweetheart—he fucks every woman he meets." She winks at me and anger surges through my chest. I jump on her, my nails clawing at her neck. She throws me off and stands before putting her guard up again. "There you are." She grins at me. "Let's do this."

I act on instinct, forgetting that Jax and Benji are watching, forgetting that she is a woman who Jax has obviously fucked. This isn't about any of them. This is about me proving that I am good enough. That I am worthy enough. She is a freaking MMA champion for fuck's sake. There is no glory for her being able to beat me up, but there is plenty of glory for me when I knock her on her ass, because I will.

For the next twenty minutes we fight. My lip is bleeding but so is her eye where I caught her with a right hook. She has put me on my ass at least half a dozen times but each time I have got back up and held my ground. At one point we were rolling around the canvas and I managed to pin her until she threw me off.

Every muscle in my body is aching but I won't give up until her ass is on that mat.

"Come on, princess. Jax is watching," she snarls and I lose my shit, bringing my arm back and hitting her with everything I have left. My right hook connects with her jaw and she staggers backward before she stumbles and falls flat on her ass.

I stare down at her, smiling, as I wipe the sweat from my eyes. I vaguely hear Jax cheering from the sidelines but I don't care.

That was for me. I feel like I just won the heavyweight title as I stand there looking at her sprawled on the canvas. I raise my guard though, expecting her to bounce back up and knock me out, but she smiles at me and I blink in shock.

She pushes herself up holds her hands up in surrender. I drop my guard and she wraps an arm around my shoulder. "You did good," she whispers.

"I did?" I blink at her.

"You know how many people have ever knocked me on my ass?" she laughs. "Not many. A few more sessions with me and you'll be able to hold your own with anyone."

I look up at her. "But..." I stammer and she laughs. "You called me princess. You were horrible to me."

She puts her hands on her hips. "You know how many people I train like this?"

"No."

"None. Zero. But when your father asked me to do this—"

"My father?"

"Yes." She nods. "I wouldn't waste my own, or your, time by taking it easy on you, Lucia. No one out there is ever going to take it easy on you. You want to learn to fight then I'll teach you, but I won't hold back, and I'll say anything I need to say to push you. So maybe next week, you come ready for a fight and I won't have to tease you so much." She nudges me playfully before she walks away and climbs out of the ring. "Someone see to that cut before Alana sees it and kicks my ass."

I climb through the ropes and Jax walks toward me. "Let's get that cut looked at," he says as he puts a hand on my shoulder.

I shrug him off and lick the blood on my lip. "I'm fine."

"I got some iodine in my office," Benji offers. "You don't want it to get infected now, do you? No one will want to kiss those pretty lips if they're oozing green pus."

I can't help laughing at the face he pulls when he says that.

"Okay. Thanks," I say and follow him to his office.

I shower and change back into my regular clothes before I leave the gym. Toni is sparring with Benji and they both stop to say goodbye to me as I leave.

"Thank you, both," I say, aware I wasn't exactly pleasant when I first got here.

"My pleasure, princess," Toni replies with a wink. "Can't wait for next week."

"Take care of that lip," Benji adds.

Jax is leaning against his truck waiting for me when I get outside.

"You did good in there, Rocky," he says with a smile.

I ignore him and start to walk around to the passenger door

but he steps out and stops me in my tracks. "Lucia!" he frowns at me.

"Please get out of my way," I snap as I glare at him.

"I will when you tell me why you're so pissed at me."

"You don't know?" I shake my head in disbelief.

His Adam's apple bobs in his throat as he swallows.

"You enjoy watching your girlfriend beat me up in there, did you?"

"What?" He narrows his eyes at me.

"You heard me."

"Well, I assume I misheard you because she is not my girl-friend and you honestly think I enjoy watching you get hurt?"

"You seemed pretty happy in there when I was getting my ass handed to me," I snarl.

He takes a deep breath in through his nose and then he steps out of my way. "Just get in the truck," he snaps.

"Maybe I'll just walk."

"You're going to walk ten miles to get home?" He arches an eyebrow at me.

"It's preferable to spending time with you."

He grabs hold of my arm as I go to walk away, pulling my body close to his. "Get in the fucking truck. Now!" he hisses.

"I can't do this, Jax," I shake my head. "I can't pretend like what we did never happened."

He runs a hand through his hair and sighs. "I'm sorry, Luce. I shouldn't have—"

"Shouldn't have what?" I glare at him. "Brought me here?"

"No. Toni's methods might be unconventional but she's the best."

"She insinuated that you and she..." I don't finish the sentence.

"I told you that she fought dirty."

"So you haven't?"

"No. She's not my type and I'm definitely not hers. You're much more her style."

"Oh." I blush remembering the fire in her eyes when I was straddling her earlier.

"Friday night shouldn't have happened though, Luce. I'm sorry," he whispers, taking a step closer to me until his breath dusts my cheek.

"Do you regret it, Jax?" I blink at him.

He brushes the hair back from my face. "Yes."

The word is like a sliver of ice slicing through my heart. I step back from him, pulling out of his embrace. "Oh."

"Luce."

"We'd better get going," I say, tossing my hair over my shoulder as I walk around the truck to the passenger side. Jackson Decker can go to hell.

CHAPTER 16

JAX

I stifle a yawn as Alejandro drives us through the streets of LA. It's two a.m. and I've already done a full day's work with Lucia but we needed to collect on a debt that he was owed and this is the kind of business I much prefer. It's been a long time since we've handled something so trivial ourselves, but sometimes one of us needs to blow off some steam and beating up people who have fucked him over is a good way to do it. Tonight, it was him who called me, but I can't deny that I've been feeling a lot of pent up frustration myself these past few days.

"I forgot to ask, how did Lucia do today?" he breaks the silence.

"With Toni?"

"Yeah."

"She was great," I reply, rubbing a hand over my jaw. Fuck, she was better than great. She was incredible. She is always incredible and I am going to burn in hell for all eternity for the things I think about doing to her—and for the things I've already done. And now all I can see is her face when I told her I regretted what we did a few nights ago. I should have told her the truth, which is that I don't regret a single fucking second of it, but how do I do that to her? Isn't it kinder to let her hate me and move on? I have nothing to offer her and she deserves everything. "She knocked Toni on her ass," I add.

"What?" Alejandro laughs out loud. "My girl knocked Toni Moretti on her ass?"

No, my girl knocked Toni Moretti on her ass. "She sure did."

"She's something special, isn't she?" he says, his face full of pride and I feel a fresh wave of guilt washing over me. What the fuck have I done?

I don't have a chance to answer him because his car is filled with the sound of his cell phone ringing and Lucia's smiling face appears on the screen on the dash of his car.

"Speak of the devil," he says as he frowns at the screen. What the hell is she doing calling at this time of night?

"Hey, *mija*," he says when he presses the button to answer.

"Papi!" Her voice trembles and my heart almost stops beating. "I'm sorry it's so late."

"It's never too late for you to call me. What's wrong?" He glances sideways at me, the worry on his face matching mine.

"Somebody just tried to get into the apartment." She sucks in a breath as though she's desperately trying to hold it together. "They picked the lock. The only reason I heard them was because I was up late reading."

"Where are you now? Are you and Matthias safe?"

"Yes, we're okay. Whoever it was has gone and Mr. and Mrs. Cates from next door are here with me. They wanted to call the cops, but I—"

"We'll be right there, *mija*. I'm five minutes away. Okay?"

"Okay."

He ends the call and then curses in Spanish. "I knew I should have made her stay at the house until she found a proper place to live," he snarls.

"She needed her independence, amigo," I remind him.

"What if someone had got to her, Jax? To both of them?" he whispers and I recognize the fear in his voice because it's the same fear I feel in my bones. The thought of anything happening to her and Matthias makes me feel like I can't breathe.

Alejandro drives to Lucia's apartment as fast as his old Mustang will take us, cursing the fact that he's not driving his Bugatti. As soon as he screeches to a stop outside her apartment building, we jump out of the car and to the door as her neighbor buzzes us in. I have never taken stairs so fast in my life as I do running up to the fourth floor where her apartment is. Her door is open and her neighbors Mr. and Mrs. Cates are waiting in the hallway. Alejandro nods to them in greeting and appreciation but rushes past them. As soon as she sees him, she falls into his arms, as though she's been holding everything together until he got there.

"Papi," she breathes and he hugs her, smoothing her hair.

"It's okay, *mija*. We're here now."

"Thank you for everything," I tell her neighbors. "We can take it from here."

"If there's anything she needs at all..." Mrs. Cates says, worry etched on her face. "We should call the police."

"Mr. Montoya is handling it, dear," Mr. Cates says as he puts a reassuring arm around his wife's shoulder.

As soon as they're gone, I inspect the front door. There is clear damage to the lock where someone has tried to pick it, but none to the rest of the door. I close it behind me and walk inside. Alejandro looks at me over Lucia's shoulder, a frown on his face.

"The lock's still working but we'll get it replaced obviously just to be sure. No other damage to the door. I'll get the security footage from the building and I'll check the feeds from anywhere else around her that might help us."

He nods his agreement and then he turns back to her. "What happened to your face?"

She brushes her fingertips over the cut on her lip. "That was just Toni."

"Oh, yeah. Jax told me you were great," he says proudly.

"He did?" She glances at me but I don't meet her eyes.

"Yeah," he says but then seems to remember why we're here. "Now you're coming home with me."

"No. Matthias is asleep. He doesn't even know anything happened. I'm okay now. I overreacted. I just got so scared. I heard him breathing at the door, Papi." She shudders. "But he was probably just looking for something to steal. If you could just check around outside and downstairs, then I'll be fine."

"But what if he wasn't just looking for something to steal?" I ask.

Alejandro shoots me a warning look but Lucia is a grown woman and this is the reality of our world. We have many enemies.

"You think he targeted me?" she whispers.

"It's a possibility," Alejandro agrees but we both know it is way more than a possibility.

"Has anything else strange happened?" he asks her.

"Like what?" she shrugs.

"Anything weird or unusual. Meet anyone new?" I ask.

She scowls at me.

"No. I haven't met anyone new." She folds her arms over her chest.

"Have you upset anybody? Rejected someone's advances?" I probe further.

"No." She shakes her head but then her expression changes.

"What?" Alejandro snaps.

"There's this guy on a social media app. He keeps messaging me and I keep blocking him—"

"Lucia! What have I warned you about social media?" Alejandro barks.

"It's one app, Papi. I don't put any personal information on there. There are billons of users on it. It's probably just some creep."

Alejandro glares at me and I nod my understanding. "I'll look into it. I'll need all of your passwords, Lucia."

"Okay," she swallows.

Alejandro rolls his eyes in frustration. "Right, well if you won't come home tonight, I'll stay here."

"No," she shakes her head. "Mom will be worried about you. Nobody is going to come back here tonight. I'll be fine."

He stares at her—Lucia is right that Alana will worry if he stays out all night—then he looks at me. *Fuck!* "Okay. Then Jax will stay, right?"

"No," she snaps. "I'm fine, Papi. I'm sorry I called you."

"Hey." He takes her face in his hands. "I am your father. You always call me. No matter what. You got that?"

"Yes."

"Jax. Can you stay here?" he asks me again.

She glares at me, but how do I say no to him? Then I would have to explain why I don't trust myself to be alone all night with his daughter. Except that we won't be alone. Matthias is here. Thank fuck!

"Of course I will," I say, because what choice do I have? Besides, I don't want her here alone any more than he does.

"Fine," she snarls but then smiles sweetly at her father. "Thank you, Papi."

He wraps her in a hug. "I'll check outside before I leave. Jax will look after you until the morning and then we're going to discuss your living arrangements."

"But—" she starts but then closes her mouth again. She can

wrap him around her finger about most things, but when it comes to her and Matthias' safety, he will stand his ground.

"Goodnight, *mija*."

I walk him into the hallway. "Thank you for this," he says.

"Any time, amigo."

"I don't know what I'd do without you." He gives me a quick hug and another wave of guilt slams into me. "You're the only man I would trust to protect her like I would."

Fuck!

"I would do anything for you and your family. You know that," I say.

"Because we're your family too, right?" He frowns at me.

"Yeah," I nod because that's true. No matter what happened between Lucia and me, they are my family.

After Alejandro has gone, Lucia hands me some spare blankets and a pillow. "The couch isn't all that comfortable actually. You can take my bed if you'd prefer?" she offers and I almost choke on my breath.

"I won't be in it, Jax," she says with a roll of her eyes. "I could sleep with Matthias."

"The couch will do fine," I tell her. The thought of sleeping in her bed, surrounded by her smell and her warmth while I wonder at what she might do in it when she's alone, or even worse when she's not, is too much.

"Fine," she snaps and turns on her heel but before she reaches the hallway she turns to me. "Thank you," she whispers and I hear a crack in her voice that makes me walk over to her. And against all of my better judgement, I wrap her in my arms.

"It's okay, Luce," I breathe against her hair. "I'm always here for you. Nothing will ever change that."

She nods against my chest. "I know, Jax."

My cock twitches at the way she says my name and the feeling of her soft body in my arms. I could pick her up and carry her to bed right now. I could bury myself inside her until both of us felt better. But that would make me an even bigger asshole than I already am.

So instead I kiss the top of her head and let her go. "Night, Luce."

"Night, Jax."

I lie on Lucia's sofa, listening to the soft ticking of a clock somewhere. I'm so tired but I can't sleep. I keep picturing her lying in bed. Alone. Half-naked? Is she still upset? What if she needs me?

She doesn't!

But what if I need her? What if the throbbing in my cock can only be fixed by burying myself in her hot, tight cunt and making her whimper my name as her walls squeeze me tighter? The memory of her soft skin, the way she squirmed when I kissed her all over, the way she looked up at me when I made her come, the taste of her sweet pussy—I can't get any of it out of my head. I will my cock to stop twitching. I can't even give myself any relief because the idea of her or Matthias walking in here and catching me jerking off is unthinkable. So I close my eyes and try to think of anything but her.

The sound of high pitched shrieking pierces my ears followed by a tiny human ball of energy jumping on my head.

"Matthias," Lucia warns him. "Please be careful."

"Jax," the kid shouts, unable to contain his excitement. "You had a sleepover."

I blink in the sunlight. I must have fallen asleep after all.

"Hey, buddy. I sure did," I push myself up and pull him onto my chest, tickling him and making him squirm and giggle hysterically.

"I'm sorry," Lucia mouths.

"No problem at all," I reply with a wink. I mean, I love this kid. "Any chance of some coffee?"

"Sure." She ruffles Matthias' hair. "Don't wear out your Uncle Jax, munchkin," she says before she disappears out of sight.

"Why didn't you wake me up when you got here?" Matthias says when he's finally stopped giggling.

"It was very late and you were sound asleep," I tell him.

"You should have come got me. You could have stayed in my room." He grins at me.

"I could have, huh?"

"Yeah. Next time you sleep over will you stay in my room with me?"

"Sure, buddy," I smile at him, but all my deviant brain is thinking about is how much I'd love another sleepover with his mom.

CHAPTER 17

LUCIA

My father called me first thing this morning to tell me he wants to meet to discuss my living situation. If I'm honest, last night did freak me out a little, but that doesn't mean I'm ready to move back home. I love my apartment and I don't want to live anywhere else. It's so close to Matthias' school and we've made friends with our lovely neighbors, but I know that my father isn't going to let this go without a fight. Perhaps there is something we can do to at least make my apartment more secure—something that doesn't involve Jackson Decker sleeping on my sofa every night.

I mean there was a time that would have been like a dream come true, but now it just reminds me that I can never have him. I hardly slept at all thinking about him lying out there, remembering the miracles he can perform with his tongue.

I feel a blush creep over my cheeks and I focus on the road ahead as I drive to my father's hotel with Jax sitting beside me.

"So, tell me more about this asshole who's been stalking you," he says, breaking the silence.

"I never said he was stalking me," I say with a roll of my eyes.

"He just sent me a bunch of messages. Weird guys do that kind of shit all the time. Women are constantly fending off dick pics."

"Okay." His eyes narrow. "So what makes this guy different then? Why did you mention him and no one else?"

I frown. Why is he any different from the other fishing messages I get on a regular basis? "Because he is persistent. No matter how many times I block him, he creates a new account and messages again."

"Like a stalker." He arches an eyebrow at me.

"Semantics," I mutter under my breath.

"How do you know it's the same guy?" His brow is furrowed as he glares at me but I know this is Jax's process. I can almost see the cogs in his brain working.

"Because he always calls me chica and he always signs off with the same thing."

"Which is?"

"Your one and only." I shake my head because saying that out loud makes me cringe.

"Some guy you've slept with then, who maybe thinks he was the only guy?" he asks. Heat creeps over my chest and neck at the question, but Jax is working and this is business now.

"I don't see how that's possible. I mean there have only been five guys my whole life. Two of them are dead. The other two were guys from college who knew I had a child and the other one..." I swallow. Well, he's sitting here in my car grilling me about my sex life.

"Why does he call you chica? He knows your parents were Spanish?" he frowns at me.

"My user name is Chica21," I say.

"That's not exactly anonymous Lucia?" he scowls at me now.

"Oh come on!" I shake my head.

"Can I have your phone?"

"Why?" I whisper.

"So I can look at the accounts. I'll start a trace later but right now I just want to have a look."

I hesitate. There is so much personal stuff on that phone. Messages to Archer about my night with him last week. Oh, God. What if he sees them?

"I won't look at anything except them. I swear," he says, sensing my hesitation.

"Fine. You know where it is," I say with a shake of my head.

He pulls it from the center console and puts in my passcode.

"How do you know that?" I frown at him.

He frowns right back. "Because I set it up for you." He frowns right back.

"Oh, yeah. Of course. I could have changed the passcode for all you knew though," I add.

"But you didn't." He holds up the phone as evidence.

"You think he's going to make me move home?" I ask quietly.

"He'll certainly try."

"I don't want to, Jax. I love my parents, but I love my independence, too."

"I know," he replies with a nod, because he gets it. He's lived alone since his mom died when he was seventeen.

"Will you back me up?" I whisper.

"Luce," he sighs. "Don't ask me to come between you and your father."

"I'm not. I'm just asking for you to be the voice of reason when he starts foaming at the mouth. Because you know he will."

The faintest smile plays on his lips. "If he gets completely loco, I'll help you talk him down."

"Thank you." I smile.

· · ·

By the time we reach my father's office half an hour later, he's pacing the floor waiting for us.

"Papi," I say as walk into the room.

"Mija," he pulls me into a hug.

"Hey amigo," Jax says as he takes a seat.

My father simply nods in greeting, his attention focused on me. "I've spoken to your mama, and we both want you to come home—"

I shake my head. "No."

"At least until we can find out who tried to get into your place last night and Jax can find out who this creep is who's sending you messages."

"That could take months!" I reply.

"Hey!" Jax interrupts us. "When has finding some asshole online ever taken me that long?"

"That app has billions of users, Jax." I frown at him; he's supposed to be on my side.

"So?" he scowls and I realize I have insulted him, because he is the best at what he does. I have no doubt he could hack into the White House if he wanted to.

"I don't want to uproot mine and Matthias' life, Papi." I turn back to him.

"And I'm not asking you to, *mija*. All I'm asking is that you stay with us for a few weeks until we figure out who was behind this."

I look between him and Jax.

"Think of it like a vacation. The boys are going to be thrilled to have you and Matthias around."

There he goes, playing his trump card. He knows I would die for those boys.

"Two weeks, Papi," I agree because I know I'm not going to

win this argument, and also because last night, along with all the talk of stalkers in the car with Jax, has me spooked.

"Perfect!" He winks at me. "I'll have someone move your stuff."

"No," I shake my head. He will have my entire apartment moved in the blink of any eye. "I'll get our stuff together. This is just a vacation, right?"

"Okay. I'll get someone to help you."

"Fine."

He stares at me and I sense he has something else on his mind. "I do have one more condition."

"What?"

"Jax is going to be busy on this for the next week or so." He looks at Jax who nods his understanding, but I don't know where this is going yet. I do know that the thought of not spending every day with Jax makes me feel like my heart has been ripped from my chest. It feels like a punishment, even though my father cannot possibly know that. "So, while you're not working with him, you'll need a bodyguard."

"Papi!"

"Yes, Lucia. This is non negotiable."

"So moving back home was?"

"Yes, but you've agreed to that now, so—" He shrugs and grins at me.

"Why do I feel like I've just been completely played?"

Jax laughs softly. "You know better than to give in to his initial demands, because there's always more."

"How could I forget?"

"Hey!" My father laughs too. "Is it so bad to live with your parents and be spoiled for a few weeks? And to have a father who worries about you so much?"

"No." I roll my eyes because he speaks the truth.

"Why don't you go get your stuff now and take it home? Your

mama is working from home today and then you can surprise Matthias when you pick him up from kindergarten later."

"But what about work?"

"Jax is going to be busy today and I have nothing for you to do, *mija*. Just take a day off."

"Okay," I agree because this is another argument I'm not going to win.

"Take my car. Raoul is downstairs."

"Raoul?" I arch an eyebrow at him. Raoul is one of my father's most highly trained men. A skilled assassin, but he barely speaks.

"I told you you'd be having a bodyguard, *mija*."

"But Raoul though?" I pout and I see Jax chuckling to himself from the corner of my eye.

"He's the best," he replies with a shrug.

"He's mute," I reply.

"He's not there for conversation, Lucia. He's there to stop a bullet from entering your body or some psychopath from running away with you."

"You're so dramatic," I sigh and then I kiss him on the cheek. "I'll see you later then."

"Bye, *mija*."

"Bye, Lucia," Jax adds.

I give him a faint smile and a wave of my hand. Why does it feel like I'll never see him again? That's ridiculous, right? I'll still see him all the time. So, why does my heart ache like this, just because we're not working together for a while?

I take the elevator down to the lobby and see Raoul waiting in the huge black sedan. It's the armored one and it makes me wonder if there is something else going on that I should know about. Upon seeing me, Raoul jumps out and opens the door for me.

"Thank you," I smile.

He nods and grunts in response.

"I see you'll be my babysitter for the foreseeable future," I say once we're both seated and he pulls the car away from the curbside.

Nothing. Not even the hint of a smile.

I miss Jax already.

CHAPTER 18

JAX

I stare out of the huge floor-to-ceiling windows of Alejandro's office. Lucia left an hour ago. I've started a trace on the IP address of the last account to message her on that stupid social media app and now Alejandro and I are going to speak to some people about the attempted break in at her place last night. I know she's safe. Raoul is one of the best, but I would still feel better if she were with me.

"You ready, amigo?" Alejandro asks as he ends the call he was on.

"Yeah," I reply as I turn back to face him as his cell starts to ring again.

He rolls his eyes but when he sees the name on the screen he frowns.

"Raoul?" he says when he answers.

I can't hear the other part of the conversation and all I can do is watch as the expression on his face tells me that something is seriously wrong. I stare at Alejandro, willing him to hurry the fuck up so he can tell me that she's okay.

"Where are they taking her? We'll be there as soon as we can," he says and then he ends the call.

"What is it?" The words catch in my throat. I've never been a man of God but I say a quick prayer to him anyway. If he'd just let her be okay, then—

He blinks at me. "It's Lucia."

Yeah, I got that. "What about her?" I snap as my heart hammers in my chest.

"Someone tried to run the car off the road. They're taking her to the hospital."

I suck in a breath as the blood rushes in my ears. "Is she okay?"

Time stands still as I wait for him to answer.

"Yeah." Finally he nods and I breathe again. "Raoul managed to keep the car on the road but he hit a stop sign. He said she's a little banged up but fine."

"Fuck!" I run a hand over my face.

"Someone just tried to kill my daughter, Jax!" he snarls now, as though the reality of what he just heard is sinking in.

"I know," I nod, but right now I have an overwhelming need to get to her and check over every inch of her body. "Let's go see her and find out what happened and then we can decide what to do next, okay?"

"Yeah," he nods at me. "Let's go."

CHAPTER 19

JAX

Alejandro makes several calls while I drive us to the hospital, jumping at least two red lights and committing every traffic violation there is to get us there as fast as possible. First he called Alana, who was only around the corner with Hugo. She is sitting beside Lucia's bed when we arrive, holding her daughter's hand, but the two of them are deep in conversation about something and they are smiling.

The relief at seeing her sitting there, safe and relatively unharmed, almost knocks me off my feet. I have to stop myself from going straight over to her and checking her over myself. I want to run my hands over every inch of her skin to check for scratches or broken bones then wrap her in my arms. I imagine the looks on her parents' faces if I did that, and so I hang back, standing awkwardly with my hands stuffed in my pockets because I feel kind of out of place here. I'm family but not quite. I have no right to touch her like that but that doesn't stop a memory of my hands and my mouth on her skin from popping into my brain and making my cock twitch in my pants. *Not now, Jax!*

Raoul is sitting in the corner, stony faced as usual, and you can hardly tell he was just in a car accident. Alejandro walks straight to his wife and daughter, hugging and kissing each of them in turn before he turns to Raoul.

"What the fuck happened?"

"We were at a crossing. A car jumped the light and hit us. It was headed for us though, Boss. It was a targeted hit."

"Why are you so sure of that?" Alejandro frowns.

"It swerved around two other cars to get to us," Raoul replies matter-of-factly.

"It was only because Raoul acted so quickly that we weren't run off the road," Lucia adds. "He swerved just in time and we missed the worst of the impact."

"Thank you," Alejandro says to Raoul, who simply nods in response.

"Did you see anything? Remember any helpful details?" he asks both Lucia and Raoul.

Lucia shakes her head but Raoul speaks, reeling off the information he has for us. "A silver Dodge pickup. California plates but they may have been stolen. Driver had a black cap on. That's all I got."

"We can check security and traffic footage. I'll speak to the LAPD and see if they got anything," I add.

"Yeah," Alejandro says absent-mindedly.

"Do you need me for anything else, Boss?" Raoul asks as he stands. "I can wait outside."

"Can you accompany Hugo when he takes the girls home shortly?" he asks.

"Of course." Raoul nods, then excuses himself.

"I can't go back to the house now," Lucia says. "What if I put Mom or the boys in danger?"

"Lucia!" Alana frowns at her.

"You won't." Alejandro frowns at her too. "There is nowhere safer for you than the house."

"No." She shakes her head. "What if something happened to one of you because of me?"

"Lucia. This is not up for discussion!" Alejandro barks.

"What if they're just waiting, Papi? What if next time Matthias is with me?"

She looks up at him and it's then that I see she is terrified. I mean that's completely understandable but I have never seen her like this before. The instinct to protect her is so overwhelming that I have to force myself not to speak and suggest that I become her personal twenty-four seven bodyguard and take her far away from the danger that is here in LA.

"I can't just hide out in your mansion. I'll go crazy," she adds.

Alejandro rubs a hand over his jaw and then he looks at me. "Any ideas?"

Fuck! "What if I got Lucia and Matthias out of the city until you can figure out who was behind this?"

His eyes light up and I feel as guilty as fuck for suggesting this. But I am just trying to protect her. I mean that's what I keep telling myself anyway. And it's not like we're going to be alone. Matthias will be with us, not to mention my family.

"I think it's perfect. I mean if they're not with me, Jax, then the safest place is with you. Nobody outside of this room knows about the ranch, do they?"

"No." I shake my head. Ten years ago I bought the ranch I was raised on until the age of thirteen, but it's all in my aunt's name. Even the people working there believe it's her place and I just visit once in a while.

"You think you could protect them there?" he asks.

"Yes." If there is one place on this earth I could keep them safe it's the ranch.

"So Jax is going to take Lucia and Matthias to Texas?" Alana asks with a frown.

"Yes," Alejandro nods. "Until I can find out who is targeting

Lucia and why. Nobody will know who she is there and nobody but us will know where they are."

"Lucia, what do you think?" Alana asks but Lucia just sits staring at her parents, still in a state of shock—or maybe she is wondering why the hell I just suggested taking her and her son away from everything they know.

"Are you sure about this, amigo?" Alejandro asks me, ignoring the fact that Lucia hasn't answered her mom yet. His brow is furrowed and his eyes are full of concern as he waits for me to speak. I glance at Lucia. Her cheeks are pale and her eyes red. I have never seen her looking so vulnerable and fragile, and it breaks me.

I'm doing this to protect her though. Surely I can be alone with her for a few days until Alejandro finds out who was behind this? I have some self-control, don't I?

"As long as it's okay with Lucia," I say. There's no way she's going to accept this anyway—I'm definitely not her favorite person right now—but to my surprise she nods.

"Yes" she whispers, and I wonder if she would agree to anything right now because not only is she terrified for herself, but for Matthias too.

"I'll need all of your focus on them," Alejandro runs a hand over his jaw. "But I got no one who knows this tech shit as well as you do."

"Then we ask the second-best hacker we know?" I suggest.

"Jessie Ryan?"

"Yep. I'll call Shane and get her the information she needs." Shane and his brothers are friends of ours and I looked into Jessie for them a few years earlier and discovered she was the best hacker I've ever come across. We've done some bits of work together since and I know that she's as capable of finding Lucia's online stalker as I am.

"Shall I go and pack you and Matthias some things?" Alana asks Lucia.

"Please, Mom," Lucia says softly.

"I'll ask Hugo and Raoul to take me to your place now," she says before giving Lucia a hug. I know that she will feel better doing something practical and keeping her mind off the fact that someone just tried to kill her daughter.

"Pack some jeans, tanks and sweatshirts," I suggest. "The ranch can get kind of messy." That is true, but the idea of Lucia walking around in nothing but a summer dress with all of the ranch hands hanging around isn't a particularly welcome one.

"Will do," Alana says and before she walks out of the door she shoots me a look that tells me she wants to speak to me. I follow her into the corridor.

"I know you're a professional, Jax, but these are my babies," she says, her words catching in her throat.

I place my hand on her arm. "I know, Alana. You guys are my family too, you know?"

She smiles up at me. "I know."

"I'll protect both of them with my life. I swear."

"I know you will. And if you get them both back safely to me, I'll even forgive you for sending my husband a hooker on our wedding night."

"You know about that?" I feel heat creeping over my neck. I'm never rattled but she just pulled the rug from under me.

"Yes. We don't keep secrets about that kind of stuff." She arches an eyebrow at me.

"Alana! It was... I mean you and him... When you got married..." I stammer, trying to offer a justification but there is none. The truth is their marriage was a business arrangement and was supposed to be nothing more. So Alejandro had spent their wedding night in his hotel, and I had thought it was only right that he didn't spend it alone and had sent him a gift. He turned her down and obviously I regret it now, because I love Alana and she is the best thing that ever happened to my best buddy, but back then it was no big deal. He was never supposed to fall in love with his wife. "I'm sorry," I say eventually because that's all I really can say.

"I know." She smiles at me. "But please take good care of them."

"I will. You have my word."

She leans up onto her tiptoes and kisses my cheek. "Thank you."

CHAPTER 20

LUCIA

As soon as Matthias is settled with his tablet and juice box in the back seat of the rental truck, we set off. The kid was so excited when I told him we were going on a mini vacation with Jax. He threw his arms around Jax's neck and has had a huge smile on his face ever since. He chattered away excitedly all the way to the airport and then during the entire three-hour plane journey. He should be tired out by now but he's still full of energy. His excitement is kind of infectious and it almost made me forget about this morning and last night

But now the feeling of dread and terror in the pit of my stomach is back. Somebody tried to kill me. If it hadn't been for Raoul's quick thinking, they just might have succeeded.

I glance at Matthias again and my heart aches. He's sitting smiling at the cartoons without a care in the world, which is exactly how every four-year-old should feel, but I almost left him without a mother today and the thought of leaving him behind in this world without me is the most terrifying thing I have ever faced. I know he has family who love him. He would be taken care of by my parents, but there is no one on this earth who can love him the way that I can.

A tear runs down my cheek as I think about my own mom. She wasn't perfect, but she tried her best. She was so worn down by her husband that she turned to pills and booze to get through the day, but I felt her love every single day she was alive. I only wish that I could have saved her. I swat the tear from my cheek before Jax sees it, but it's too late.

His fingertips brush my cheek too.

"It'll be okay, Luce," he says softly. "I won't let anyone hurt either of you."

I turn and look at him. He is a good man. He cares for me and Matthias in his own way. I know that, but it's not enough. It will never be enough.

"I know." I sniff. *Get a grip, Lucia!* "It's just been a weird day, that's all. I'm fine."

"You don't have to pretend to be fine, Luce," he frowns at me. "You were almost—" he doesn't finish that sentence because of Matthias, but he doesn't need to.

"I'm fine," I snap at him. Being mad at him is so much easier than facing up to the truth right now. I can't keep letting him rescue me. I can't keep relying on him because one day he is not going to be there and it will break me. I should never have agreed to this, but it seemed like the best way to keep me and my son safe.

"We'll be at the ranch in time for supper," he says as he leans back in his seat.

"Okay."

"You'll like it there. You both will."

"Yeah," I mumble as I stare out of the window, wondering how long it will be before I can go home and get on with my life.

.   .   .

After an hour's driving we turn down a dirt road.

"Are we there yet?" Matthias pipes up from the back seat.

"Almost, buddy," Jax replies. "You see that huge house up ahead?"

My son leans forward, craning his neck to see out of the front window. "Yeah."

"That's it."

"Wow! Did you grow up here?"

"Sure did."

I look at the impressive house as it comes into view. It's beautiful and the surrounding land is vast. It seems so peaceful and serene. "How do you ever leave this place?" I ask him we drive through the gates.

"I have plenty to go back to LA for," he says with a shrug.

When the truck rolls to a stop outside the house, the screen door opens and a woman comes rushing out. She looks to be in her late-forties and has dark blonde hair tied up in a bun, tanned skin and a huge smile. Jax climbs out of the truck and she runs to him.

"Jackson," she says, throwing her arms around him.

"Who is that, Momma?" Matthias asks.

"Let's go find out," I say and the two of us climb out of the truck.

As she sees us, the woman steps back from Jax and walks toward Matthias and me. "You must be Lucia and Matthias?"

I don't even have time to answer before she pulls me into a hug too. She smells of sandalwood and fresh air and there is something comforting about her. I like her already.

"This is Aunt Molly," Jax says as he shakes his head. "As you can see, she doesn't get many visitors here."

"Oh, Jackson," Molly says dismissively.

"It's a pleasure to meet you," I smile. "Thank you so much for having us."

"The pleasure is all mine, sweetheart," she says before she crouches down to Matthias. "Do you like blueberry pie?"

Matthias grins at her. "I like any pie."

"Then come with me. I made some special, just for you." She holds out her hand to him and he looks up at me seeking permission to go off with this stranger.

"Go on, munchkin. I'll get our bags." I wink at him and he takes Molly's hand and walks toward the house. Before they reach the door, it opens again and a huge bloodhound lumbers out and plods down the steps with his tail wagging.

"Momma," Matthias shrieks.

Oh damn. The dog at the park the other day really freaked him out.

"Blue," Jackson calls him and the dog pads over to him while Matthias clings to Molly's leg.

"Come on inside. That old dog won't hurt you," Molly says.

"I'll make sure he stays outside," a deep, croaky voice adds as another figure appears in the doorway. He looks slightly older than Molly and I assume it's her husband. He has a beard and kind eyes. Jax looks remarkably like him actually—Molly must be his aunt through marriage, then?

Molly glances back at Jax before she takes Matthias inside. Jax releases the dog's collar and he goes off into the yard, sniffing at the floor.

"The kid's scared of dogs," Jax says sharply.

"I'll make sure Blue doesn't bother him."

"I'm sure he'll get used to him," I say with a smile as I make my way to Jax's uncle. "It's just that—" I don't get to finish my sentence because Jax interrupts me.

"I think it's best if you and your dog just stay out of every-one's way while we're here," he snarls.

I frown at him, wondering what the man could have possibly done to make Jax so mad at him.

His uncle nods solemnly and my heart breaks for the look of hurt on his face. "Okay, son," he says.

"Do not call me son," Jax snarls.

Son? This is Jax's father? I thought he was dead? What the hell?

He winces as though he just made a huge mistake. "Of course." He looks to the bags in the back of the truck. "You need a hand?"

"Not from you."

"It's a pleasure to meet you, Miss." He tips his hat and then walks down the yard after Blue.

I wait until he is out of earshot before I speak. "Jax? Is that man your father?"

"He's the man whose DNA I share, but he has never been any kind of father," he snaps as he grabs some of our bags. "And while we're here, you will stay the fuck away from him. Do you understand me?"

"Yes," I swallow because the tone of his voice tells me this is not the time for arguing or asking for an explanation.

Jax walks into the house carrying most of our bags and I grab the rest. I stop at the doorway and look back at his father. Blue rubs himself against his legs as they walk through the over-grown grass. I don't know much about Jax's childhood but obviously his father wasn't around much and I wonder what their story is. He's clearly not all bad because that dog seems to adore him, and animals are good readers of people, right?

I carry the bags inside and as I reach the door, Jax is making his way back through it. He takes the bags from my hands. "I'll show you to your room and then Molly has supper ready."

"Okay." I smile at him but he's still rattled and he doesn't smile back.

I follow him down the hallway and up the stairs and along a huge corridor which has at least half a dozen rooms leading off it. We walk to the end before he kicks open the door. "This is your room," he says and I walk inside. It's beautiful. A huge floor-to-ceiling window floods the room with the light from the sunset. It has polished hardwood floors and a huge bed in the center. Jax indicates another door on the far wall. "That's an adjoining room for Matthias," he says.

"It's perfect. Thank you," I turn around and he is in the doorway, filling it as he leans against the doorframe. My breath catches in my throat at the sight.

"Where do you sleep?" I whisper and then silently admonish myself because that sounded so much more loaded than I meant it to be and now there is a tension in the room that there shouldn't be.

He clears his throat as though he feels this too. "Across the hall."

"Good. I'm glad you're close by," I say honestly.

"For anything you need, Luce," he says and my pussy walls contract as heat flushes over my cheeks. "Molly will be waiting for us. Let's have some supper and I'll show you around." He winks at me and just like that the tension is gone. He's Jax again —my father's best friend—and not the man who I spent one incredible, sinful night with.

After a delicious meal, I take a sleepy Matthias to bed. I smile at his beautiful face as I tuck him in. We had such a lovely time at supper. Molly is fabulous. She is funny and smart and she makes Jackson squirm when she talks about his childhood. There is a genuine love and affection between them that is wonderful to witness. His father—who I learned is Harvey,

Molly's brother—didn't make an appearance, although I'm not surprised the way Jackson warned him off.

After closing Matthias' door I walk back to the kitchen to find Molly and Jackson leaning against the kitchen counter sipping a beer each.

"Shannon will be here tomorrow. I hope that's okay?" I hear Molly say before they realize I've come back into the room. The hairs on my neck stand on end. Who the hell is Shannon?

Jax takes a sip of his beer before he replies. "It's fine."

"Okay," Molly shrugs. "Just so you're prepared."

"Prepared for what?" I ask with a smile as I walk toward them both.

Jax holds out a beer for me and I take it from him; my fingertips brush his hand, reminding me of the things he can do with those fingers. *Stop it, Lucia!*

"Well, Jax and Shannon always had kind of a thing." Molly whispers.

"Oh?" I keep the smile plastered on my face but I don't like the sound of this.

Jax shakes his head but he lets her go on talking.

"But now Shannon is engaged to the local veterinarian. They get married next month."

Now this I do like the sound of. "Oh?"

"I'm just making sure Jackson here isn't going to find it too awkward," she winks at me.

"We were never anything serious, Molly." He frowns at her.

"Well you and she used to hook up every time you came down here, so you know..." Molly shrugs. "I bet she'd have married you if you'd asked her."

Wow! Now I don't like this again and I've already decided that I don't like Shannon.

"No she wouldn't," he shakes his head and takes another sip of his beer. "But more importantly, I don't want to marry her."

"Oh of course. Jackson Decker. The eternal bachelor." She rolls her eyes but she smiles at him. "My only nephew. I have no children of my own. I will never get any babies to spoil, will I?"

"I'm sorry I'm such a disappointment to you." He leans in and kisses her cheek.

"You could never be," she chides him. "I'll make do with my horses."

I watch the two of them. They share such a close bond that I wonder again why Jax doesn't spend much time here.

"You should show our guest around the place," Molly says, "while I wash up."

"Oh, please, let me wash up," I insist as I take one of the plates from the counter.

"No guest of mine washes up after their supper," she says as she slaps my hand away. "Well, at least not on their first night here." She winks at me and I laugh.

"Come on. I'll give you the tour," Jax says before he finishes off the last of his beer.

I place my bottle on the counter and follow him outside. We walk through the huge yard at the front toward the stables.

"So you grew up here?" I ask.

"Yup. Until I was thirteen."

"Why did you leave?"

He frowns and sucks on his lip.

"I'm sorry. If you'd rather I didn't know, that's fine."

"It's not that." He shakes his head and sits down on a wooden bench.

I sit beside him. "What then?"

"I just don't talk about it much. It hurts, you know?"

"Yep," I agree.

"Of course you know," he says with a soft sigh. "Being a kid sucks, right?"

"Depends," I say. "I hope Matthias never thinks so."

"He won't. Because you're an amazing mom."

"Thank you," I lean back on the bench and watch the sun setting over the fields. "It's beautiful here."

"It sure is," he agrees. "You see that huge oak?"

"Yeah?"

He laughs. "I had my first kiss under that tree."

"You did? With Shannon by any chance?"

"No, with Amy-Lou Wainwright."

"Amy-Lou?" I arch an eyebrow at him.

"She had long auburn pigtails." He shakes his head. "And the greenest eyes I've ever seen."

"Where is she now?"

"I have no idea. Probably married with a dozen kids."

"Was she just your first kiss?" I bump my shoulder against his.

"Jesus, yes! I just told you I left when I was thirteen."

"Okay. Some people have sex that early."

He frowns at me. "Did you?"

A memory of my thirteenth birthday almost steals the breath from my lungs. I jump up from seat. "When you said you were showing me around, I thought you meant the horses and such. Not where you and Amy-Lou got your freak on."

He pushes himself up off the bench. "We did not get our freak on. Don't taint the memory of my first kiss." He pushes me gently and then walks past me toward the stables.

I admire the beautiful horses as Jax introduces me to each one by name. I've never seen one up close before.

"I didn't realize they were so big," I say as I rub the nose of Zena, one of the mares. "Is it scary to be up there riding one?"

He comes up behind me, the heat from his body makes goosebumps prickle along my forearms. "A little, if you're not used to it, but there's nothing else like it. I can teach you while you're here if you like."

"Could you? I would love that?"

"Sure," he whispers, his face so close to me that I feel the warmth of his breath on my neck. I imagine his lips dusting over the delicate skin there and think of how good it would feel if he unzipped my jeans and slid his hand inside. We stand like that, our bodies so close together but not quite touching—hearts pounding, breathing getting deeper and faster.

"You want to meet my horse?" He steps away and walks to the next stall, breaking the spell.

"Sure," I follow him until I come face to face with a beautiful black horse. He clearly recognizes his owner as he dips his head and rubs it over Jax's chest, making him laugh.

"This is Bastian," he says.

"Hey, handsome," I say as run my hand over the silky smoothness of his neck and for a second Jax's eyes lock on mine and there it is again. That tension that seems to follow us wherever we go.

I stare at him, licking my lips as heat pools in my core. He wants this too, I can see it, how much he's holding himself back. He likes me to ask for what I want, right?

"Jax?" I whisper.

"Lucia," he growls.

"Jackson!" A high pitched squeal cuts through the air making me jump and him blink in surprise.

I turn on my heel to see a tall woman wearing jeans, a tank and cowboy boots strolling toward us. She has long wavy blonde hair. Not the kind of untamed waves I have either, but those perfect beach waves that take me an hour in the salon to get. I bet she rolls out of bed looking that good.

"Hey, Shannon," he says with a smile.

Shannon? This tanned goddess with perfect teeth and a tiny waist is Shannon. Well, of course it is.

"Harvey told me you were back. I just dropped off Blue's ear meds so I thought I'd say hi." She looks at the two of us as though she's waiting for him to introduce me.

"Hi," I say with an awkward wave.

"Shannon this is Lucia," he says, clearing his throat.

She arches one perfect eyebrow. "Lucia?"

"Remember my friend, Alejandro? She's his daughter. She needed out of the city for a few days," he says. *His friend's daughter. Not his friend. Or his work colleague. Or the woman he was just about to throw on the floor and fuck until you walked in here, Shannon.*

The two of them stare at each other and then at me like I'm in the way. I feel like such an idiot when I realize that I am. When will I ever learn?

"I'll leave you two to catch up." I wipe my hands on my jeans. "It was great to meet you, Shannon," I lie.

Then I walk out of the stable.

"Luce," Jax calls after me but I keep walking with my head high.

As soon as the warm evening air hits my face, I start to cry, even though I hate myself for it. He's broken my heart for the last time. It's my own fault. He warned me it was one night, didn't he?

As I walk toward the house, I feel a soft wet nose at my hand and look down to see Blue at my side. He's licking my salty tears from my fingers where I just wiped them.

I drop to my knees. "Hey, buddy," I sniff and he licks my face too, making me smile.

"I'm sorry. Come here, boy," Harvey says.

"It's fine. He's adorable," I sniff.

"He has a sixth sense for people being upset."

I stand and wipe my face again.

"Are you okay?" Harvey asks, his face full of concern.

No. Because your son is an ass! But of course I don't say that. Jax has his reasons for not wanting Harvey in his life and I would never betray him like that. "I'm fine. Allergies, I think."

"Yeah. They can get you this time of year," he says with a wink. "Come on, boy."

Blue wags his tail and the two of them wander off away from the house.

CHAPTER 21

JAX

"So how long are you here for?" Shannon asks as I watch Lucia walk out the door.

"A few days, maybe longer," I reply absent-mindedly. She was upset. I should go after her. But then what would I do, because I was about two seconds away from fucking her right here in the stables before Shannon walked in. It seems like I'm always just moments away from fucking her. One word from her would be all it would take, but this was the closest I'd come to just taking her anyway.

Fuck!

"Well, it's good to have you around," she goes on. "Lucia seems nice."

I shake my head and focus on Shannon. "Yeah. She is."

She pops one eyebrow. "Something going on with you two?"

"No," I shake my head.

"Jackson Decker. You can't fool me," she laughs as she pats Bastian on the nose. "Don't you break that girl's heart, though."

"What?" I blink at her.

"She is so in love with you. Don't tell me you can't see that?"

"What? No. She likes me, yeah, but it's like a crush."

Shannon smiles at me. "I was only in here for a minute with you two and that was way more than a crush."

"How is Ed anyway?" I ask, changing the subject.

She lets out a long, slow breath. "That man. He is wonderful. I damn well adore him."

I smile at her. "I'm happy you found someone, Shan."

"I know that you are," she grins back at me. "And I would be for you. Because we really do just like each other. But tell me, Jackson, how would you feel if your friend's daughter found someone else?"

"Fuck you." I shake my head and she laughs again.

"Hey. If you're intent on hiding your feelings, how about you help me give Zena her injection?"

"She hates those," I frown at her.

"Exactly. And I'm the poor soul who has to give them to her once a month. I was going to do it tomorrow, but as you're here now?"

"I ain't distracting that crazy horse while you stick a needle in her ass."

"She is not crazy," she says with a hand on her hip. "She's just cranky because she gets sore eyes sometimes. And you have a way with her."

"Now I know you're fucking with me."

"You do," she laughs. "You get it from your daddy."

"Shan!" I warn her.

She shrugs. "Like it or not, he has a gift with animals. You do too."

"Yeah? It's a pity that gift didn't extend to his wife and son, isn't it?" I snarl.

"Come on." She puts a hand on my arm. "You gonna help me give this horse her shot or what?"

"Fine," I snap. At least it will stop her talking about my father.

Shannon grabs the medicine from her bag and we step into Zena's stall.

"Just keep her calm," she says and shoots me a look of fake terror.

I stand close to the mare, one arm on her neck while I stroke her nose with my free hand, from her ear to the tip of her nose, the way she likes it. Her ears flick and she snorts as she feels Shannon behind her. Zena's not stupid and she knows what's coming.

"Don't you dare let her knock me on my ass, Jackson," Shannon warns.

"I won't. Just get it over with."

"Here goes," she says and she must have given the horse her shot because Zena rears up, knocking me flat on my ass instead, and straight into a pile of fresh horse shit.

"Fuck!" I snarl as Shannon peers over Zena's back and sees me sitting there.

Zena snorts as if to tell me I got exactly what I deserved, while Shannon almost pees in her pants as she laughs hysterically.

I stand up, my jeans and shirt covered in horse shit and shake my head. "It's not fucking funny." I scowl at her but she is too busy laughing her ass off.

"It kinda is though." She takes a breath before she goes off again.

I let myself out of Zena's stall and Shannon follows me. "Good girl," she says to the crazy horse before she falls into step beside me.

"You stink." She wrinkles her nose as she looks at me. "Molly will kick your ass if you go into the house like that."

"Damn!" I hiss. "Are there any spare clothes around here?"

"No." She shakes her head. "You're wearing underwear, right?"

"Yes."

"So just walk back to the house in your pants. It's nothing I ain't seen before." She laughs again as she walks out of the stable.

I look down at my clothes. Fuck, I do stink. I'd forgotten how bad horse shit smells living in LA. I pull my t-shirt over my head and toss it into the pile of trash. My jeans aren't too bad though and the smell from them not quite as close to my nose. I can take them off in the house.

I walk out of the stable a few minutes later and Shannon is waiting for me.

"Oh that is a shame," she says as she looks down at my jeans.

"Does your fiancé know that you like to look at other men?" I ask as we walk to the house.

She grins at me. "He knows I am one hundred percent in love with him, so he wouldn't care."

"He seems like a good guy."

"He is," she says with a contented sigh, "though he doesn't have your way with animals."

"Fuck you."

"When I looked up ... and you were just sitting on your ass..." She snorts with laughter now and it's so fucking infectious that I laugh too. We're both still laughing when I open the door leading from the backyard to the kitchen. I stop when I see Lucia is sitting there alone at the table nursing a cup of Aunt Molly's famous herbal tea.

Fuck!

She doesn't even speak to me. She just stands up with her mug and walks out the room. I should go after her and tell her that this is not what it looks like, but maybe this is the kinder thing to do? Let her think I'm a complete jackass so that she can stop looking at me like I'm the only man she'll ever want and I can focus on doing what I'm supposed to be doing, which is protecting her and trying to find out who tried to kill her.

CHAPTER 22

LUCIA

I wake to the sound of Matthias giggling to himself as he sits on the end of my bed watching cartoons on his tablet. I swear this kid is better with technology than I am.

"Morning, munchkin," I smile.

"Morning, Momma. What are we doing today?" He grins at me.

"What would you like to do?"

"Can we go see the horses with Jax?"

Jax. His name is like a knife slicing through my heart. Seeing him and Shannon last night—it wasn't even that he was half-naked, it was the way he was with her. Like he was being his true self. I've seen him laugh plenty, but not like that. He has never looked at me the way he looked at her and he never will.

"Maybe later. I think Jax is busy. How about me and you do something? Just us?"

"Can we go dinosaur hunting?" he asks with a goofy grin.

"Yes." I clap my hands. "I'll bet there are lots of T-Rexs around here. How about we grab some breakfast and go find some?"

"Yes," he shrieks, jumping off my bed. I smile at him as he

walks back to his room, pretending to be a T-Rex. He is all I need. As soon as we get back to LA I'll tell my father I can't work for Montoya Inc any longer. The sooner I start to cut Jackson Decker out of my life, the happier I will be.

M olly made us fresh pancakes with blueberries for breakfast and we ate our fill before we came out exploring the fields. To my relief, there's no sign of Jackson anywhere. No doubt Shannon is keeping his bed nice and warm for him. We have walked a fair distance from the house, but I have made sure to keep in sight of various landmarks on my way so we don't get lost. That would be the last thing I'd need, having Jax come to my rescue like some white knight, when in fact he is the fire-breathing dragon.

"Momma. I found a dinosaur footprint. Come see." Matthias shouts from beneath a tree a few yards ahead of me.

"Wow. Really?" I laugh. This kid's imagination is something else. He makes even the most mundane things seem fun. I run over to him, not seeing the rock jutting out from beneath the grass. I catch my sneaker on it and fall, twisting my ankle as I hit the ground.

"Momma." Matthias screams as he comes running over to me.

"I'm fine, munchkin." I force a smile as I push myself into a sitting position. "I should look where I'm putting my feet, huh?"

"You need me to go for help?" he frowns, his little face so serious.

"No." I shake my head. "I'm okay. I just need to get up and then maybe we should head back. Okay?"

"Okay," he nods. "Then we can go see the horses with Jax."

"Yeah." I resist rolling my eyes, because this kid loves his

Uncle Jax. That damn asshole! I push myself up, but my ankle throbs and pain shoots up my calf when I put my weight on it.

Damn! It must be at least a two mile walk back to the house. It's going to take me forever.

"You can hold my hand, Momma," Matthias says as he holds out his chubby little hand to me.

"Thanks, munchkin," I say as I take it. "We'll just have to walk a little slower, okay?"

He nods his agreement. "Okay."

CHAPTER 23

JAX

I t's after ten by the time I wake up. The last few days must be catching up with me. I pull on my jeans and head downstairs. Aunt Molly is in the kitchen with one of the ranch hands, Cody.

"Morning, sleepy head," she says with a smile.

"Morning," I say as I eye the remainder of some fresh pancakes. "Any of those left or did this guy eat them all?" I pat Cody on the back.

"I didn't get no pancakes," Cody grumbles. "Only for guests, apparently."

"Cody Jessop!" Molly says as she gives him a slap around the ear. "You had four eggs and half a pack of bacon, you ungrateful ass."

"Sorry, Molly," he chuckles as he stands and takes his plate to the sink.

"Lucia and Matthias are up?"

She smiles at me. "Yep. Up with the birds, those two."

"And where are they now?" I frown because I don't hear Matthias and that kid is always laughing or chattering.

"They went off exploring."

"Exploring?" I frown. "Where?"

"Beats me. They took a backpack with water and some fruit and said they'd be back for lunch."

"You just let them go wandering off on their own?" I snap as my heart starts racing in my chest.

"She's a grown woman," Molly snaps back, "and she seems pretty capable of taking her son for a walk if you ask me."

I shake my head. I shouldn't have snapped at her like that. "She's in danger, Molly. Why did you think I brought her here?"

"What?" Her hand flies to her face. "When you said she was in some trouble, I assumed..."

"What?" I frown.

"I don't know, maybe she was pregnant and wanted to hide it from her father or something? Or she had a bad break up?"

"Fuck!" I run my hands through my hair.

"I'm sure she's fine. We could take a couple of horses and go look for them?" Cody offers.

"Yeah. They're just out exploring. We'll go find them."

As our horses stroll through the fields, I see the outline of two unmistakable figures up ahead and my heart starts to pound in my chest. Matthias is holding onto his momma's hand as she limps beside him.

Fuck. She's hurt.

I squeeze my thighs and give Bastian a nudge with my heels and he picks up his pace as we head toward them. Cody spots them too and he follows me.

Lucia looks up as we approach, squinting in the bright mid-morning sun. I jump off my horse and walk over to them.

"Jax." Matthias squeals.

"Hey, buddy. What happened?" I direct my question to Lucia but Matthias answers.

"Momma fell over."

"Let me take a look," I say.

"I'm fine," she snaps as she hobbles on.

"Clearly not. Now sit your ass down and let me take a look."

She rolls her eyes and I shake my head at her stubbornness, but she sits on the floor and I crouch down and take hold of her calf. I pull off her sneaker and she winces.

"It's just a sprain," she insists as she tries to jerk her foot away but I hold her in place.

I run my hand over her ankle. "Hmm. It doesn't feel broken, but we'll get you checked out anyway. We should head back to the house." I stand up and wipe the dust from my jeans. "You fancy a ride on a horse, little guy?" I wink at Matthias and ruffle his hair.

"Yeah." He grins at me. This kid is fearless—just like his mother.

I hold my hand out to Lucia but she ignores it, fixing her shoe back on before she pushes herself up off the ground.

"You fancy a ride, Lucia?" Cody says with a grin as his eyes roam over her perfect body.

"Sure." She smiles back as she goes to limp toward him, but I put my arm out and stop her.

"Not a fucking chance," I whisper, my eyes narrowed as I glare at her. There is no way I'm having her pressed up against him for the ride home. She glares back at me but she doesn't disagree.

I turn to Cody. "Your horse isn't as jumpy. You take the little guy."

"Sure. Come on, sport," Cody laughs as he lifts Matthias up by his waist and plonks him on top of his horse.

I offer my hand to Lucia but she ignores it. "You ever climbed on a horse before?"

"No!"

"Then let me help you."

"I'm sure I can figure it out, Jackson," she snaps. Damn! I hate it when she calls me that. I pick her up by her waist, hoist her over my shoulder and plonk her on my saddle.

"There," I snarl at her and she glares at me. It should make me pissed but all it does it make me want to put her over my knee and spank her ass until she begs me to fuck her.

I climb on behind her. She bristles at my touch, but there isn't much place for her to go. I take hold of Bastian's reins, my arms encasing her and we start to head back to the house.

She keeps fidgeting in the saddle and it's driving me fucking crazy.

"Will you sit still?" I whisper in her ear.

I know she's doing it because she can't stand me touching her, but her ass keeps rubbing over my groin and my cock is becoming painfully hard.

"Fine," she sighs but she stops squirming.

Beside us, Matthias asks Cody question after question about riding horses and Cody answers them all good-naturedly. Cody is a good kid, but if I catch him looking at Lucia like he just did again, he'll be looking for a new job.

"How is your ankle?" I ask her.

"Fine."

"Is that the only word in your vocabulary today?"

"Fuck you! How's that?" she hisses.

"I'll take it for now," I growl in her ear. "But you ever speak to me like that again and I'll put you over my knee and spank your ass."

"You wouldn't dare," she growls but I hear the breath catch in her throat and see the heat flushing over her neck.

"Take Matthias back to the house," I nod to Cody. "And don't take your eyes off him for a second."

"Sure thing," Cody replies.

"Be careful with him. Please?" Lucia says and Cody smiles at her.

"I'll take good care of him for you. Promise." He tips his hat and then gives his horse a nudge until she canters off in the direction of the house.

I hold onto Bastian's reins, my arms squeezing around Lucia as she sits between my thighs. There's no disguising the fact that my cock is as hard as iron sitting this close to her, so I don't bother even trying to.

A soft breeze ruffles through her hair. Almond and cherry. She always smells so fucking good. I bend my head to her ear. "You want to come for a ride with me?"

"No," she snaps. "Why don't you take Shannon for another ride instead?"

Wow. That fucking hurt. But what did I expect when she thinks I spent last night fucking another woman.

"I might ask your permission sometimes, Lucia, but I don't need it," I growl.

"What does that mean?"

"Hold on." I grip the reins tighter, making sure she is caged in by my arms, before I give Bastian a sharp nudge in the flanks, signaling he should run like the fucking wind. She gives a yelp of surprise when the horse bolts but then she leans back against me, smiling, resting her hands on the top of my thighs.

CHAPTER 24
LUCIA

I've never been on a horse before, but as Jax's horse, Bastian, races through the fields, I know that it's something I'm going to grow to love. Despite the fact that I'm pissed at him, I lean back against his chest and close my eyes. The sun on my face and the wind in my hair, it feels like there is no one in the world but me, him and this magnificent animal. I can't deny that being encased in his arms doesn't feel good too.

Jax pulls Bastian to a stop near a stream and under the shade of a huge tree. He climbs off and turns to me, placing his hands on my waist.

"Jax," I protest but he's already lifting me and suddenly I'm in his arms. "Put me down!"

"Steady on, wildcat," he chuckles. "I'll put you down now—just be careful on that ankle."

My ankle. I was having so much fun that I forgot about my sore ankle. As if to remind me, it throbs as he sets me gently on my feet.

"How is it?" he asks as he looks down at my foot, his face full of concern.

"Fine, but it would be better if you'd taken me back to the house and let me ice it instead."

His Adam's apple bobs in his throat as he swallows. I shouldn't give him such a hard time, but he drives me crazy with his constant mixed messages.

"I'll take you back soon if that's what you really want. Just let Bastian have a quick breather. He's not as young as he used to be." Then he sits on the floor and leans back on his hands and I have to avert my eyes from his thick thighs and his stiff cock encased in those tight jeans.

"Why did you bring me here, Jax?"

He licks his lips but he doesn't reply.

"Why wouldn't you let Cody give me a ride?"

That seems to provoke something in him and his face darkens. "You know why."

I sit beside him on the ground. "No, I don't. Is he a bad guy?"

"No," he snaps. "Why? You like him?"

"He's funny. Kind of cute, too," I say with a shrug.

"Yeah, well I didn't bring you here so you could fuck some random cowboy. I brought you here to keep you safe," he snarls.

"But you get to fuck whoever you want while we're here though?" I turn to him and frown. "So, why can't I?" I have no intention of having sex with Cody or anyone else for that matter, but Jax's double standards make me pissed.

He moves so quickly that I gasp out loud as he rolls on top of me, taking my wrists and pinning them to the ground. "If you're looking to be fucked, Lucia, you come to me. You got that?" He rocks his hips against me and I feel his hard cock pressing against my pussy.

God, I want him so bad, but I'm not going to be another notch on his bedpost—at least not for a second time.

I close my eyes because if I keep looking at him, he'll know how much I want him.

"One of the horses needed a shot so I helped Shannon keep it calm," he says, his breath skittering over my cheek and making me shiver. "I fell on my ass and into some horse shit. That's what you saw, Angel. The aftermath of that. Nothing more."

I open my eyes again and look at him. "Really? You and she never—?"

"No. You think I would do that? While I'm here with you? After what we did?" He frowns at me.

"But you and me—you said that was just one night?" I breathe as the heat builds in my core.

He sucks in a breath. "One night that I can't stop thinking about, Luce. I replay it over in my head every single moment I'm alone."

"You do?" I blink at him, because I do too.

"I can't stop fucking thinking about you," he growls. "How you smell. How good you taste. Your hot, tight pussy squeezing my cock. The way you moan my name when you come for me."

"Jax," I whisper as a rush of wet heat surges between my thighs.

"I'll say it again, Angel, just so we're crystal clear, you want fucking, you come to me. I am the only man on this ranch who gets to touch you. Okay?"

"Okay," I breathe as he pins my wrists with one hand while his other skims over my breasts and down to the waistband of my jeans before tugging open the button and zipper and sliding his hand inside my panties. His fingers circle over my clit before he slips them between my slick folds.

"Jax," I groan.

"Why are you soaking wet, Angel?" he growls. "You like riding with me?"

"Yes," I pant, because how can I lie? Being wrapped in his huge arms and encased in those muscular thighs while his horse galloped at full speed was so freaking hot.

"You have any idea how much restraint I've had to show these past few days?" He dips his head and starts to trail soft kisses along the base of my throat. "Being so close to you and not being able to touch you. Not being able to do this," he growls as he slides two thick fingers inside me and I arch my back in pleasure, coating him in a rush of slick heat. "Especially when I know how much you want me too, Luce."

"You're an arrogant asshole," I hiss as he curls the tips of his fingers inside me and presses on a sweet spot that makes me want to whimper.

"All this sweet cum for someone else, then is it, Angel?" he chuckles. "You wish Cody had his fingers buried in your cunt right now instead of me?"

"You know I don't," I groan as I rock my hips into his hand.

"The ranch hands are out here today," he whispers in my ear. "If they weren't, I would strip you naked and take you right here in the open."

"Please, Jax?" I moan. I need something from him, because he has me on the edge already.

"I got you, baby," he soothes as he works his fingers expertly, the palm of his hand rubbing against my clit with delicious friction as his hand is encased in my jeans. "I'll make this quick so we can get back to the house."

He keeps my wrists pinned above my head as he finger fucks me in the long grass. My walls squeeze around him as I try to draw him deeper inside me.

"I am so desperate to fuck you," he groans against my neck. "It's killing me not to bury my cock in your pussy right now."

"Jax." I try to wrench my hands free as my orgasm rips though my body, making me shudder against his hand.

"That's my good girl," he whispers as he rubs out the last few tremors. When my body has stopped shaking he pulls his hand from my panties and places his fingers in his mouth, sucking them clean as he stares into my eyes and making a fresh well of heat pool in my center.

I open my mouth to say something but he jumps up quickly, holding out his hand. "Come on, before someone sees us out here."

My eyes roam over his body. His thick shoulders and broad chest, encased in the tight fitting flannel shirt, then his strong thighs stretching the denim of his jeans so incredibly taut, but not as taut as the material over his zipper which looks fit to bust under the strain of his impressive erection.

I look up at him, ignoring his outstretched hand as I lick my lips. "What if I'm not done yet?" I grin at him.

"I just told you we are done, Angel," he snaps and I feel the sting of his rejection. "So, get your ass up now, or I will pick you up."

"I can get myself up." I plant my hands on the ground to push myself up, but before I can he bends down and scoops me up as though I'm as light as air before hoisting me over his shoulder.

"Hey!"

"Don't act like a spoiled brat, Lucia," he growls, "or you'll be treated like one."

"I wasn't—" I start to protest but then he smacks my ass hard and I squeal.

"You think I would let some ranch hand see me fucking you?" he snaps as he walks us toward Bastian. "You think I would let anyone see you coming for me?"

"No," I whisper. "You said we were done, and I thought you meant..."

He reaches his horse and sits me on the saddle before wrapping his arms around my waist. "Not even started, Angel, but you need to learn a little patience." He winks at me before climbing on behind me.

.   .   .

I lean against his chest as we ride back to the house; this time we go slower and he keeps one hand around my waist while he holds the reins with the other.

We ride in silence and I wonder if he is feeling as nervous, excited and confused as I am. Jax Decker is everything I have ever wanted and suddenly he feels so close, but so far away. He is my father's best friend and I can't help but wonder if that is where his loyalty will always lie.

CHAPTER 25

LUCIA

Matthias is waiting for us on the porch by the time we get back to the house. Jax helps me down from his horse then carries me inside.

"I can walk," I protest but he glares at me, so I stop. Being held by him isn't all that bad, after all.

"Let's get some ice on that," Molly says as soon as Jax puts me down. "Take off her shoes," she barks to Jax and I smile at how he so easily complies.

He kneels on the floor in front of me, his head bent low as he removes my sneaker. This time when his hands brush over the skin of my ankle I feel tingles of electricity skitter up my leg. He looks up at me, a wicked glint in his eyes as his fingertips trail over my skin.

"Stop that," I whisper.

He looks around the room. Matthias skipped after Molly to get ice and Cody is taking the horses to the stable. There's nobody else here.

He dips his head low and presses a single soft kiss on my foot; it sends a surge of pleasure straight through me.

"Here we are," Molly says loudly as she comes back into the

room and hands me some ice wrapped in a dishtowel. "This is all I could find, sorry."

"It's perfect. Thank you," I say with a smile.

"Let me," Jax takes it from me and presses it against my skin. It feels so soothing against my inflamed ankle. I try not to look at him because then Molly will see that I'm completely besotted with him and that he just made me come in the middle of a field.

"Will you be able to walk soon, Momma?" Matthias asks as he sits beside me on the sofa.

"Most definitely," I assure him.

Jax winks at me and I swear the rush of heat between my thighs almost makes me pass out.

The rest of the day is much more uneventful. Molly insists that I sit on the den with my foot up and watch TV while Jax agrees to take Matthias to see the horses. I know he'll be teaching him how to ride but I try not to think too much about the possibility of him falling off. I know that Jax will look after him.

By suppertime, my ankle is much better and I can walk on it without much pain at all. I help Matthias wash up for dinner and I change into a summer dress because the evening is hot and humid. The ranch hands join us too, as well as Harvey. Jax sits at the opposite end of the table to his father and they barely make eye contact. Matthias sits next to Cody, who seems to be his new best friend, and that leaves a seat for me next to Jax.

Everyone is eating and talking when I feel Jax's warm hand on my knee. I carry on my conversation with Cody as I try not to react while it slides between my thighs.

"So the Bulls or the Lakers?" Cody asks me.

I blink at him, so distracted by Jax's wandering hand that my brain can't form a word.

"Lucia?" he frowns at me and I remember that we were talking about basketball and the fact that I grew up in Chicago but now I live in LA.

"The Bulls," I say. Glancing at Jax from the corner of my eye I see him grinning wickedly.

Cody starts talking about his high school record as Jax's hand slides higher until his fingers brush my panties.

I almost choke on my own breath. How the hell does he expect me to maintain my calm here?

"Wow," he mumbles and Cody and Molly look at him.

"I just didn't expect it to be so hot and sticky is all." He coughs loudly as he pulls his hand from beneath my dress. "The weather," he adds but my cheeks flame with heat because that is so not what he meant and what if they know it, too?

Molly looks confused. "It's always like this at this time of year."

"Hmm," he smiles to himself

I can barely breathe by the time supper is over. I stand beside the kitchen counter watching Matthias helping Molly as Jax walks over to me.

"What was that?" I hiss.

"Sorry," he grins at me. "I couldn't resist. And you need to stop coming to dinner in that dress. Cody couldn't take his eyes off you."

"What about you?" I grin at him.

He bends his head lower until his lips are close to my ear and whispers, "Well you already know that I can barely keep my hands off you. I just almost finger fucked you at the dinner table."

I close my eyes as the thought of him doing that and the memory of him in the field earlier today makes the wet heat surge between my thighs. "Jax," I mumble.

"Jackson can you help me?" Molly shouts across the room. "My current helper seems a little sleepy."

I look over and see Matthias yawning. I laugh. "He's had an eventful day. I'd better take him to bed. Come on, munchkin." I hold out my hand to him and he walks over.

"Night little buddy," Cody, Harvey and the other ranch hands shout to him.

As I'm walking down the hallway, I hear footsteps behind me. I turn to see Jax and my heart skips a beat. "As soon as he's settled"—he looks down at Matthias—"I'm across the hall if you need me."

"Okay," I whisper and then he winks at me and goes back to the kitchen.

CHAPTER 26

LUCIA

I blink in the dark room and for a second forget where I am. It's not until I hear Matthias' baby soft snores that I realize I'm in his room. I stretch my arms. I must have fallen asleep in here with him. I haven't gotten much rest lately with everything that's been going on.

I look at the clock on the nightstand. It's two a.m.

Oh no! I was supposed to go to Jax's room. What if he thinks I've changed my mind? What if he thinks I don't want him when that couldn't be further from the truth?

I climb out of Matthias' bed, giving him a kiss on the head before I walk out of the room and close the door. I go across the hallway and stand outside Jax's room. The house is so quiet that I imagine everyone can hear my heartbeat as it pounds in my ears right now.

The door creaks as I open it and step inside the dim room.

"Everything okay, Angel?" he asks in the low, gravelly tone that turns my insides to jelly.

"I'm sorry. I fell asleep with Matthias," I say as I see him lying in bed with his arms behind his head, the covers resting just below his abdomen, giving me a wonderful view of his glorious torso.

"I know. I didn't want to wake you."

"You should have," I whisper as I stand a few feet from the bed. My thighs tremble with nervous excitement. I have spent the night with this man before and it was the most incredible night of my life. Even if that's all he wants again, I can handle it. I would rather have that than nothing. Ever since the incident in the field earlier today, I have thought about nothing but having his hands on me again.

We stare at each other and I wonder if he has changed his mind, but then he speaks.

"Come here," he growls.

I step closer to the bed and as soon as I'm within touching distance, he reaches for my hand and pulls me to him until I'm straddling him. The cover is resting just below his abs now and I feel his cock twitching to life through the thin fabric.

Without another word, Jax reaches for my t-shirt and peels it off over my head before tossing it onto the floor, then his hands slide over my hips and stomach until he's cupping my breasts. I moan as he squeezes gently, rubbing the pads of his thumbs over my pebbled nipples.

"These are fucking beautiful," he groans as he squeezes harder.

I plant my hands on his abs to steady myself, my fingers flexing against his hard muscles as he kneads and rubs. I have never been so turned on by having them played with before but the wet heat is already pooling between my thighs.

When one of his hands coasts down my body and dips into my panties, I groan loudly.

He pushes his fingers between my thighs and a low growl rumbles through his chest. "You're fucking soaking, Angel. How do you get so fucking wet when I've barely touched you?"

"I ... don't ... know..." I gasp as he drives a finger inside me.

"Why did you come in here, Angel?" he growls.

"You know why, Jax," I groan as I roll my hips over his cock, which is now rock-hard.

"Say it."

"I want you to fuck me."

"I want to fuck you too, but I have no condoms here at the house. I can go down to the ranch hands' bunk house and ask the guys. I'm sure they'll have some," he says as he works his finger in and out of me, making me wetter and more needy with each passing second.

"I'm on birth control, if you're clean?" I whimper, because the thought of him stopping what he's doing and having to walk down to the bunk house and back again would be like torture.

"I've never fucked anyone without a condom before," he hisses as he adds a second finger and I coat him in a rush of slick heat.

"Really?" I blink at him. "Never?"

"Never," he grunts as he rocks his hips upwards and grinds his cock against me.

"I haven't since Blake," I groan. Blake was Matthias's father and the only man I've ever not used protection with. Not there have been many men since him. He was kind of enough to put me off for life. Not to mention that having a toddler when you're my age can be kind of a mood killer for a lot of guys.

Jax slips his fingers out of my pussy and I groan in frustration. He places his hands on my hips and stares up at me.

"Did I say something wrong?" I whisper.

"No," he says and then he flips me over, so I am flat on my back and he is nestled between my thighs. The cover has fallen away completely now and his hard cock is pressed against me. "If I take you like this, you're mine, Lucia," he growls. "That doesn't just mean no man on this ranch gets to touch you—it means no man on this earth ever puts his hands on you again."

"I'm already yours, Jax," I breathe.

"It means we do this. For real. We don't hide it from anyone. Not Matthias. And not your father."

His cock twitches against my throbbing pussy and I whimper with need. I have never wanted something so much in my whole goddamn life. Sure, telling my father is terrifying, but it's a risk worth taking if it means being with Jax.

"Yes," I nod my head.

"Are you sure? Because there is no going back. If I fuck you bare, I am the only man who will ever fuck you again. You sure you're ready for that?"

"Yes. Please, Jax?" I am so desperate for him to fuck me right now, I would probably agree to anything he suggested, but I want this as much as he does. He's the man I want to spend the rest of my life with.

He brushes the hair from my face as he stares into my eyes. "You're still so young, Angel." He narrows his eyes at me. "I can be back in five minutes with some condoms."

"No, Jax," I beg as I lift my hips up, grinding myself on him and making him groan softly. "I want this. I want you. Only you."

He makes a noise that is somewhere between a growl and a groan as he starts to trail kisses over my throat, down over my breasts and stomach before he reaches the waistband of my panties. "You will never wear panties in my bed again, you got that?" he says as he hooks his fingers into the band and begins to peel them over my hips and down my legs.

"Yes," I breathe, lifting my ass to help him get them off me faster.

He kneels between my thighs and taps them lightly. "Spread wide open, baby. You know what I want to see."

I do as he tells me, spreading my legs wide and laying myself bare for him.

"Damn, that is the prettiest pussy I have ever seen," he growls. "And I have almost forgotten how sweet it tastes."

I curl my fingers in his hair as I lift my hips, desperate to feel him between my thighs.

He dips his head lower, his breath dusting over my pussy before he licks the length of the slick folds.

"Fuck, Lucia!" he growls as he begins to suck and lick me, rubbing his nose over my clit, driving me to the brink of orgasm and then letting me fall back down again.

"Please, Jax," I hiss. "I need you."

"Aw, I know, Angel. Soon," he teases me as he moves to my opening and pushes his tongue into my hot channel, causing a rush of wet heat. Then he adds two thick fingers, plunging them deep inside me as he rims my clit with his tongue. My back arches in pleasure as my climax tears through my body. I shudder and tremble as he keeps on finger fucking and eating me, drawing out my climax so that it washes over me in long, rolling waves.

When he finally comes up for air, I lie beneath him, panting and breathless, trying to recover from the most incredible orgasm I have ever had.

He is nowhere near done though and positions himself between my thighs, his hard cock nudging at my opening.

"Are you sure you want this, Angel?" he growls, "Because I swear once I get my cock inside you, there is no going back."

I wrap my arms around his neck as our bodies are pressed together "I'm sure, Jax. All I want is you."

"I am definitely going to hell for this," he growls right before he drives his cock deep inside me.

"Jax," I cry out as pleasure rockets around my body.

"Fuck!" He groans loudly in my ear. "Your pussy feels so

fucking good like this," he hisses as he buries his face against my neck. "I am going to fuck you all night long."

"Promises, promises," I challenge him.

"I'm so fucking hard for you right now and your hot little cunt is squeezing my cock so tight. This first time might be a little quick, but then I'll take my time with you, okay?" he growls.

"Yes," I pant as I wrap my legs around his waist, drawing him deeper inside me.

He rails into me, nailing me to the bed as he fucks me harder than I have ever been before in my life. "Your cunt is so fucking sweet," he growls. Our bodies grind together, slick with perspiration as we take everything we can from each other.

"Jax," I whimper as he drives against the spot deep inside me that makes me want to live in this moment forever.

"You're mine, Luce. Mine," he growls as he comes inside me, spurting hot and heavy and driving into me until he tips me over the edge with him.

We lie together, panting for breath until he pushes himself up and stares into my eyes. "Emptying my cum into you was so fucking hot." he grins at me.

"It was," I agree with a smile.

"You realize you're gonna be spending a whole lot of time with my cum dripping out of you." he arches an eyebrow at me and I giggle as the heat flushes over my chest. That sounds pretty damn perfect to me.

CHAPTER 27

JAX

I trail my fingertips over the soft skin of her back as she lies in my arms. Whenever I reach the spot near her hips she squirms and giggles.

"What time is it?" she whispers.

I check my watch. "A little after four."

"I should go back to my own bed," she says with a sigh, "or Matthias will wonder where I am if he wakes up."

"In a little while," I wrap my arms tighter around her. "I think I got one more round in me before you go."

"Jax," she giggles. "We need to sleep."

"There will be plenty of time for sleep when we're dead."

"You already fucked me three times," she whispers.

"Yeah, but the first time didn't count," I laugh. Her hot pussy felt so good bare that I hardly had time to make her come before I blew my load in her.

"It did for me. It was incredible," she says with a sigh.

"You're incredible." I kiss the top of her head.

"I know you said before about telling people, but can we wait?" she whispers.

"Why?" I meant what I said earlier. She is mine now. No other man will ever fucking touch her again.

"I think we should tell my father first and I don't want Matthias to have to keep our secret. It's not fair."

"Okay," I agree because she's right about it being unfair on the kid.

"Besides, isn't it kind of fun sneaking around?"

"No," I squeeze her ass. "It might be fun for a day or two but I don't want you to have to sneak out of here so nobody catches us. I want to wake up next to you, Luce."

She looks up at me. "You do?" she purrs.

"Yes, mostly because I always wake up with morning wood and it would be so much more convenient to slide my cock into you than have to jerk off." I grin at her.

"Jackson!"

I roll on top her, pinning her to the bed. "You know I hate it when you call me that." I nip at her neck and she squeals as I trail tiny bites all over her.

"Yes. That's why I do it," she purrs.

I look up at her, my eyes narrowed. She's so inexperienced and there is so much I want to teach her. "You know that now you're mine, I will follow up on my promise to spank your ass?"

"I'm counting on it," she bites on her lip and my cock hardens. How does she act so fucking sweet yet so wickedly sinful at the same time?

"You know if you want something, you only have to ask?" I remind her.

"I know," she breathes. "Why do you make me ask for what I want, Jax, when you already know?"

"Because you're so much younger than me, baby, and I want you to feel confident in asking for what you want."

"Oh," she breathes.

"That doesn't mean I won't just give you it anyway," I brush her hair from her face. "Because sometimes I don't want you to ask. Sometimes I just get the urge to fuck you into oblivion and now that you're mine I'm gonna be doing a lot of that."

"That sounds hot," she breathes.

"But the more confident you are, the more I'll be able to push you. Does that make sense?"

"Yes. Does it bother you that I'm not very experienced?" She blinks at me.

"No. Not even a little. I love that I'll get to be the one to teach you what turns you on and gets you off. I'll enjoy testing your limits with you, Angel."

"You turn me on and get me off," she giggles. "I think anything you want to do to me is fine by me."

I narrow my eyes at her. "That's a dangerous statement to make, Luce. You don't know half of the things I'd like to do to you yet."

"I'm sure I'll love all of them." She reaches up and curls her fingers in my hair. "But I love that you want me to be more confident. I've never been good at asking for what I want. At least not when it comes to sex." She blushes at the word.

"You're blushing saying the word sex to me?"

"Yes." She flutters her eyelashes.

"Even though I just had my face buried in your pussy?"

"Yes." Her breath catches in her throat.

"You like it when I eat your pussy, baby?" I growl as I start to pepper her throat with soft kisses.

"Yes," she purrs like a kitten.

"What else do you like?"

"I like your fingers in me," she groans as she rocks her hips, grinding herself on my cock. "I like it when you talk about spanking me."

"Hmm. Wait until I actually spank you. I have a hunch it's going to make you super fucking wet."

"Jax," she groans, grinding harder. "I love when you talk dirty to me."

"Hmm," I mumble as I head south. The smell of her cum mixed with mine makes me feel like burying my cock deep inside her again. I have never come inside a woman before. I've tasted myself in a woman's mouth before, but never on her pussy. "Your cunt is so fucking good, I'm gonna eat you every day, Angel."

"Yes," she whimpers as she writhes beneath me and my cock is weeping for her. I bury my face between her thighs and brush my tongue over her dripping folds.

"Fuck," I growl. There is something about tasting her when she's full of my cum that brings out something primal in me. I want to mark her beautiful soft skin so that everywhere she goes people will know that she's mine.

"The thing I love most though, Jax," she groans as she rides my mouth.

"Hmm?" I mumble as I suck her clit into my mouth.

"Oh! God!" she hisses as I bring her to the edge. "Is when you fill me with your huge cock."

Fuck me! I've created a monster.

I push myself up again, positioning myself between her thighs so I can give her what she loves the most. I'm a gentleman, after all.

I ease the tip inside her and my eyes almost roll into the back of my head. I will never tire of the silky smooth wetness of her pussy. "This what you really want, baby?"

"Yes." She wraps her arms around my neck and her legs around my waist and I fuck her hard until she shouts my name so loud I have to put my hand over her mouth.

"I thought we were keeping this a secret?" I groan as I drive deeper into her. It will never be enough though. I will never be deep enough inside her that I don't want more.

She moans against my hand as her orgasm hits and her walls squeeze my cock in a vise-like grip until I empty every last drop of cum I have inside her.

"Jax," she pants when I move my hand from her mouth.

"Hmm." I lie on top of her, only half holding myself up on my forearms because I'm completely spent.

"I never want you to stop doing that. Promise me that you won't," she whispers and there it is. That part of herself that never feels good enough. The part that thinks she doesn't deserve a man like me, when the opposite is true. She is far too good for me but it's too late now. She sold her soul to the devil and I'll never return it.

"I promise, Angel," I say before I kiss her soft lips and swallow her gentle moans.

CHAPTER 28
LUCIA

It's been a lovely day at the ranch. Jax took Matthias and me riding and he said we were both naturals, then when Matthias went to pick some berries with Molly, Jax and I sneaked off to his room and he fucked me twice in an hour. Now he is reading Matthias a bedtime story.

I smile as I wander through the house. I could sure get used to living like this.

I walk out into the yard and see a lonely figure sitting near the campfire. The huge lump of lovable bloodhound at his feet tells me it's Harvey. I go over and sit on the small wooden crate beside him. He seems lost in his own thoughts but he snaps out of them when I sit down.

"Come on, Blue," he says as he rests his hands on knees and goes to push himself up into a standing position.

"Please don't go, Harvey," I say, placing my hand on his arm. "I just came out for a little fresh air. I won't stay long."

He considers it for a second and then he sits back down.

"Jackson won't like you talking to me," he says.

"Well, he's not here right now," I smile at him. "Besides, I'll tell him I was talking to Blue." I reach down and scratch behind the dog's ear and he licks my hand.

"I don't blame him," he takes a sip of his tea. "Not wanting me around you and your little boy. He has his reasons."

"And they are?" I ask because Jax hasn't told me anything about his father and whenever I ask he shuts me down.

"I've been sober for ten years now," he says with a shake of his head. "Before that, well I was pretty useless."

"Ten years? That's an achievement."

"Is it?" he frowns at me.

"Don't you think so?" I ask.

"Not much of an achievement when your only son still hates you and you'll never get the chance to tell the only woman you ever loved how sorry you are."

"I'm sure Jax doesn't hate you, Harvey."

"He does," he says matter-of-factly. "And I don't blame him. Not even a little. He has grown into a fine man though, and that makes me proud every damn day."

Lots of people say stuff like that but don't really mean it, but I believe Harvey. There is no resentment or malice in his words, just a deep sadness.

"He's a good man. I'm sure one day he'll be able to forgive you."

"I did some things that were unforgivable, Lucia. By the time I fixed my drinking, it was too late. He's already done far more for me than I deserve."

"Like buying this place?" I ask.

"Yup. This land has been in my family for six generations and I almost lost it. Jackson found out through Molly and he bought it up. Put it all in Molly's name. It should have always been half hers anyway, but our Pa was kinda a traditionalist, believed everything should be passed down to his son. And well,

I never really thought about what was right or fair back then, so I just took it."

"And she lets you live here?"

"Yeah—it was one of Jackson's conditions that she always gave me a roof over my head. Like I said, he's a fine man."

I smile as I think about that fine man. He would make a great father himself some day.

"My biological mom was an alcoholic," I say as a memory of her pops into my head.

"I'm sorry about that. It must have been tough."

"It was, but not as tough as being without her. She died when I was eight."

He doesn't offer false condolences, he simply nods.

"I miss her though. Even though my parents are amazing, she'll always be my mom too. You know?"

"I get it. It's nice that you still think of her fondly." He smiles at me and I'm struck by how much Jax looks like him.

The sound of footsteps behind us makes Blue sit up and wag his tail. I spin around to see Jax storming toward us with a murderous look on his face.

"What the fuck?" he snarls at Harvey when he reaches us. "I thought I told you to stay the hell away from her?"

Harvey stands and opens his mouth to speak but I jump up and stand between them. "It's my fault, Jax. Harvey and Blue were already here when I came and I asked him not to leave."

"I'll go," Harvey mumbles.

"There's no need. She's leaving." He takes hold of my arm. Harvey looks down at his son's hand gripping me tightly and a strange look, like regret mixed with anger, flashes across his face.

"Don't you dare fucking look at me like that," Jax growls. "I am not you, old man."

"I never..." Harvey shakes his head.

"Let's go." Jax grumbles as he leads me back to the house.

"I'm sorry," I mouth to Harvey as we walk away.

He gives a slight shake of his head and a faint smile but I feel guilty for making things worse between the two of them.

We are back inside the house before Jax speaks to me again. "Can you ever just do as you're fucking told?" he snaps as he runs a hand through his thick hair.

"I was only talking to him," I protest.

"I told you to stay the hell away from him," he glares at me. "It was the one thing I asked you to do."

I fold my arms across my chest. "Well maybe if you told me why I had to do that, I would have."

He narrows his eyes at me. "I shouldn't have to explain myself, Lucia. If I tell you to do something—"

"I'm just supposed to obey you without question, is that it?" I interrupt him.

"Yes."

I close my eyes. There's no reasoning with him when he's in alpha asshole mode so I try a different tactic. "Is he dangerous?"

For some reason that makes him laugh and he shakes his head. "Not anymore."

"But he used to be?"

"Lucia! I don't want to talk about it," he barks at me and I take a step back from him. I have spent the last four years doing my best to push every button this man has. I've thrown up on him and in his car, called him names, teased him relentlessly, but I've never been the recipient of his anger like this before.

"Okay. I guess we're done then," I turn around and walk away but I have barely taken two steps before he pulls me back to him, spinning me around until I'm facing him again.

"We're done?" he growls, glaring at me with such fire and fury that it makes my legs tremble, but not in a bad way.

I swallow hard before I answer, momentarily unable to speak. But before I can utter a word, his lips crash onto mine and he kisses me so fiercely that I struggle for breath. His hands fist in my hair as he grips me tighter, pushing his tongue into my mouth and devouring me like a starving predator who has finally caught its prey. I wrap my arms around his neck as he lifts me and walks us toward the huge wooden table before sitting me on it. His lips don't leave mine as he pushes my thighs apart and settles himself between them. The unmistakable sound of him unfastening his belt and zipper makes wet heat pool in my core. I should push him away. Anybody could walk in on us here, but I am powerless to resist him. Then his hands are on me again, one on my hips while the other slides up my inner thighs until he reaches my panties and tugs them to one side.

He lets me up for air as he drives his cock into me and I gasp loudly. I'm not quite ready as he stretches me wide open.

"Jax," I whimper as I cling to his neck.

He kisses me again, pressing me tight to his body as he fucks me on the table. There is none of his usual finesse, this is simply about raw, primal fucking. He is claiming me and I love it. I love him. Every facet of him. My fingernails claw at his back as I fight to pull him deeper. My walls squeeze around him as I try to take more. He shifts my hips so I'm leaning back slightly and the new angle ensures that he hits that perfect spot deep inside me.

I wrench my lips from his as I struggle to breathe and then I groan his name, no longer caring who might catch us. I need this like I need air.

He buries his face in my neck, growling obscenities in my ear. "We will never be done. You belong to me, Angel. I will never stop fucking you. Your juicy cunt was made for me."

When he slides his hand between us and rubs my clit with his thumb, I feel the familiar tingling in my core as the heat and pleasure spreads through every nerve in my body.

"Fuck," I hiss in his ear as I lose all sense of time and space.

"Come hard for me, Luce," he growls and I do exactly that,

whimpering and shuddering in his arms as he goes on fucking me until he finishes too.

He pants for breath and I rest my head on his shoulder as my heart races. We stay like that for a moment before he cups my chin in his hand and tilts my head so I can look into his eyes. "Done?" he frowns at me.

"I meant the conversation," I whisper.

He narrows his eyes at me.

"But I'm so glad you misunderstood me, because that was next-level hot." I arch an eyebrow at him and he chuckles softly.

I rest my hands on either side of his face. "I wish you would share some of your past with me, Jax. I get that it hurts, but…"

"But what?"

"It feels like you don't give me all of you."

He looks down at our joined bodies. "I'm still inside you, Angel. I just gave you everything I have."

I swat him in the chest, making him laugh again. "I don't mean like that."

He pulls out of me and zips up his jeans. "We should get out of this kitchen before somebody walks in on us," he says with a wink and holds out his hand to help me down from the table.

I take his hand and sigh inwardly. Once again, he has managed to avoid telling me anything meaningful and it hurts me more than I could have imagined. He takes my hand as he starts to walk out of the kitchen, expecting me to follow, but I stay rooted to the spot.

"You talk about how different we are in age, Jax. How much more experienced you are than me. But this right here, this is the biggest imbalance in our relationship."

"What?" he frowns.

"You say you want me to act like a grown up—to ask for what I want—but you only mean when it comes to sex."

"Luce?"

"It's true though, isn't it? You know everything about my past, Jax, even though I didn't tell you. I had no choice because you went digging into my family history on my father's behalf."

He shakes his head. "I..."

"And I don't blame you for that. It was your job. But at least do me the courtesy of giving me a little something back in return. Because until you do, then we will never be on an equal footing."

He blinks at me but he doesn't say anything further. What was I expecting anyway?

"Night, Jax," I whisper and then I walk out of the kitchen alone.

CHAPTER 29

LUCIA

I stare out of the huge window into the darkness. It is so peaceful here. I wonder if I could ever get used to not living in the city though. The door to my room creaks open and I spin around to see Jax standing there.

"Hey," he says quietly.

"Hey," I whisper.

He walks to the bed and lies down. "Come here." He holds out his hand to me.

"I need to shower," I say, turning back to the window.

"Luce! Come here," he orders, his tone a little firmer now.

I close my eyes and will my feet to stay right where they are even though I want nothing more than to lie there with him.

"I'm sorry," he says and that's when my treacherous body betrays me and I walk over to the bed and lie beside him. I don't lie on his chest the way I usually would though. I mean, I have to show a little restraint here, right?

He pushes himself up onto one elbow and looks down at me, his fingers trailing softly over my stomach.

"I don't want you talking to my father because I don't want him to be a part of my life. Even knowing a little about you or

Matthias means that he gets that little bit closer to me. I know that sounds crazy..."

"It doesn't. I understand that."

"He doesn't get to share my life now. He doesn't get to share you," he says, his voice thick with emotion.

"Okay. I won't talk to him again."

"Thank you," he whispers and then he lays his head on my stomach and I run my fingers through his hair. "My mom did everything she could to stop him drinking, but it was never enough. She wasn't enough and neither was I. When he started beating her she decided that was it. She packed up mine and her things in her truck one day and we drove to LA to stay with her older sister. Just like that. No looking back. We went from this huge ranch in the middle of this beautiful country to sharing a one-bed apartment with my aunt."

"That must have been tough."

"My mom worked three jobs to get us our own place. It was a shitty apartment with no air con and no hot water half the time, but it was opposite a basketball court, so..."

"That's where you met my father, right?"

"Sure is. His mom used to visit her old neighbors and he used to go with her."

We lie in silence before he speaks again. "He never even tried to find us, Luce. He didn't even get off his drunk ass to see where we'd gone. How can you just let your wife and your only son slip away from you like that? My mom stayed in touch with Molly. He could have just asked her where we were. He could have got himself cleaned up and come for us, but he didn't even try."

I curl my fingers in his hair and let him go on talking.

"When I was a kid and he was sober he used to talk to me about all his grand plans for me and him. How we'd train horses and expand the ranch. But he was full of bullshit. He could never see past the bottom of his next bottle. Even when Mom got sick he didn't care. Not even a phone call. So, the fact that he got sober ten years ago, when neither of us no longer needed him is the biggest insult he ever gave me. If he could do that, why didn't he do it when it really fucking mattered? "

"I'm sorry, Jax."

He looks up at me. "Don't be. I have a better life now than I could have imagined. If I hadn't moved to LA, I'd never have met your father—and then I'd never have met you."

I smile at him. "Well that would have been a damn shame now, wouldn't it?"

He pushes himself up until he's lying on top of me. This is where he feels in control again and I know that's what he needs. Leaning down, he runs his mouth over my breasts through the fabric of my dress.

"Jax," I breathe. "I really do need a shower. I stink."

"You smell incredible," he mumbles against me.

"I smell of fire," I whisper. "And sex."

"Hmm." He looks up at me. "You smell of me."

"I do." I bite on my lip.

"I like you smelling of me, Angel. I'd have you walk around permanently dripping in my cum if I had my way."

"You're a bad man, Jackson Decker," I giggle.

He flips me over until I'm lying on my front and smacks my ass, making me squeal. "You've seen nothing yet, Lucia," he growls as he starts to peel my clothes off. "Now be a good girl and try to be quiet while I fuck you."

CHAPTER 30

JAX

"You still know nothing about this guy?" Alejandro asks as I sit at the desk in my study, his concerned face filling the screen of my laptop. It's been four days since we arrived in Dallas and I've spoken to him at least twice a day, but I've avoided a video call because looking him in the eye while I'm spending every spare second I have either fucking—or thinking about fucking—his daughter is killing me.

"No. I swear this guy has at least two dozen fake accounts, all of them with different IP addresses. He uses a sophisticated VPN—"

"Jax," Alejandro interrupts, shaking his head. "This is me you're talking to. English?"

"He basically knows what he's doing and is good at covering his tracks."

"Fuck."

"He's not that good though. I spoke to Jessie earlier and she's on this guy too. We'll find him."

"Hmm," Alejandro rubs a hand over his jaw. "That's if it is the same guy. This could just be a random creep from the internet. Alana tells me there are loads of guys who do this kind of shit to women."

"Yeah, unfortunately so. Where are you at anyway? Any leads your end?"

"Nothing new," he shakes his head in frustration. "I have shaken down every single asshole we know. So he's either someone or no one."

"Yep," I nod my agreement. In my experience, if Alejandro hasn't found this guy in a matter of days then it it's because they are either so big they have the resources and the reputation to cover things up or they are so insignificant that nobody knows who they are.

"As soon as I have something more, I'll let you know," he adds.

"Same."

"How are Lucia and Matthias?"

I try to keep my voice as steady as I can. "Good."

"I spoke to them earlier, but you know Lucia, she always puts on a brave face."

"They're both fine, amigo. I promise you."

"Good. Matthias is loving those horses." He laughs. "You better be prepared to take him back out there on vacation."

"Yeah." I laugh too. If I have my way that kid will be coming here every single year with his momma and me.

"I need to run. It's way past the twins' bedtime and I can hear them causing hell out there," he says, rolling his eyes.

"Say goodnight to Alana and the boys for me."

"Will do." He leans over and switches off the screen and I lean back in my chair, hit by a wave of guilt. I have been far too distracted by Lucia and not focusing on finding out who tried to kill her.

My job here is to protect her though, right? And what better way to do that than be by her side every possible second? With that in mind, I stand up and head outside to find her.

I t doesn't take me long to find Lucia. She is sitting around the campfire with the ranch hands. My father is there too, but I suppose I can't be too pissed about that because he does this almost every night.

I take a seat beside her and the way she smiles at me makes my cock twitch in my jeans.

"You want a cold one?" Cody asks her, holding up a bottle of beer, and she nods before taking it and twisting off the cap.

"So, you work for Lucia's dad, right, Jax?" Cody asks as he takes a seat opposite us.

"Yeah," I say before taking a slug of my beer.

"And you're learning the family business?" He flashes his eyebrows at Lucia.

"Yep," she says with a nod and a smile.

"So, you'll probably take over one day?"

"I hope so," she replies.

"And then you'll be Jax's boss?" Cody grins.

She gives me a sideways glance. "I guess so."

"You kind of already are," one of the other guys—Caleb—interrupts. "I mean if Jax works for your dad and it's your family business, right?"

She chuckles softly as she takes a drink of her beer.

"Yeah," Cody agrees. "You're Jax's boss."

"I guess I am." She turns and arches one eyebrow at me.

I narrow my eyes in warning but she turns back to her captive audience.

"Wow! Jackson Decker taking orders off a girl fresh out of college." Caleb starts to laugh. "No offense, Lucia," he adds quickly.

"None taken." She smiles sweetly and I remain silent, sipping my beer and letting them talk shit.

"Can you tell him to go get us some more beers?" Caleb laughs louder now. "We're running low." He's drunk so I let it go.

She bites on her bottom lip and turns to me. "Hmm?" she purrs. "What do you think, big guy? Is that in your job description?"

I remain silent. I don't give a rat's ass what these jackasses think of me. They don't know that this is my ranch and I could toss every single one of them out on their asses if I wanted to. I'm secure enough not to care who they think I take my orders from. The truth is, if Alejandro were to hand over his empire to her tomorrow, then she would be my boss, and that would be fine by me.

So, I let her be Lucia—the spoiled daughter of Alejandro Montoya—because that is her armor. It's who she pretends to be when she's around people she doesn't really know or trust. When she is the spoiled little princess of one of the richest and most violent men in California, then she is invincible and nobody can hurt her. But when she is just Lucia, the little girl from Chicago whose family made her feel like an outcast, who never felt good enough for anything or anyone, well then the whole world can get to her.

"I don't think he wants to," she says, turning back to the guys.

"But you could make him though? He has to follow your orders, right?" Caleb says.

She turns to me and grins, her full lips dusting over the top of her beer bottle as she prepares to take another drink. She looks me right in the eyes. "He sure does," she purrs.

I arch one eyebrow at her as I down the last of my own beer. I know the game she's playing. I know exactly what she's looking for. If she's lucky, I'm feeling just about annoyed and horny enough to give it to her.

CHAPTER 31

LUCIA

I feel the heat of Jax's gaze on my skin and it's even fiercer than the flames of the fire a few feet in front of me. I glance sideways at him, not daring to look him full in the eye for fear of what I'll see. Maybe I took the whole being his boss thing too far. I mean, I live to push his buttons, but sometimes I don't know when to stop.

He picks up the two empty beer bottles beside him and then stands, wiping dust from his jeans. "I'm going to call it a night. Sleep tight, assholes," he says in his low rumbly growl.

I look up at him and can't determine how pissed he is at me because his face is unreadable. He turns and starts to walk away.

Shit! I did go too far. He's going to bed without me. He takes two paces then says one word and it proves to everyone sitting around this campfire who is really in charge. "Lucia."

I place my empty bottle into the trash can beside me and stand. "Night, guys."

"Night," they chorus. Cody flashes his eyebrows at me, as though he knows exactly how much trouble I am in.

My cheeks are already warm from the fire, but now they blaze with heat of an entirely different kind. I follow Jax as he remains two steps ahead of me. He stays silent and I do too, unsure what I can say that won't make him any angrier than he already seems to be. He continues walking and I frown as we pass the house.

Where the hell are we going? I daren't ask in case maybe he didn't want me to follow. I want so much to be close to him, so I continue walking behind him in silence.

When we reach the small barn a few hundred yards from the house, he stops outside the door. He turns to look at me, his eyes narrowed. "You trust me, Lucia?" he growls.

"Yes," I whisper, because I do, and he is one of the very few people in the world I can say that about.

He nods and then he opens the door and holds it wide. I take that as my cue to step inside. I look around the small space. It's dark, illuminated only by the light of the full moon. It smells of wood and oil and I see the long workbench in the center of the room. Jax flicks on a small lamp and the room is filled with a soft amber glow. There is a tractor in here, an old Chevy with no hood on it, a Harley Davidson, and various vehicle parts.

"Is this your workshop?" I ask, my voice barely a whisper. I know that he likes to tinker with engines when he has some downtime, not that he ever has much.

He doesn't reply. Instead he walks toward the bench and places the two empty bottles on it. I almost forgot he was carrying them and wonder why he didn't toss them into the trash. But I don't have time to unpick that thought as he crosses the small space between us. He wraps his hand gently around my throat and I gasp. I look up at him expectantly, licking my lips as I wait for him to kiss me, but he spins me around and walks me over to the bench. As we reach it he slides his hand to my back, pushing between my shoulder blades until I'm bent over the wooden table.

"Jax?" I whisper.

"If you're going to act like a spoiled brat, Lucia, then you're going to be treated like one," he growls. My insides contract and goosebumps prickle along my forearms.

He picks up a length of rope and then reaches for my hands, pulling them over my head and securing my wrists to the wooden support beam the bench is pressed against.

I shiver in anticipation and a whisper of fear dances up my spine as he goes on working in silence. When he has tied me securely, his hands run over my back until they reach the waistband of my jeans. With deft fingers, he undoes my button and zipper and starts to pull them off over my hips, hooking his fingers into my panties and taking them along too. He pulls them to my knees and stops.

I suck in a breath as my bare ass is exposed to the cool air but warmth spreads through my center. Why does this feel so damn hot?

Jax rubs his hand over my ass cheeks before he draws it back and slaps me.

"Ouch!" I yelp, but is one of surprise rather than any real pain. I know how strong he is and he held almost everything back.

"Isn't this what you want, Lucia?" he spanks me again and this time I moan.

"Isn't this why you put on your little show for the guys?"

Smack.

"Testing me?"

Smack.

"Wondering how far you could push me?"

Smack. This time it's harder and I yelp for real. "Yes," I gasp, because that is the truth. I do want to see how far I can push him. Ever since he joked about putting me over his knee, this is what I've wanted from him. I have never explored this side of myself before, but I want to with Jax.

"Thought so," he growls but he doesn't spank me again. Not yet.

I feel his warm hands on my knees as he starts to work my jeans and panties off over my calves, pulling them down and tugging them off along with my socks and sneakers until I am completely naked from the waist down.

My heart hammers in my chest as I lie with my face pressed against the cool wooden bench and wait for whatever it is he has planned next. Surely it has to involve him fucking me? Oh God, I hope so.

He slides a finger into my hot entrance and my cheeks flush with shame as the wet sound of my arousal is clearly audible in the quiet barn.

"You're soaking, Lucia," he groans softly.

"Jax," I whimper as he adds a second finger and rubs at a spot deep inside.

He chuckles softly before he stops and pulls his fingers out of me.

"I have a challenge for you, Boss," he says and my cheeks flame with heat as he taunts me with my earlier words. He nudges my legs wider apart with his knees. "If you can pass my test then I won't punish my little brat. Do you accept?"

"Yes." Of course I do. I'm not a brat and I will pass any test he can think of, not that punishment doesn't sound fun too.

"Good. Spread those legs as wide as you can for me."

I shuffle my feet along the wooden floor and stretch my thighs as wide as they'll go.

"Come on. You can do better than that, Angel," he growls.

"I can't," I protest. Not without being uncomfortable anyway.

"Hmm?" He gently taps each of my ankles with his foot and I edge wider until I'm standing on my tiptoes. "Told you so."

My thighs tremble as my limbs are stretched to their limits

and I wonder if he's going to tie my legs too, because I'm not sure how long I can hold this position if he doesn't.

"I wish you could see yourself like this," he hisses as he runs his hands over my ass and pussy. "So fucking beautiful." He spanks me again harder this time and my thigh muscles clench instinctively.

Damn! My muscles are already trembling with the effort of holding myself up on my tiptoes.

"Jax," I gasp.

He chuckles softly as his hands rub over my skin again before he slides a finger through my slick pussy lips and up the seam of my ass. "You ever been fucked here, Angel?"

"No," I whimper.

"Damn, Luce," he groans.

Then his hands are gone and I watch as he takes the two beer bottles from the bench. My racing heart goes into overdrive. What the hell is he going to do with them? I suck in a deep breath and close my eyes. Nobody would even hear me scream out here, would they? What the hell was I thinking, letting him tie me up?

Get a grip, Lucia! This is Jax. I breathe deeply, inhaling and exhaling to the count of four until my heart stops hammering. I trust him completely.

I strain to look behind me but I can't see what he's doing now.

The next thing I feel is one of his hands running over my ass again before it glides down my thigh and over my calf as he crouches down behind me. I hear the soft clink of glass against wood as he places one of the bottles on the floor next to the inside of my right ankle, so close that the cool glass rests against my skin. Then he does the same with the second bottle so that it sits against my other foot before he stands again and leans over me, his hard cock pressing against the seam of my ass through his jeans, his hot breath on my ear.

"Those bottles better not fall over, Angel," he growls. "Because as soon as they hit the floor..."

"But..." It's impossible. They're so light and I have no doubt he's about to make my legs shake violently. The thought of how he's going to do it makes wet heat slick my pussy.

"But what, Angel?"

"Nothing," I breathe. I'm going to pass his damn test if it kills me.

"Out there you might be the heir to the Montoya empire, Lucia, but don't forget that you still belong to me. This"—he slides his hand between my thighs and palms my pussy—"belongs to me. Your body is mine, Angel, and I will use it whatever way I choose. Understand?" He slides one finger inside me and my knees almost buckle.

"Yes, Jax," I whimper.

"Good girl," he whispers before he stands tall again. "I'm going to keep finger fucking you just the way you like it. I'll even make you come." He adds another finger and I groan loudly as the bottle beside my left foot wobbles precariously. "This will be all about your pleasure." He spanks my ass again with his free hand and a rush of wet heat coats his fingers.

"Jax," I groan loudly. Damn! How the hell am I going to stop those bottles from falling when he's doing this?

"Fuck, Luce, your pussy is loving this spanking?" he groans. "But as soon as one of those bottles falls..."

"What?"

"Then your punishment will begin," he chuckles softly as he slides his fingers in and out of my pussy while spanking my ass every few seconds. My walls clench around him as my orgasm builds.

My thighs are trembling. Calves burning. Knees shaking as I

try to keep those damn bottles from falling over. My ankles bump them slightly as a rush of heat pulses throughout my entire body and they wobble but they don't fall.

"You're doing so well, Angel," Jax chuckles. "But I've barely even started on you yet."

"Jax," I groan in frustration as he eases me back down from the crest of my climax before beginning again. When he sweeps the pad of his thumb over my clit, I cry out.

"How you doing there, Angel? Is this too easy for you?" he chuckles.

"No," I groan.

My entire body trembles now and my legs ache with an exquisite pain as the stretch burns through every muscle in my lower body. I almost want to kick over the damn bottles just to get this over with, but then I won't get the high that he's deliberately withholding and I need it. My body needs a release like it needs air. As I feel like I'm unable to take any more, he pulls his fingers out of me and a wet sucking sound fills the room, making my cheeks flush with heat. Is this it? Did I pass?

"So fucking wet," he hisses as he slides his fingers up to the seam of my ass, coating me with my juices before rubbing the pad of his thumb over my asshole. I realize I haven't passed—he's upping the stakes! He edges the tip in slightly and I moan so loudly, I think everyone on this ranch must have heard.

"You like that, Luce?" he groans.

"Yes," I gasp as he pushes in a little deeper and the feeling of fullness makes my walls clench around him. My legs shake violently as he pushes his thumb into my ass while he finger fucks my pussy and rubs on my clit. I close my eyes, trying to focus on my breathing and keeping my toes planted firmly in place, but all I can feel is the pleasure rocketing around my body as Jax's fingers take me to the brink of oblivion over and over again.

"Jax! Please!" I moan and then it happens. My foot spasms and one of the bottles clatters to the floor.

"Oh, Angel," he laughs softly. He slowly withdraws his fingers and the climax that was just a breath away retreats, fading from an impeding explosion to a flicker of a flame, leaving me feeling like crying in frustration.

"I'm sorry," I whimper. "Please, Jax."

"I know you are, Luce," he soothes, "but a deal is a deal, right."

Damn! I'm too tired and dazed to argue that his test was unfair.

The sound of his belt buckle being unfastened sends more shivers skittering around my body and I feel a wave of relief as I wait for the sound of his zipper too, but it doesn't come. Instead, it's the sound of the soft leather sliding against his jeans that I hear. Oh, God. I hold my breath as I lie here waiting for this to hurt.

"Jax," I whimper.

"I got you, Angel," he reminds me just before the leather cracks down over my ass.

Holy fucking shitballs! It burns, but it sends a current of lightning electricity through my pussy and around my body. I shiver as the aftermath skitters through my nerve endings.

He does it again and I stifle a moan. This is everything I didn't even know I wanted. It hurts, but in the most incredible, delicious way possible. It is sinful and erotic and... I have no words left.

Jax slides a finger inside me again, coating it in my wet heat. "You still enjoying this?" he chuckles before he spanks my ass again.

"Yes!" I breathe, unable to lie to him. I know this is supposed to be punishment but it feels like my reward.

"Good girl," he growls as he lands the next blow and I swear I almost pass out.

I have no idea how many times Jax spanks me with his soft leather belt. I lose count after six because I can hardly remember my name let alone what number comes next. When he finally drops the belt to the floor, he stands directly behind me, his strong hands running over my burning skin, generating a whole different kind of pleasure. Then the sound I have been waiting for—his zipper being opened—makes me whimper against the bench.

"This what you need?" he asks as he presses the tip of his cock against my opening.

"Yes, please."

He takes hold of my hips and drives into me, pummeling me against the workbench so hard that my feet lift off the floor. "Fuck, Luce, I've never felt you so wet," he groans. "Your ass looks so fucking beautiful when it's striped from my belt." He pushes his thumb into my ass again.

"Jax," I whimper as I draw my thighs closer together.

"I'm going to fuck this one day, Angel, but not right now."

"Okay," I breathe.

"You're so fucking close, Luce," he groans as he slides his thumb deeper inside, holding it there as he rails into me.

When my orgasm finally comes, it crashes into me like a freight train, shaking the breath from my entire body. Jax fucks me through it, leaning over me and whispering what a good girl I am in my ear. I tremble and shudder beneath the weight of him as the last waves wash over me. When I have stopped groaning his name, he unties my wrists and pulls me up, turning me in his arms and lifting me onto the bench.

I shuffle back, trembling as my orgasm ebbs away, but he narrows his eyes at me. "I'm not done with you yet. Come here."

Wrapping his arms around my waist, he pulls me close to

him, until our bodies are pressed flush together, before sliding his cock into my pussy again.

"Oh, fuck! Jax," I groan.

I can hardly take any more, but I need more anyway. My walls squeeze around him, pulling him deeper as I claw at his back. I'm still so sensitive that it only takes him a few thrusts before he has me teetering on the edge again.

"You're so fucking greedy for me, Angel," he growls. "Your tight little cunt loves my cock."

"I know."

"You want to come again?"

"Yes."

He drives in deeper and harder. "You think you deserve to?"

"No," I whimper.

He cups my chin in his hand and tilts my head so he can look into my eyes. "You took your punishment so well, Angel. Why don't you deserve to come again?"

"I knocked the bottle over," I breathe. "I failed your test."

He laughs softly. "You honestly think I was going to let you pass, Angel? It was an impossible task. I was about five seconds away from kicking those bottles over myself."

I want to yell at him and call him an asshole, but I can't. All I can do is breathe and feel him as I wait for his body to give mine exactly what it needs. My walls pulse around his cock and my head spins as a rush of arousal coats him, making him hiss out a breath.

He bends his head low and kisses my neck, sucking on the tender flesh on my throat that makes me quiver. If I have buttons, then Jackson Decker knows how to press every single one, and he is currently pressing them all at the same time— well, almost. When he slips his hand between us and circles two fingers over my clit, I may have well just handed him the launch codes because my climax rips through me like an atomic bomb just went off in my pussy.

"Easy, Angel," he growls in my ear as my body shudders in his arms. "I got you."

He grinds out his own release while I'm still riding the high of my own and when he's done, he presses his forehead against mine. "Who owns you?" he whispers.

"You, Jax. Only you."

CHAPTER 32

JAX

I roll out of bed, planting my feet on the solid wooden floor as I realize I've overslept. I stayed in Lucia's bed until after four because I couldn't tear myself away from her. I wish I could wake up next to her every morning, and to my surprise it's not because I want to fuck her every second of every day—although there is that. But I want to be a part of every bit of her life. I imagine Matthias climbing into bed with us and chattering about dinosaurs or superheroes and it brings an unexpected smile to my face.

I've never thought about having kids of my own. It's not that I'd decided not to have them, but I've never met anyone I wanted to be attached to for the rest of my life before. But now there is Lucia and the thought of her pregnant with my baby inside her brings out something primal in me. Not to mention the kid she's already got is pretty fucking awesome and I'm as much in love with him as I am with his mother.

I pull on my jeans then run my hand through my hair and sigh. The sooner we tell Alejandro and Alana about us, the better—though hiding in the shadows was fun for all of two days, now I want the whole fucking world to know that she's mine.

She's not in the kitchen when I go to check, or the den. The house is eerily quiet and it makes the hairs on the back of my neck stand on end. I open the back porch door and hear Matthias scream and my heart races in my chest. I run toward the sound but when I get to the edge of the yard, I see him with Lucia and my father. He is clinging onto my father's leg while Blue stands beside him wagging his tail. I feel a rush of relief quickly followed by anger at Harvey.

Matthias is scared of dogs and that asshole has his old hound running around here.

I look at Lucia wondering why she's not putting a stop to this and I notice she is smiling as she looks at her son and my father. I look back and watch as Matthias gingerly reaches out his hand and scratches Blue behind the back of his ear, and that old dumb dog stands as still as a statue and lets him. My father bends down and whispers something in the kid's ear that makes him smile. Then he lets go of my old man's leg and steps closer to the dog. He is hesitant at first, but Blue drops his head slightly, allowing Matthias to pat his fur. If there's one thing my father has done right in his life, it's train that dog. He is the most obedient mutt I've ever come across.

I lean against the tree, my arms folded across my chest as I watch the scene before me and Matthias slowly grows braver with each passing second. When Blue lays down and rolls onto his back, the boy squeals with laughter and drops to his knees to rub the dog's belly.

Lucia laughs too. Fuck she is beautiful when she smiles like that. She walks toward Harvey and wraps an arm around his waist before giving him a soft kiss on the cheek. He nods politely but then he steps away from her and she steps back too, as though she is hurt by his rejection. A pang of guilt gnaws at my chest. He's not rejecting her, simply keeping his distance because I warned him to stay the fuck away from her and Matthias. She is so fucking hard to stay away from though. They both are. Like little magnetic rays of sunshine.

I walk over to them.

"Jax," Matthias shouts. "Blue is letting me rub his belly."

"He sure is, buddy." I crouch down and ruffle his hair. "You want to come for a ride with me and your mom?"

He looks up at me, huge brown eyes shining with happiness. "Can I stay with Harvey and Blue?"

"Harvey might have things to do, Matthias," Lucia replies.

"I got all the time in the world," my father says but then he looks at me, knowing he should have kept his mouth shut.

"Can I stay with Harvey, Momma?" Matthias asks.

Lucia opens her mouth to reply, but then she looks at me instead, and now the three of them stare at me waiting for my response. My approval.

"Please, Jax?" Matthias asks.

"Can I trust you to stay here and look after him?" I ask my father.

"Sure. We'll be right here in the yard playing fetch with Blue."

I suck in a breath. "It's your call," I say to Lucia.

"If he won't be a bother, Harvey," she says with a smile.

"Not at all," he smiles back at her. "This kid is the best company I've had for a long time."

"Then of course you can stay." She leans down and kisses his head. "But you behave and do as Harvey says, okay?"

"Okay. Thanks, Momma."

We walk away, leaving Matthias and my father to play with Blue.

"That was incredible the way your dad did that," she says as she smiles at me, her eyes sparkling in the sunshine. "Matthias was so scared when Blue licked his hand, but then your dad just really calmed him down."

"Yeah? Well he always was good with animals."

She reaches for my hand and squeezes it in hers. "Thank you for letting him stay, Jax. I know that wasn't easy."

"He's your kid," I say with a shrug and immediately feel like a complete jerk.

"Of course, but I know that you're just looking out for us both," she replies, taking no offense.

"You want to come for a ride with me? I need some exercise."

She bites on her lip and looks up at me through her long dark lashes—my cock throbs at the sight.

I slide my arm around her waist. "I wasn't talking about that kind of ride, or that kind of exercise, Angel," I growl.

"I know," she purrs, "but my ass is kinda delicate this morning. I'm not sure a ride in the saddle is going to help matters."

"Well, that's a damn shame, because I was looking forward to having a reasonable excuse to have you pressed up against me for an hour or two."

I almost forgot that her ass would be tender after our adventure in the barn, but the memory of her tied up and spread wide open for me while I spanked her with my belt makes my cock weep. She presses her body closer to mine.

"Well, I don't want to ride your horse, but I could definitely be persuaded to ride you."

"Lucia," I warn as I look around to make sure there is nobody who can see us before I palm her ass in my hand. It fits perfectly. She fits perfectly.

"Jax," she breathes. "Please take me to your bed and fuck me."

"Fuck," I groan. She knows how much I love it when she asks me for what she wants. "Do you have any idea what you do to me?"

She glances down at the outline of my hard cock in my jeans. "I have a pretty good idea," she giggles, then chews on her lip again.

"Then you'd better get your fine ass in the house. Now." I slap it lightly and she bites down on her lip and groans my name. Fuck! Me! This woman is going to be my complete and utter ruin.

I lie back on the bed and watch her peel off her clothes for me. Mine were off within ten seconds of getting into the room. She has the most beautiful body I've ever seen, with soft, sensual curves and fullness in all of the places that make my cock throb in appreciation. I take my cock in my hand, stroking the shaft as I stare at her. Pre-cum beads on the top because she makes me so fucking hard and desperate to be inside her. When she's completely naked she grins at me.

"Get your ass over here, Lucia," I growl.

"You're so bossy," she giggles as she approaches the bed.

Reaching up, I grab her hand and pull her down on top of me. "You have no fucking idea, Angel."

I fist my hand in her hair and crush her lips against mine, pushing my tongue into her mouth and tasting her sweetness. She moans softly and the sound vibrates through my bones. I pull back and she gasps for air.

"You said something about riding me?" I arch an eyebrow at her.

"Did I?" she purrs.

"Yes. So slide that hot pussy of yours onto my cock right now, because if you make me wait any longer for you, I'll be forced to bend you over the end of this bed and fuck you into oblivion."

"Jax," she groans, "that sounds so freaking hot though."

"Later, Angel. Make me come first and I'll reward you for being my good girl."

"Yes, Sir," she purrs as she shifts her hips back, rubbing her wet pussy lips over me.

I grab hold of her hips, pulling her down onto me but she jerks away, grinding her pussy on me instead. "Patience, Jackson," she teases me. "Maybe I should tie you up?"

"I'd like to see you try, Angel," I flash my eyebrows at her.

"Hmm?" She flutters her eyelashes at me.

So she wants to play? "I can wait." I loosen my grip on her hips. "You keep on rubbing that sweet pussy on me and we'll see who caves first?"

"Okay." She flashes her eyebrows at me. "You're on, Decker."

She goes on rolling her hips over me and my cock throbs. I grind my teeth. Who the fuck am I kidding? I am desperate to be inside that sweet pussy right now. I know exactly how silky, hot and wet she will feel when I bury myself in her. I slide one hand between her thighs and rub her clit. She arches her back and groans softly.

"You like that, Angel?"

"You know I do," she hisses.

"Yeah and you know it'll feel so much better when my cock's in you too."

"I know," she groans and bears down, grinding her hips until I'm coated in her juices.

"So slide onto it, baby." I rock my hips up, nudging at her opening and she places her hands on my stomach, her eyes locked on mine as they burn with fire.

"Jax," she purrs and my balls draw up into my stomach. I love the sound of my name on her lips when she's about to lose control.

I reach up and grab her hair, pulling her down with my free hand while I keep working her clit with the other. I press my lips against hers so I can tongue-fuck her mouth the way I want to be fucking her pussy. She's going to win, isn't she? I'm going to fucking die if I don't get inside her soon.

Our bodies bead with perspiration as we grind against each other. I'd call it dry humping except that Lucia's pussy is dripping wet and she has soaked my cock with her cum now too.

"I really need inside you, Angel."

"Then do it, Jax," she groans. "I want you to fill me with your huge cock. I need you to fuck me real hard, cowboy. My pussy is desperate for you."

Dirty talk now, too. She's going to fucking kill me. But if that's how she wants to play. "I know, baby. I can feel your cum dripping all over my cock," I growl as I rub soft circles over her clit. "I'm going to stretch your tight little cunt wide open when you sink your hips onto me. It will feel so good when I'm inside you, fucking you hard the way you like it. Won't it?"

"Yes," she whimpers.

"So just slide onto me and then I'll take care of you," I plead with her.

"Just fuck me. Please?" she moans.

I grab onto her hips just as she shifts them slightly and we move together; I drive into her as she positions herself at the perfect angle, neither of us caring any longer who held out the longest because it doesn't matter. Later if she asks, I will insist it was a tie, but right now all that I care about is this sweet pussy gripping my cock for dear life.

She sits up, rolling her hips over mine as she sinks deeper onto me, then she looks down at me through her dark lashes, her eyes almost black with desire.

"Oh, God!" she breathes as her wet heat soaks me.

My cell starts ringing loudly in my ear and I glance at it on the nightstand. I usually keep it on silent but I'm expecting a call. I pick it up and glance at the screen and my heart sinks when I see Alejandro's name on the screen. I press the button to end the call but I must be distracted by Lucia fucking me or my fingers are too slippery with cum, because I press the answer button instead and it goes straight to fucking speaker phone.

"Hey, amigo."

Fuck!

I clamp my hand over Lucia's mouth—she looks at me wide-eyed as she presses both of hers over mine and shakes her head. She's going to come. Her father is on the phone and his little princess is about to come all over my cock—and my girl is not quiet.

I fumble with the phone and it almost slips out of my fingers. If I just end this call he'll worry there's something wrong. But I can't speak to him while his daughter is riding me like she's about to win the Kentucky Derby.

"I'll call you right back. Just … busy…" I manage to grind out the words before I press the right button and cut him off.

I toss the phone onto the floor and a few seconds later it beeps to signal he sent me a text message instead.

I move my hand from her mouth and she moans my name so loudly it vibrates through the entire house. I thank Christ there is no-one home because our secret would be out. I forget all about the phone call from her father as her pussy squeezes around me and I am so close to the edge I feel it pulsing through my entire body.

But I need more.

I flip her over onto her back, pinning her wrists beside her head as she looks up at me with a huge post orgasmic smile on her face. "I love fucking you, Angel," I growl as I nail her into the bed until I can't hold off any longer and I fill her with my cum.

.   .   .

We lie in bed, Lucia draped over me and our bodies pressed together as we catch our breath.

"I need to call your father before he sends a drone down here to see what's going on," I say as I trail my fingertips over her back, making her shiver.

"Don't go," she says as she buries her head into my chest. "Call him from here. I'll be quiet."

I press a soft kiss on her forehead. "As much as I would prefer to stay in here with you for the rest of the day, I can't speak to him while you're dripping cum onto my leg, Angel. Lying to him is one thing, but doing it while your naked body is pressed up against me is another."

"I suppose you're right," she says with a sigh. "I need to check on Matthias anyway."

I tap her on the ass. "Come on. Let's get up."

She rolls off me and climbs off the bed and I can do nothing but stare at her as she picks up her clothes from the floor. She catches me looking and blushes.

"What?" she whispers.

"You are fucking beautiful."

"Jax!" Her cheeks turn an even deeper shade of pink.

"It's true," I say as I jump off the bed and slide my arms around her waist. "You need to learn to accept a compliment, Angel."

"Then thank you," she whispers.

I wait until I am far away from Lucia before I call Alejandro back.

"Hey, amigo, Sorry about before," I say as soon as he answers.

"What the fuck were you doing? You sounded out of breath."

"Nothing. Just sorting the horses," I lie.

"Nothing or sorting the horses?"

"Does it matter?"

He starts to laugh. "You were fucking someone weren't you?"

"No."

"Is Shannon available again?" He laughs harder.

"Alejandro."

"Okay. I hope you're still keeping an eye on my daughter and grandson while you're *sorting the horses.*"

Fuck! If only he knew. "Of course. They are my number one priority."

"How are they anyway? I tried Lucia's cell a few times but it was off."

Double fuck! Any second now, he's going to realize what we were both doing.

"Can you tell her to charge the damn thing and call me back?"

"I will." I breathe a sigh of relief. Of course he's not going to suspect anything, because the idea of me fucking his daughter is unthinkable to him. I'm going straight to hell for what I've done to her these past few days. "Is everything okay?"

"Yeah. We got the guy who tried to run Lucia off the road."

"You did?"

"Yeah. So you three can get your asses back here as soon as possible."

"Who was it? Why did he go after her?" I frown as I think about the reason we're here at the ranch. I'd almost forgotten there was a far more serious motive for me bringing Lucia here than simply fucking her senseless.

"Some kid. We're holding him for now and I haven't had a chance to question him yet," he growls and I know he actually means that whoever it is will be tortured into speaking. Alejandro is skilled at making people talk. Not that the stupid fuck doesn't deserve what's coming to him. "You want me to wait until you get back?"

"Yeah," I snap. I want to watch him die myself.

"I'll send the plane. It can be there tonight."

"Yeah." I swallow hard. "Thanks." Tonight? That means our time here is over. What if this doesn't work back in LA? What if being here at the ranch allowed us a freedom that we just won't have when we get back?

"Jax?" Alejandro snaps and I realize he's been talking to me but I was too lost in my own thoughts.

"Yeah, sorry," I stammer.

"Can you tell Lucia and get her to call me?"

"Of course," I say, snapped from my daze.

"Great. I'll see you both by morning then?"

"Sure."

"You don't sound too thrilled about getting back here?"

"I am," I answer a little too quickly.

He's quiet for a few seconds. "Once this is all sorted, maybe you could take a few weeks vacation and go back for another visit?" he offers.

"No. I'm good. I'm looking forward to getting back. I'll see you soon."

"Good. I'm looking forward to seeing you all."

"Bye, amigo." I hang up the phone.

I am looking forward to seeing him too, and Alana and the twins, but I am not relishing telling him about me and Lucia.

I walk into the yard to find Lucia, but before I can search for her, I see Matthias and my father sitting on the old wooden bench. Each of them holds a glass of lemonade while Blue lies at their feet.

I don't mean to eavesdrop, but I hear my name and I freeze.

"Are you Jax's daddy, Harvey?"

"I sure am."

"Why doesn't he call you Daddy? Or Papi?"

My father sighs and I wonder if he's to going fob the kid off with some lame ass excuse. "Because I'm not a very good dad, Matthias," he says.

"Why not?" Matthias looks up at him all wide-eyed and innocent. "You make me laugh."

My father laughs at his response. "Ah, well. That's a good thing, isn't it?"

"Why aren't you a good daddy then?"

My father draws in a deep breath before he speaks. "I didn't used to be a very nice man."

"I think you're nice," the kid says sweetly.

"Why, thank you," my father ruffles the kid's hair. "But back when Jax was little like you, I was mean and not much fun at all."

"Why?"

I wonder when my father is going to tire of Matthias' constant questions, but he goes on answering them. Even the difficult ones. Even though Matthias doesn't always understand what he means, he tries to explain it in a way the kid will get most of it.

"I don't have a daddy," Matthias says and his little voice sounds so sad that it breaks my heart.

"I know. Some of us don't," my father agrees.

"I'd like a daddy though," he beams as he swings his legs on the seat.

"You would, huh?"

"Yeah. One just like Jax."

"Well, you couldn't go wrong with a dad like my Jackson. He's the best kind of man there is." My father wraps his arm around the kid and they sit in silence as my heart feels like it's going to turn into a puddle of mush. What the fuck is wrong with me?

"Hey," Lucia sneaks up behind me and slides an arm around my waist. "Don't those two look cute together?" She nods toward my father and her son.

"Yeah," I say, the word sticking in my throat.

"I took them some lemonade but then Matthias told me I could go back inside. I felt like I was being dismissed by my own four-year-old," she laughs softly. "Is everything okay, Jax?"

"What?" I blink at her.

"You seem distracted."

"Oh yeah. I just spoke to your father. He found the guy."

She sucks in a deep breath. "He did? Who is he?"

"I don't know yet. He's holding him until I get back. He's sending the plane for us now, so we should pack up. We'll need to leave in a few hours."

"Oh." She looks as disappointed as I feel.

I pull her back so we're hidden by the house and wrap my arms around her waist. "I have loved every second of being here with you, but we have to go home, Angel."

"I know." She places her hands on my chest. "I was just starting to love it here. Your aunt Molly is so nice. Matthias loves the horses and he's even conquered his fear of dogs. I'll miss it."

"That's all you're going to miss?" I arch an eyebrow at her.

"Well, I won't have to miss you, will I?" she purrs and my cock stands to attention. I swear she has a direct line to him.

"No, Angel."

"Nothing is going to change is it, Jax?"

"We have to tell him. I can't lie to his face, Luce."

She smiles at me. "I know, but not as soon as we land though?"

"No," I shake my head. I'll have much more pressing matters

to deal with, such as torturing the cunt who tried to run my girl off the road.

"I'd better tell Matthias we're leaving," she says with a sigh.

"Tell him we'll come back in the fall," I say, brushing her hair back from her beautiful face.

Her eyes widen in delight. "Will we?"

"Yes." I lean down and press a quick soft kiss on her lips and then I have to pull away because whenever I have my hands on this woman I want to carry her to my bed and get a part of my body inside her.

CHAPTER 33

LUCIA

As the plane lands on the runway at LAX I turn to Matthias and squeeze his hand. He's looking out of the window—he cried when I told him we had to leave. Molly cried, too. Then I cried. I even saw a tear in Harvey's eye. Jax promised that we can go back in the fall and I really hope that we do. I love the ranch; it felt like home to me in a way that I never thought possible. Even though I was only there for a few days, I feel like I've left a piece of myself back there.

"Are you ready to see Papa, Nana and the boys?" I ask my son, plastering a huge smile on my face and feigning my excitement. It's not that I'm not looking forward to seeing my family, but I know that as soon as we get off this plane, Jax is going to disappear somewhere with my father and I don't know how this thing between us is going to work in LA. He spent most of our journey back making calls and checking his laptop. I feel like he's slipping away from me already.

The stewardess helps us collect our things and just before the plane door opens, Jax puts an arm around my waist. "I'm sorry I've been distracted," he says quietly.

"That's okay."

"No, it's not," he sighs. "Now that your father has the man responsible for trying to kill you, well my life just got as hectic as it used to be is all."

"I know," I lean against him. "We'll figure this out though, won't we?"

"Of course." He winks at me, then the plane door opens and we pull back from each other. My father is waiting on the runway beside two cars and I know that one is for me and Matthias and one is for him and Jax. I might be part of their organization now, but it's clear this is still their domain and I don't have the energy to argue with them about it right now. It's early morning and I haven't had any sleep. Matthias slept a little but he'll be tired and cranky soon and I need to get him home. I don't think I want to come face to face with the asshole that tried to kill me today anyway.

"Matthias," my father shouts, holding out his arms.

"Papa," my son replies as he begins to clamber down the steps.

"Be careful," I say but he is way too focused on his grandpa and a few seconds later he's being scooped up into my father's arms and swung around in the air.

As I reach the bottom, my father wraps his free arm around me and kisses my forehead. "It's so good to have you back, *mija*."

"It's good to be back, Papi."

"Your mom is waiting for you at the house." He nods to the silver SUV behind him where Raoul and another of his security team sit waiting for me.

When he hands Matthias to me, he hugs Jax briefly. "I have missed you the most, amigo," he laughs. "Doing this job without you is no fun at all."

Jax laughs too but I know he is feeling as guilty as I am right now.

"I'll see you tonight, *mija*," my father says to me. "You're staying at the house, right?"

"Actually, Papi. I'd like to go back to my apartment," I say, avoiding looking directly at Jax—I can see him watching me and if our eyes meet then we just might give ourselves away.

"But..." he starts.

"You have the man responsible now. Jax said you put in some additional security. I just want my own bed. Please?"

"As you wish." He frowns at me. "I'll have a man outside the building too."

I roll my eyes.

"Just until we speak to this cabrón today and find out why he targeted you. You could still be in danger, Lucia."

"Okay," I sigh.

"Come on," he says to Jax who nods. As they walk to the other car Jax turns and glances at me and it is a look full of longing and desire and everything that we can't say out loud, and I almost melt into a puddle on the asphalt.

CHAPTER 34

JAX

I sit on the backseat of the SUV beside Alejandro as his driver takes us to the warehouse where the guy who tried to kill Lucia is being held.

"So, what do we know about this guy?" I ask.

"His name is Owen Kincaid. Worked for the Ortegas a while back."

"Those Ortegas again," I snarl.

"After we had our run in with them a few years ago they had a change of leadership."

"Yeah. I remember," I say. "The younger brother took over, right?"

"Yeah. He had a shakeup and Kincaid was one of the casualties. It seems he has been a little down on his luck ever since. Lost his apartment. Wife. Kid."

"Any idea why he targeted Lucia, though?"

"Not yet. But he used to work in that club she used to go to sometimes," said Alejandro. "That awful place you picked her up from."

"Deemon?"

"Yeah, that's the one. Maybe he knew her from there?"

"Maybe? You got his cell or anything?"

"No," he grins. "It got smashed when we picked him up."

"Smashed with what?"

"Kincaid's face," Alejandro replies with a shrug.

"Fair enough."

"Anyway. We got him on camera getting into the car that ran into Lucia and Raoul outside an IHOP about two miles up the road. He was wearing a black cap. Raoul took a look at the footage and identified the car and him as the ones that he saw too. So—"

"We definitely got the right guy then!"

"We sure do," he said. "I don't know about you but I haven't tortured anyone in a long time and I'm itching to break out every single trick I know on this motherfucker!"

"A long time being like what, six weeks?" I arch an eyebrow at him.

He frowns at me. "Six weeks?"

"Yeah. We went to Phoenix, remember?"

"Oh fuck yeah. Well six weeks is a long time."

"Whatever, amigo. I am up for giving this piece of shit everything we got."

He nods and smiles at me. "I love when you let your inner sadistic fucker out to play."

F ive hours later we are in the warehouse with Owen Kincaid. He's tied to a chair and I am holding a blowtorch to his nuts while he screams in agony. The smell of his burning flesh fills the large space and makes one of Alejandro's newer recruits throw up in the corner.

"Get him the fuck out of here!" Alejandro snarls and he gets escorted from the room by the scruff of his neck.

I turn off the torch and step back, watching as tears, blood and snot pour down Owen's face.

"Please just kill me," he groans as his eyes roll in the back of his head.

"You want to give him a shot?" I ask Alejandro. This guy is about to pass out from the pain he's in. We've been at this on and off all day. I've already cut off so many parts of him that he looks almost unrecognizable from the man who we met when we first came in here, but all he keeps telling us is that we ruined his life, he's sorry and he never meant to hurt her, in between begging us to end his life. One of Alejandro's tactics is to give people morphine so that they can endure more pain for longer and then when it wears off every part of their body screams at the same time. I have to admit it's pretty twisted.

"You think he deserves any?" he asks.

"No." I kick him in the nuts and he retches but there is nothing left in him to throw up. He puked up his guts ten seconds after I cut off his first toe. "But he's going to be out soon though. I'm not sure how much more he can take."

"So fuck him. I want him to hurt so bad that the memory of his screams will haunt this place for the rest of time."

"I do too, but we've got nothing from him yet."

"Maybe there's nothing to give?" Alejandro shrugs. "Maybe he's told us all there is. Because I gotta say I don't think this piece of shit has it in him to withstand this level of pain without cracking, do you?"

I look back at the pathetic figure of Owen Kincaid. "No." I frown. He was definitely the guy in the car that day. But why target Lucia?

I grab him by his hair and try one more time. "Why her?" I ask him again. "Why did you try to run her car off the road?"

"I didn't," he wails.

"What?" I snarl at him. He's fucking delirious. He's already admitted that it was him driving the car and now after everything he's endured he's trying to claim that it wasn't. Alejandro walks over and punches Owen in the side of the head. His head snaps back and stays there.

"What the fuck?" I shake my head at him.

"I knocked him out. Wake him up."

"Owen." I shake him but there is not a flicker of life. "Owen!" Still nothing. I take my knife and hold it to his lip, slicing into the delicate flesh but he doesn't flinch. "You fucking killed him."

"So? That was the plan. I just did it a little sooner than expected."

I drop the blow torch to the floor. I suppose he's right. But fuck I was enjoying torturing that fuck way more than I thought I would.

As I walk out of the warehouse, I wipe my blood-soaked hands on an old rag and toss it to one of Alejandro's security before I take out my cell phone. "Fuck." I have no battery.

Alejandro walks up behind me.

"Can I borrow your cell?"

"Sure." He takes it from his pocket and tosses it to me but he stays right by my side as we walk to the car. I can't call Lucia because he'll ask questions. I enter his passcode and dial Shane Ryan's number instead.

"Hi, buddy. What's up?"

"Hey, amigo. We found that guy that Jessie was looking into for me."

"You did? I'll let Jessie know she can stand down."

"Thanks, and tell her thanks for her help."

"I will. I'm glad you got everything sorted. How is Lucia?"

"She's fine. There was no permanent damage from the crash."

"Ah, that's good."

"Yeah. Thanks again, Shane."

"No problem, Jax. I'll catch up with you soon."

"Bye, amigo."

I end the call and hand Alejandro his cell phone back, wondering if Lucia is expecting me or whether she's sleeping because we were traveling almost all night. I also remember that Alejandro has a guy stationed outside her apartment; how will I explain my visit? I'll just say I'm checking in on her after our trip. She must know I'll come to her place, right?

I should go home first and wash this asshole's blood off me but all I can think about is touching her, tasting her, burying myself inside her until the rest of the world fades away. Rage and adrenaline and fury burn through my veins and I need to do something to release it. I need her. She is the light to my darkness.

"You ready?" Alejandro holds open the car door for me and I climb inside and count the seconds until I can get to her.

CHAPTER 35

LUCIA

I look out of the window and watch the droplets of rain run down the pane. Matthias is asleep. Jax's cell phone is switched off. I spoke to my mom half an hour ago and she told me my father wasn't home yet. I don't know how she does this, knowing he's out there, possibly in danger, and not being able to reach him.

I can't focus on anything other than the knot of anxiety in my stomach. I don't even know if Jax is coming back here. We didn't get a chance to discuss plans once we landed at LAX.

A black truck drives past and I hold my breath, waiting for it to stop, but it drives right by.

I sigh and walk into the kitchen to make a cup of Molly's famous calming tea—she gave me a box before I left. The water has only just boiled when I hear a knock at my front door. I run out into the hallway and look through the peephole. My heart almost bursts with relief when I see Jax standing there. Opening the door, I throw my arms around his neck.

"Thank God you're okay," I breathe as I pepper his jaw and face with kisses.

He wraps his arms around me and walks me through the door, kicking it closed behind him. It's only once we're inside my apartment that I see his shirt is covered in blood.

"Are you hurt?" I look down at his blood-soaked clothes.

"It's not mine," he growls and keeps walking me back through my apartment until we get to my bedroom. Once we're inside he kicks that door closed too and spins me around until I'm pressed up against it.

"Jax," I whisper, taking his face in my hands. "What happened?"

"He's gone, Luce. He can't hurt you anymore." He drops his head to my neck and starts kissing me. He is rough and hurried and his stubble scratches my skin but I pull him closer.

"I need you so fucking bad," he growls in my ear as his hands run over my hips until he reaches the edge of my dress and he pulls it up until it's bunched around my waist.

"I'm right here," I breathe as I reach for his zipper and tug it open. Sliding my hand into his jeans, I squeeze his cock. It's hard and smooth, like hot stone.

"Fuck," Jax growls as he squeezes my ass, lifting my legs and wrapping them around his waist. I have to grab onto him for support as he rolls his hips against me. I groan as wet heat sears between my thighs. He presses me against the door, holding me up while he reaches beneath my dress and tears a hole in my panties.

"Jax," I gasp.

"I want in your hot cunt right now, Angel," he growls as he thrusts himself inside me and I gasp as he stretches me wide open for him. It burns but it feels so damn good.

"You are everything I need," he groans as he buries his face in my neck. I claw at him, wanting him deeper and harder and he responds by driving further into me, nailing me to the door.

"Jax. I love how you fuck me," I whimper and it seems to

spur him on even more. He fucks me harder than he ever has before, while he is soaked in the blood of the man he just killed — for me. And I love every single second of it, because the animal inside me recognizes his and it knows that this is the best kind of salvation there is.

CHAPTER 36

JAX

I t's been five days since we got back from Dallas and Lucia
and I are working together again. We still haven't told her
father about us and I understand her reservations. The
timing needs to be right and she and Matthias are my priority.
We have settled into something of a routine though—that
routine being I fuck her anywhere and any chance I get. I go to
her apartment every night after Matthias is in bed and I tear
myself away from her before sunrise.

There's something addictive about fucking her in secret and
the added thrill of being caught, but I also feel an overwhelming
sense of guilt that I'm lying to Alejandro. I've avoided him as
much as I can and it's only a matter of time before he becomes
suspicious.

Lucia smiles at me as she opens the door to her father's hotel
suite that he uses as a base for his business. There are no armed
guards today because he's not here. I follow her inside and as
soon as I close the door she wraps her arms around my neck.

"You know there's a huge bed in this place, right?" She
arches an eyebrow at me.

"I do." I kiss her quickly as I take her arms and place them by her side. "But we're here to pick up some papers—besides, I draw the line at fucking you in your father's bed, Angel." I slap her on the ass and she giggles.

She follows me to his office. I can't resist her and she knows it. There's every chance I'll be fucking her in this suite before we leave.

I find the brown envelope with my name written on the front on Alejandro's desk and pick it up. "This is all we came here for," I say. "Let's go."

"But, Jax," she pouts.

"Don't be a brat, Lucia." I try to scowl at her but I can't. She's wearing a tight fitted dress today. It covers her skin but it does nothing to hide her delicious curves.

"It's been so long since you touched me though," she purrs.

"It's been less than six hours," I remind her as she walks toward me, taking the envelope from my hand and placing it back on the desk.

She presses her body against mine and I suck in a deep breath. We have twenty minutes to spare and I do hate to leave my girl in need of attention.

I slide my hand beneath her dress and up the soft, supple skin of her thigh until I reach her panties. Brushing my fingertip over the fabric I smile against her neck as I find them damp.

"You're already wet, Lucia." I growl, my teeth grazing the sweet skin of her throat.

"I know, Jax," she pants and the sound makes my cock twitch in anticipation.

I tug her panties aside and circle the tip of my finger over her clit, making her hiss out a breath.

"You're fucking insatiable, you know that?" I whisper and she whimpers. Sliding my fingers through her folds until I reach her hot opening, I push the tip inside her and she shudders, clinging onto my forearm. "Is this what you want, Angel?" I push deeper inside.

"Yes," she groans as she rocks her hips against me, grinding herself onto my hand.

"You want to come?" I breathe, my lips dusting over her the shell of her ear.

"Yes."

"Say please." I chuckle softly as I add a second finger and she wraps her arms around my neck.

"Please, Jax," she moans softly.

"You'd better be quick, Luce, because if one of your father's men catches me with my fingers buried in your cunt then our secret will be out," I tease her, because there is no risk of anyone walking in on us in here. Alejandro is at home with Alana and the twins and nobody else but Lucia and I have access to this suite when he's not around.

"Your fingers?" she pants but she looks up at me, flutters her thick dark lashes and smiles. "Hadn't you better hurry then, Jax, because if they catch us with your cock buried in me, then they would probably just shoot you on sight."

So, my girl wants to play? I sink my fingers deeper inside her, making her groan softly as she coats me in a rush of slick heat. "You want me to fuck you on your father's desk, Luce?"

"Yes," she grins at me. "Unless you're too worried about him finding out."

I don't know where my senses have gone, but I have clearly lost them because I start undoing my suit pants with my free hand. She reaches down to help me, wrapping her hand around my cock and squeezing.

"You want that?"

"You know I do, Jax," she gasps as I pull my fingers out of her and lift her onto the desk. I pull her thighs wide apart before I drive my cock into her, making her gasp out loud.

"Fuck, Luce. You're going to get me killed," I groan as her pussy grips me like a vise. Even if someone walked in here right now, I wouldn't stop. I am addicted to her. Isn't that the only reason that would account for the complete craziness of fucking Alejandro Montoya's daughter on his desk?

"Jax," she gasps as what I've just said hits home. "He has cameras in here."

"I know, Angel." So, she does care about getting caught. I'm relieved about that, because I do too. This is not how I imagine him finding out about us. "I turned them all off before we got here. Don't worry."

"So you knew this would happen?" she purrs.

"You and me alone in a room? Of course this was going to happen."

"But what if he realizes you've turned them off?"

I arch an eyebrow at her. She knows better than anyone what I do and how good I am at it. "I'm deeply offended that you would even ask me that."

She bites on her lip, her eyes dark with lust as she pulls my face closer to hers. "Of course. I forgot you're the great Jackson Decker, hacker extraordinaire."

I push her back so she's lying flat on the desk, leaning over her as I drive my cock deeper inside her. "You forgot who I am?"

"Uh-huh," she pants.

"Really?" I drive harder.

"God! No, Jax!" she shouts.

"That's my girl. Who do you belong to, Luce?"

"You, Jax," she whimpers. "Only you."

"Damn right, baby. Now come on my cock like a good girl so we can get back to work."

Her walls squeeze me deeper and she rakes her nails down my back as she comes hard and loud for me. I keep on railing into her until I find my own release. I kiss her forehead and she purrs like a contented kitten. That was incredibly stupid, but she makes me want to do completely reckless shit like this. I can't think clearly when she's around and that's dangerous for a man in my line of work.

As soon as she stops shaking, I stand up and zip up my pants before helping her with her clothes.

"I'm just going to the bathroom to freshen up," she says breathlessly.

"I don't think so, Angel."

She blinks at me. "What?"

I wrap and arm around her waist and press my lips against her ear. "You just made me fuck you on your father's desk. Maybe spending the rest of the afternoon with my cum dripping out of your pussy will teach you not to do it again."

She opens her mouth to speak, no doubt to argue with me, but maybe it's the wicked grin on my face that makes her stop and think. "You really want me to go to our next meeting like that? With my panties damp?"

I slide my hand to her ass and squeeze possessively. We're only going to meet with the city council about some parking issues involving the club. "Fuck, yes," I growl. "I love marking you with my scent. And after our meeting, I'm going to peel them off you again and fuck you in the back of my truck."

"Jax," she sucks in a breath and grabs onto my shoulder as her cheeks flush pink. "Did you used to kiss your mother with that filthy mouth?"

"Only on Sundays after church," I wink at her. "Shall we go?"

I can't help the feeling of pride that surges in my chest when she takes hold of my arm and we stride out of the door with my cum leaking out of her pussy.

CHAPTER 37

JAX

Listening to the sound of Lucia's steady breathing as she lies wrapped in my arms is so fucking sweet and relaxing. My eyelids flutter closed for a second before I jolt awake.

"What is it?" she mumbles sleepily.

"I almost fell asleep. I should go."

She drapes her thigh over mine and squeezes me. "No," she purrs. "Just stay a little while longer. Please?"

I press a soft kiss on top of her head. "I can't, Angel. I'm fucking exhausted and if I fall asleep here, Matthias might come in and find us."

"I'm sorry for having you sneaking around at night and not getting enough sleep."

"Hey." I cup her chin in my hand and tilt her face to mine. "I'm sneaking around of my own free will. And I would rather be here than anywhere else, but—"

"Matthias," she finishes my sentence.

"Exactly."

She pushes herself up and straddles me. "I miss you when you're not here," she whispers.

I reach up and brush my fingertips over her cheek. "I miss you too, Angel, but there's only one way to fix it." I don't want to pressure her to tell her parents before she's ready, but I can barely look her father in the eye and I hate being apart from her. "I want to wake up every morning with you in my bed. I want to wake you up in the middle of the night just so I can fuck you."

"Jax," she breathes as she grinds her wet pussy over my cock.

"Any mention of sex makes you horny, doesn't it?" I chuckle as I slide my hand down her body and hold onto her hips.

"You're the one who started talking about fucking," she whispers.

"Hmm," I roll her hips over me and my cock hardens against her.

"But I know you're tired," she purrs.

"I am never *that* tired, Angel," I smile at her. "Besides, I might just lie here and let you do all the work."

She laughs softly. "I'm happy to, but you can't help yourself from taking control."

"Well, slide your hot pussy onto my cock and we'll see." I wink at her, but she's right. It's only a matter of time before I take over in one way or another. I can't help myself. I love to dominate her as I make her whimper and moan my name.

A fter I have fucked her for the fourth time tonight, I drag myself out of her bed and grab my clothes and start to get dressed.

"I think we should tell my father about us, Jax," she whispers.

I sit on the bed beside her. "Good. Let's do it tomorrow."

"Okay," she breathes.

"It'll be fine." I take her hand and squeeze it in mine.

"I'm not worried about me—I'm worried about you and

him," she says, the words catching in her throat. "You won't fight, will you?"

"Lucia," I say with a sigh. I can't lie to her and tell her that we won't because I know without a doubt that when Alejandro Montoya finds out I am fucking his daughter, his immediate reaction will be to tear my head from my body. "I can't make that promise, Angel. But I can promise you that it'll be worth it."

"Not if either of you get hurt," she whispers.

I roll on top of her, taking hold of her hands and entwining my fingers with hers. "We can't go on sneaking around or we're going to get caught and that will be a million times worse. I can't go on lying to his face whenever I see him. I told you back in Dallas that we were going to have to do this all the way. I've given you a week, Angel, but now we need to be open about what this is between us. I can't go on pretending that you don't mean everything to me."

"Jax," she gasps.

"What, Angel?"

"Do you mean that?" she blinks and her eyes brim with tears.

"That you mean everything to me?" I frown at her.

"Yes," she whispers.

"Lucia," I growl. "You think I went into this with you lightly? I told you that this was it for me, didn't I? That no one else would ever touch you?"

"Yes."

I stare at her, waiting for her to tell me that she feels the same, because the fact that this has come as a shock to her makes me nervous.

"I..." She blinks at me. "This feels like a fairytale that I'm going to have to wake up from."

"Why?" I frown at her. "Why is it a fairytale?"

"Because I love you so much, Jax. I've been in love with you since I was seventeen years old. Happiness like this can't be real, can it?"

"It sure feels real enough to me," I smile at her. "I love you, Angel. Your dad is going to be pissed as hell at me, but we'll all get over it. I promise." My words are full of conviction because I want her to believe them but I'm not sure I believe them myself.

CHAPTER 38

LUCIA

I stand on the doorstep to my parents' home with Matthias'
warm, soft hand held tightly in mine. I've never been so
nervous to go into this house before, not even the first
time I ever visited when I was pregnant and alone. Jax stands on
the other side of me and he gives my hand a quick, reassuring
squeeze.

"It will all be okay," he whispers just as my mom opens the
door to us.

"Why didn't you use your key, sweetheart?" she says as she
pulls me into a hug before bending down to Matthias, who
flings his arms around her neck.

"Nana," he squeals.

"I forgot it," I say with a shake of my head. "I didn't come in
my car."

"Oh." My mom stands tall again and smiles at Jax. "Did you
drive together?"

"Yeah," I reply.

"Then come on in, the two of you. Your father is in the
garden."

We all follow my mom into the house and Matthias scam-

pers off ahead to find his grandpa and the twins. By the time we
get to the garden, Matthias is playing with my little brothers and
Hugo on the lawn.

"I didn't realize you were coming over tonight, amigo?" My
father smiles at Jax and I feel a wave of fresh guilt almost over-
whelm me. He is so happy to see his best buddy here and has no
idea we're about to break his heart.

"I came with Lucia," he says and the tone of his voice makes
the hairs on the back of my neck stand on end. Dear God! He's
going to do this right now. "We have something we need to talk
to you both about."

"Okay?" My father frowns while my mom closes her eyes
and sits beside him, as though she knows what we're about
to say.

Jax looks to me and I draw in a deep breath. "Let me?" I
plead as I place my hand on his arm.

He stares at me for a few seconds before he nods his
agreement.

"Jax and I are dating," I say the words super quick as though
they'll somehow hurt less.

"What?" my father growls as he looks to Jax to tell him that
I'm completely delusional and have lost my mind.

My mom stays silent but she places her hand over his, which
is now balled into a fist on the table.

"It's more than dating," Jax says as he shoots me a look that
says I could have worded that better, but what else was I
supposed to say? We're screwing each other's brains out every
chance we get?

"No." Alejandro shakes his head and starts to laugh, but it's
not a pleasant sound. "You're both fucking with me."

"We're not, amigo." Jax replies.

My mom holds onto my father's hand as though she's trying
to channel some of her calming energy through him somehow,

but it's not working. He glares at Jax, his face full of fury—his eyes are burning so fiercely that my stomach starts to flutter, and not in that nice excited way, but in that I'm gonna throw up way.

"You had better be fucking with me," he snarls as he edges forward in his seat, every ounce of his anger directed at Jax. "Because that is my little girl you're talking about and you are old enough to be her fucking father!"

"Papi," I snap.

"Stay out of this, Lucia," he growls.

Stay out of it? Like it doesn't concern me? What the hell?

"I wouldn't fuck with you about this." Jax glares back at him. "We're not just dating, Alejandro. This is serious—"

"Serious?" he shouts, his face contorting with rage. That word seems to have been the final straw, the match that lit his incredibly short fuse because he jumps out of his seat, launching himself at Jax and landing a right hook on his chin with such force that the two of them stagger backwards and end up on the floor.

"Papi!"

"Alejandro!"

My mom and I shout in unison, but the pair of them completely ignore us as they roll around on the lawn like a pair of MMA fighters, punching and grappling to maintain the upper hand.

"Mom," I say as she stands beside me and we watch them in horror.

"Hugo," she shouts and he comes running. When he reaches us he frowns at us both and stands staring at my father and Jax fighting.

"What the hell?" He shakes his head in disbelief.

"Please stop them," my mom pleads with him.

"Fuck," he hisses but then he wades into the fight, signaling one of the armed guards to help him. They manage to pull them apart only for my father to launch himself at Jax again, grabbing him in a headlock and dragging him back to the ground.

Hugo and the guard stand with their hands on their hips, shaking their heads in defeat and confusion.

"Oh for goodness' sake," my mom hisses before she marches over to them herself. I wonder if she's going to take a nearby chair and crack it over my papi's back, WWE style, because I don't see any other way to split them up. But instead, she leans close to him and places one hand on the back of his neck, turning his face to hers with her other hand. "Alex," she says calmly. "You're scaring the boys."

He stops, fist in mid air as it was about to come crashing down on Jax's face, then he stands up, brushes the grass from his suit pants and spits blood onto the floor.

Jax stands too and wipes the blood from his nose with the back of his hand.

My father glares at him. "Get the fuck out of my house right now," he snarls.

"Alejandro?" Jax glares back at him.

"I said get the fuck out." My father's hands are balled into fists by his sides. "And stay the fuck away from my daughter."

Jax looks to me just as Matthias runs to me. "Why are papa and Jax fighting, Momma?" he cries.

"It's okay." I pick him up and hug him tightly. "They were just playing."

When I look up again, Jax is turning away and heading for the door.

"Jax," I shout, preparing to walk after him but my father stands in front of me.

"You are not going anywhere with him," he growls.

"The hell I'm not," I hiss as I cover Matthias' ears.

"Lucia. Stay and speak to your parents," Jax says.

"No. I'm coming with you."

My mom stands beside me and puts a comforting arm around my shoulder.

"No. He's right. I should leave. You need to stay here with your family."

His words tear out my heart. Why is he leaving without me? We're a team, aren't we?

"I'll have someone drop your car here and I'll see you later," he adds with a faint smile and I heave a sigh of relief. I'll see him later.

"The fuck you will," my father snarls.

"Alejandro," my mom snaps shooting him a look that says this conversation is over for now. Jax walks away, leaving through the side gate to get to the driveway. My father shakes his head and marches over to my twin brothers, scoops them into his arms and storms into the house.

"I'm sorry, Mom," I whisper as tears fill my eyes.

"Oh, sweetheart," she wraps her other arm around me now and hugs me tightly. "It will all be okay."

M y father manages to avoid even looking at me during dinner. If it wasn't for Matthias begging me to let him stay and play with the twins, and the look of concern on my mom's face, I would have left straight after Jax did.

"Can I sleep over, Momma? Please?" Matthias sidles up to me, his face covered in chocolate ice cream as he smiles up at me.

"Not tonight, munchkin," I say, brushing his hair. "I have to be up early for work tomorrow."

"Papa can take me to kindergarten," he says, his eyes shining. "Can I stay? Pleeease?"

I look at my father whose eyes finally meet mine. "Let him stay," is all he says.

I look down at my son's excited face and can't say no to him. I know my father is pissed at me and Jax, but that would never affect his relationship with Matthias.

"Fine," I say as I lean down and give him a kiss on the nose.

"If you're staying here, then you need a bath and some pajamas. You monsters are not getting chocolate ice cream all over my bed," my father says with a grin as he pushes his chair back.

Matthias and Tomás shriek with delight, but Dario has already fallen asleep on my mom's lap.

"You need any help?" my mom asks him.

"No. I got it," he says, feigning a scowl that she would question his ability to control two little kids, but then kisses her forehead and takes Dario from her arms. "I'll put him down first and then see to the other two."

"Thank you," she smiles at him.

He doesn't look at me though and I swallow down the ball of emotion in my throat. He is so disappointed in me and it is breaking my heart. He is such a great dad and even though he is in the same room as me, I miss him already.

"He's not angry with you, sweetheart," my mom says softly.

I wipe the stray tear from my cheek, annoyed with myself for getting so upset. He's being unreasonable here, not me. So I fell in love with his best friend—there are much worse things I could do. "He can't even bear to look at me, Mom."

"He's angry. He's just processing it, that's all. I mean, it was quite the bombshell you two dropped on us."

"You were shocked, but you're not acting like a jerk about it," I sniff.

"Lucia," she warns me. "I don't care what he's done, you do not speak about your father that way."

"I know," I wince. "I'm sorry. But you're still speaking to me."

"Well, it's different for me."

"Different how?"

"Well, Jax isn't my best friend." She takes a sip of water. "And I know how it feels to fall in love with someone you're not supposed to," she adds with a shrug.

"You mean, Papi?"

"Of course," she says with a smile.

"But he wasn't supposed to fall in love with you either," I remind her. "He knows how that feels too."

"Yes, but you are his daughter and it's his job to protect you, Lucia. In his eyes, Jax has betrayed his trust. You must see why he feels like that?"

"I guess," I admit. Of course I understand why he's so upset, even if I hate that he is and I don't agree with him. "What about you, Mom?"

"It doesn't matter what I think. This is between you, Jax and your father."

"Of course it matters," I blink at her. "Your opinion means everything to me."

"All that matters to me is that you are happy, sweetheart. Does Jax make you happy?"

I swallow the lump of emotion that wells in my throat as I consider the answer to that question and wonder what the best way to explain it is, because to simply answer yes doesn't feel like enough. "You know the way that you look at Papi when he comes home from work?" I say instead. "I used to think the two of you were soppy and romantic. I could never have imagined being so excited to see someone who I had only seen a few hours earlier."

"Hey," she narrows her eyes at me and laughs.

"Now I get it though. Jax makes me feel like that, Mom. Like my heart will burst if I don't see him. He makes me feel like I can conquer the world."

"Oh dear," she says softly, shaking her head.

"What?"

"I think your father is going to have to learn to accept you and Jax pretty soon. But be careful, sweetheart—you are wise beyond your years, but Jackson is a lot older and more experienced than you."

"You were a virgin when you married Papi," I remind her.

She arches an eyebrow at me. "I'm not talking about that kind of experience."

"Oh." I blush to the roots of my hair. I have just admitted to my mom that I'm having sex with Jackson Decker. I mean, she obviously knew that, but still.

She smiles. "You can talk to me about anything, sweetheart. You know that, right?"

"Yes." Before Jax, I did talk to her about this kind of stuff. She was the person I called that time I couldn't get my diaphragm out, and also when some idiot frat boy told me my ass was too fat right after we'd had sex, which had been the most disappointing sex of my life even before he said that.

"Good." She wraps an arm around my shoulder. "Everything will be okay. I promise."

CHAPTER 39
LUCIA

I pop my head into my parents' bedroom to see Matthias, Tomás and my father lying on my parents' huge bed watching cartoons. Tomás' eyes are fluttering closed so I walk quietly over to the bed and sit on the edge.

"You sure you want to sleep over, munchkin?" I whisper to my son.

"Yes," he says and cuddles against my father's chest.

"Okay." I bend and give him a kiss on the forehead. "Night, little guy."

"Night, Momma," he smiles.

"Night, Tomás." I reach over and brush my younger brother's hair.

"Night, Luch-ee," he mumbles.

"Goodnight, Papi," I say softly.

He grunts in response—actually grunts instead of speaking. I roll my eyes and stand up before walking out of the room.

After I've looked in on Dario and said goodbye to my mom, I grab my purse and the keys to my car which are now on the table near the front door. I smile at the sight of them, knowing that Jax had someone drop off my car like he promised he would. The thought of seeing him soon makes my insides warm and tingly.

"Lucia!" My father's voice cuts through the silent hallway.

I draw in a deep breath and turn to face him. So now he wants to speak to me. I had hoped to get out of here without having this conversation, but who am I kidding, right?

He walks toward me and I wait for him to speak first. "Are you going to see him?"

"Yes, Papi," I reply with a sigh.

"No." He shakes his head, anger darkening his features. "I forbid you to have anything to do with him."

"What?" I frown at him. "You can't forbid me to see anyone. This is not 1920."

He glances down to the car keys in my hand and I can almost hear what he's thinking. He bought me that car. He owns my apartment too. I plan on getting a place of my own as soon as I save enough from my paychecks. I'm not used to being so looked after and it took me a long time to accept that he and my mom would pay for things like that for me. I know that most people aren't as lucky as I am, but it was him who persuaded me to swallow my pride. It would have been hard for me to get my degree and work part-time while being a single mom too, so I accepted their generosity. As he told me time and time again, that is what parents do for their children. I suppose I spent so much of my life without a decent parent that I forgot what that looked like.

I wonder now if he's going to make me regret my decision and use any of that against me. I know he must want to. He is a man who gets what he wants by any means necessary and he's used to being the one in control of every situation he finds himself in.

It makes my heart almost burst with love and respect for him when he doesn't. He chooses another tactic instead though.

"The gates are locked. Nobody is getting through them until the morning," he snaps.

"Fine!" I pop my keys into my purse. "I'll walk."

"Over my dead body," he snarls.

"Dad," I shout and the word seems to stop him mid-rant. I have never once called him dad before. The twins call him dad or daddy, but not me. I always call him Papi and even though it means the same thing, somehow this word feels more.

Tears fill his eyes and I wonder if he is going to relent. But he is Alejandro Montoya—backing down is not in his DNA. "You are not leaving this house," he snarls.

I suck in a breath and hold my head high, just like he taught me to. "I am. I know that you're upset, but this is my life. Be mad at me all you want but it's not going to change how I feel about Jax."

He scowls at the mention of Jax's name.

"I love you, Papi, but I love him too and he's the man I want to be with."

"He's taking advantage of you, *mija.*"

"You really think that? The man who you trust more than any other person in the world?"

He glares at me. He has no real comeback for that. "He's so very wrong for you," he finally snaps.

"He's completely right for me."

"You are not leaving this house," he insists.

I sigh in frustration but then suddenly my mom appears out of nowhere—the only person in the world he will bend for. "Alex." She places a hand on his arm. "Lucia is a grown woman. As her parents, we allow her to make her own choices, even if we don't agree with them," she says softly, reminding him of what he told her when I decided to join the family business.

I see the moment he gives in. The slightest drop in his shoulders is the only outward sign as he continues to glare at me, but how can he argue with his own words? My mom steps closer to him, wrapping her arms around his waist.

"Go to bed and I'll join you shortly," she says before pressing a soft kiss on his cheek.

He looks between us both now then rolls his eyes. He kisses my mom and she releases him from her embrace. Then as I think he's about to walk away, he wraps an arm around my shoulder. "Goodnight, *mija*," he says softly before planting a kiss on the top of my head.

"Night, Dad," I whisper.

I watch him walk away, cursing under his breath in Spanish as he does.

"I'm sorry I made him so mad, Mom," I say quietly.

"I told you he's not angry with you, sweetheart. He's mad at Jax."

"I wish he wouldn't be. It's not like that is all Jax's fault and I had no part in it," I say, shaking my head in exasperation.

"I know that. He just needs some time is all."

"I hope so," I say because the thought of him always being mad at Jax breaks my heart. I would never forgive myself if I came between the two of them.

"I know so. And in the meantime, I'm always here. No matter what. Okay?"

"Okay," I whisper and she pulls me into a fierce hug.

"Love you, kiddo," she says into my hair.

"I love you too, Mom."

Once I'm in my car, I call Jax. I am so eager to see him. I need to talk about what happened tonight and how we are going to deal with my father's disapproval. There is so much to discuss, but more than that, I just want him to hug me and tell me everything is going to okay.

"Hey, Luce," he says when he answers his cell. "How are you?"

"Hey. I've just left. I'm okay. Are you at home?"

"Umm. No," he replies, sounding a little awkward.

My stomach drops and I feel a huge crushing wave of disappointment. "Oh? I thought—" I start to say but maybe I misheard him earlier when he said he would see me later. Maybe he isn't as bothered as I am about what happened at my parents' house, or maybe he has a different way of dealing with it. "Where are you?"

"Sitting in my truck outside your apartment waiting for you to get home," he replies.

"Oh?" I smile widely and warmth floods my entire body. He's waiting for me. "I'll be there soon."

"See you soon then, Angel," he says in that soft drawl that makes my heart skip a beat.

W hen I pull up outside my apartment a short time later, I feel a familiar fluttering in my stomach at the sight of his truck parked outside. Even though I knew he was there, it still hits me like a sledgehammer. By the time I park up and get out of my car, he is out of his truck, leaning against it with his arms folded. He's wearing jeans and a t-shirt that shows off his huge tattooed forearms and it takes every ounce of restraint I have not to mount him in the street.

I walk toward him and as soon as I'm within touching distance, he pulls me into his arms.

"Have you been here all night?" I ask.

"Not all night." He winks at me. "But for over an hour." He bends his head low and kisses that spot on my neck that makes my thighs tremble. When he lifts his head again, his face is full of concern. "Are you okay?"

"I am now," I whisper as I rest my head against his hard chest.

"I'm sorry that I left, but we would have just kept fighting if I'd have stayed. I don't want to come between you and your parents, Luce. I can handle him being mad at me, but not you."

I don't answer, I simply wrap my arms tighter around him and bury my head closer against his chest.

"Was it that bad?" he asks softly, brushing his hands over my hair.

"Not really. It could have been worse, I suppose. I mean my papi is pissed as hell. Mostly at you, though," I chuckle. "I'm still his sweet little girl."

"Don't," he groans as his hands slide over my back. "I already feel bad about defiling you." A soft chuckle rumbles in his chest.

I laugh too. I love how easy he makes it to be around him. Even after everything that happened tonight, he is here making me laugh. "I know you're only kind of joking, but you've done nothing wrong, Jax," I remind him. "I'm an adult."

His hands drop to my ass and he presses my body against his. "Can we talk about this in the morning?" he growls. "Because now that I know you're okay, all I want to do is take you to bed and defile you even more."

Wet heat floods my core at his words. "Yes, please," I whimper shamelessly.

"That's my girl," he whispers as he lifts me, wrapping my legs around his waist as he carries me into my apartment building.

As soon as we're inside, he sets me down on my feet but before I can move, I am pressed against my front door. He wraps one of his huge hands around my throat while the other slides beneath my dress and up between my thighs.

"Jax," I breathe as he tugs my panties to the side and rubs a finger over my clit.

"I'm not usually such a patient man when it comes to what I want, Lucia," he groans as he dusts his lips over mine. "But I've been very patient with you."

"I know," I say, thinking he's talking about waiting outside for me.

"I want to claim every single part of you, baby. I'm tired of waiting."

Oh, shit! That's not what he's talking about.

"Jax," I murmur against his mouth. Perhaps there is something I should tell him? He deserves to know, doesn't he? No. Not yet. It would spoil everything.

"Hmm?" he mumbles as his hand slides down my body and he peppers soft kisses over my throat, focusing on that one point on my neck that he knows would make me agree to anything.

"Will it hurt?" I whisper.

"I would never hurt you, baby," he growls as he starts to pull my dress up until it's bunched at my waist. "I'll make sure you're ready. My cock will be soaked in your cum before it gets anywhere near your ass. By the time I'm done with you, you'll be begging me to fuck you."

I suck in a breath as a rush of intense wet heat almost knocks the wind from me. My knees buckle but I'm held up by the weight of Jax's body against mine. When he starts to peel my panties off, I can hardly control the trembling in my thighs. As his fingers brush my skin, they leave trails of electricity and fire behind. Then his hand is between my legs again and he nudges them further open with his knee as he slides two thick fingers deep into my pussy.

My walls squeeze around him as the pleasure rockets through me. He knows my body so damn well. I know that he'll make this good, and then maybe I can forget.

"Jax," I groan. "I need you. Please?"

"Soon, baby," he soothes in my ear. "You're always soaking

for me, but I need you wetter. Your pussy was made for me. You know that, don't you?"

"Yes," I hiss as he pushes against the spot deep inside me that I hadn't even known was there until I met him.

"That's my good girl," he growls as he presses the pad of his thumb over my clit and my orgasm crashes into me like a freight train. I come so hard that I almost pass out.

When I finally stop shaking, he carries me to the bed and lays me down on it.

I reach up and stroke his hair.

"You still with me, baby?"

"Barely," I whisper. "I have no idea where that came from."

"Oh, I do." He chuckles and I make a note to ask him what he meant by that when I regain my ability to think and talk, but right now all I can focus on is him peeling off my dress and then the feeling of his lips as they trail kisses over my skin. Over my breasts and my stomach. He spreads my thighs wide apart with his powerful hands and when his head dips between them and he gets that magical mouth on my pussy, I almost come apart again.

"Jax," I moan loudly.

"Your pussy is so fucking good, Luce," he growls as he sucks and licks and nibbles me to another earth shattering orgasm.

CHAPTER 40

JAX

She's ready. We both are. My cock is as hard as iron and I've made her come four times. Her thighs and pussy are slick with her juices and I coat my finger in them before I slide it into her ass.

"Jax," she groans and my cock weeps in appreciation.

I pull my hand back and her body trembles at the loss of touch.

"On your knees, baby. Stick that beautiful ass in the air for me," I order and as I knew she would, she complies. She is so submissive in my bed and I am beyond fucking honored that I get this side of her.

I reach over and take the lube from her nightstand and sit up until I'm kneeling between her thighs. Her chest heaves with ragged breathing and her legs tremble from the orgasms I've already given her. I know her body better than I have ever known anyone else's—exactly what buttons to press to take her to the edge. I love having that power over her when I decide whether to keep her there or let her come.

There was no teasing her tonight. I let her have all of them as soon as she needed them because I need her this way—soft and boneless and compliant—ready for the first time I fuck her like this. I love her ass. It's the most perfect peach I have ever seen and I have dreamed about fucking it for far longer than I should have.

Squeezing some lube onto my hand, I rub it into my fingers to warm it before I slide one inside her, not just to the knuckle this time, but all the way in. Her muscles squeeze me tight and I can't help but imagine how they will feel around my cock shortly.

"Your ass is beautiful, baby," I growl as I work my finger in and out of her.

The sound of her soft unintelligible moans fill the room.

I squeeze more lube from the tube onto her asshole before I push it inside with a second finger.

"Jax," she hisses as I push deeper, stretching her open as much as I can so that she'll be able to take me. She pushes her hips back, looking for more, and I am more than happy to oblige, sinking both my fingers as deep into her as they'll go.

She whimpers and moans as I work them in her, twisting and stretching to make her as loose as I can.

"Does that feel good, baby?" I growl.

"Yes," she gasps. "So good."

Fuck! She's ready. She has to be because I am going to come just from watching her. I push my cock into her pussy to coat it in her juices again and then I slide my fingers out of her.

She sucks in a breath and shudders as I press my cock against the seam of her ass. "You feel how hard you make me, baby?" I growl.

"Yes," she whimpers.

"You're going to take all of my cock like a good girl, aren't you?" I ask as I rub my hands over her back and grab hold of her hips.

"Yes, Jax," she purrs. "Please?"

"That's my girl," I soothe as I push the tip inside her. Her body inches forward on instinct, but I hold her in place as I allow her to adjust to me stretching her open. When her breathing slows, I edge in a little further.

"God! Jax," she hisses, but this time she pushes herself back against me.

"You ready for more?" I groan as my fingers dig into the soft flesh of her hips. It's killing me holding off from driving my cock all the way into her, but I intend on doing this often so I need to make sure she enjoys every second of it. Besides that, I promised her I'd make her beg me for this.

"Yes. Please, Jax. Fuck me."

Fuck! I can't wait a second longer. I roll my hips, driving deeper into her and she shouts my name. I keep hold of her hips with one hand while I fuck her hard, before I reach in front with my other so I can rub her clit. Her entire body bucks on my cock as her orgasm threatens.

"Oh, God! Jax! Stop!" she shouts.

I freeze. Have I hurt her? No. She's on the edge. I can feel her ass squeezing my cock and her pussy trembling and quivering as she waits for her release.

"What's wrong, baby?"

"I feel like I'm gonna—"

"Gonna what?" I bite back a smile.

"Pee," she whispers.

Fuck! Me! I am going to blow my load in her any second. I rub my hand over her back. "You're not going to pee. I promise."

"But it feels so intense," she hisses as I start to gently rock my hips into her again. "Oh, Jax! I am," she groans.

"You're not. Just relax, Luce. I got you. Let go."

My words are all the permission she needs and as I drive into her one last time, she comes with a roar and a sweet release of her juices as she squirts all over me and the bed. Being drenched in her cum and knowing I am the only man who has ever made her do that makes my balls tighten and I follow straight after her, filling her with my own release as I hold onto both of her hips and drain every last drop into her, grinding out every second of the high I'm on.

When I'm done, I pull out of her and lie on the bed, pulling her onto my chest and brushing her hair back from her face.

We lie together, completely spent, our bodies damp with sweat as we catch our breaths.

"What was that, Jax?" she eventually asks.

"You squirted, baby. Have you never heard of it before?"

"Oh," she giggles. "I have, but I've never done it. I honestly thought I was going to pee."

I laugh with her. "It definitely wasn't pee."

She lifts her head and looks at me, her eyes all wide and innocent-looking despite what we've just done. "I kind of didn't care though," she says as her cheeks flush pink.

I arch an eyebrow at her and she chews on her lip.

"I mean. I really didn't want to pee on you, but—"

"But?"

"You told me to let go and I trusted you. That's a big deal for me," she whispers. "I have never trusted anyone like that before."

"I am fucking honored that you trust me, baby," I say before I kiss her forehead. "You have no idea how much it means to me that you do."

"Hmm," she mumbles as she nestles her head against my chest. "We need to take a shower and change the sheets."

"Soon." I wrap my arm around her. "Right now, I'm enjoying lying here in a pool of your cum."

"Jax," she giggles.

"But that's exactly what it is," I laugh. "Did you enjoy your first ass fucking?"

"Yes," she whispers. "I love you, Jax."

"I love you too," I say as I stroke her hair. She's far too good for me, but now that she's mine, I'm never letting her go.

I wake in the night with Lucia lying on me. I don't mean lying next to me, snuggled against my chest like she usually is, I mean actually lying on top of me, her arms and legs wrapped around me like a koala grips a tree. My chest feels damp too. Has she been crying?

"Lucia, baby. Are you okay?" I whisper in case she's asleep.

"I lied to you, Jax," she says.

"What are you talking about?" I brush her hair back from her face and her cheek is wet with tears.

"That wasn't my first time."

I sit up in bed, bringing her with me and scooping her up until she is sitting on my lap. What the hell hasn't she told me? I resist the urge to fire questions at her while she's upset, knowing it might only push her away.

"Talk to me, Angel," I say instead as I wrap my arms around her.

"It was the first time I wanted to do it, Jax." She looks up at me with her huge brown eyes wet with her tears and I can't help squeezing her tighter as every muscle in my body tenses. "I've done it once before, though."

"Okay," I whisper, trying to keep my voice steady and calm and not betray the anger that is bubbling in my chest.

"It was my thirteenth birthday. My oldest brother, Luca." She shudders at the mention of his name and I swear if that cunt wasn't already dead I would make him feel pain like he had never imagined possible. "When I was younger him and Sammy, well they would bully me and hit me and stuff, but when I got older and started you know, filling out, Luca started to look at me different. I didn't know what it was at first, just that it made me feel really uncomfortable. I used to do whatever I could to avoid him." She draws in a shaky breath and I sit in silence while I wait for her to go on, even though I know what she's going to tell me and the anger that I feel burns me from the inside out.

"He would corner me sometimes and press up against me, rubbing his dick on me. I used to try to fight him off, but he was so much bigger than me. He said it was my fault because I provoked him. I tried to do everything not to, but not matter how I dressed or how quiet I was, he would always find a reason to do it. I kind of got used to it, you know?" She blinks at me.

No, I don't know how it feels to have to get used to your older brother groping you every chance he got, but I don't say that. "Go on, baby," I say instead.

"This night, he'd been out drinking and I was reading in the den. I didn't get many presents but an old friend of my mom's bought me the Harry Potter books from the thrift store and I was so engrossed reading them that I stayed up too late."

My heart feels like it is going to break into a million pieces for her. Everything about what she just said makes me want to protect her and spoil her for the rest of her goddamn life.

"I must have fallen asleep because I woke up and he was pulling my jeans off." She takes another deep breath and my knuckles feel like they might pop out of my skin from how hard my fists are clenched.

"I fought, Jax. I tried but he was so strong. I scratched his face and he slapped me and called me a tease. The next thing I knew he was on top of me, his breath stinking of beer and his big ugly hands pulling at my panties. I told him I was on my period and he laughed at me. He said he would never fuck me anyway because I was disgusting and that he couldn't even bear to look at me. That was when—" She gulps loudly, a deep sob bubbling up from her throat and I pull her tighter to me, pressing my lips against her temple.

"It's okay, baby. There's only you and me here," I whisper.

She nods at me, tears running freely down her cheeks. "He turned me onto my stomach and then he pushed it inside me. It hurt so much, I thought I was going to die. It felt like a hot poker pulling my insides out. I didn't even know you could do that there. God, I was so naïve," she says with a shake of her head.

"No. You were thirteen. You shouldn't have known about that."

She leans against my chest and I wrap my arms tightly around her. I wish I'd known about it earlier. Would I have still done what I did before? Yes, at some point, but I would have checked in with her more. I would have done a little more before and after care.

"Why didn't you tell me, Luce?" I ask as I brush her hair.

"I don't think about it—I don't let myself think about any of the horrible things he did to me. I mean I know they happened, but I've buried them deep, you know? And then earlier, when you said that's what you wanted, I didn't want it to spoil anything between us."

"Lucia," I say against her hair. "Nothing about your past could do that. You should have told me."

"Are you honestly telling me that the night would have ended the same way? That you wouldn't have been thinking about him the whole time?" She sniffs. "And then I would have been thinking about you thinking about him, instead of us being able to enjoy what was happening."

"I'm sorry if you weren't ready," I say. I should have fucking checked and not assumed.

"I was ready, Jax," she snaps. "This is what I was afraid of." She pulls back from me.

"What?" I frown at her.

"That you would start seeing me differently. Treating me differently."

"Hey," I snap her from her mini tirade and pull her back to me. "That is not what this is about. But, yes I would have handled this differently."

"And that's what I'm afraid of, Jax. Because what we did before was perfect," she breathes as she places a warm hand on my cheek. "Now show me how much you still want me."

I flip her over onto her back before she can even finish that sentence. "Don't," I growl.

"Don't what?" she blinks at me.

"Don't even think about going there, Lucia." I nudge her thighs apart and settle between them, my hardening cock pressing against her slick pussy. "You think I could ever not want you?"

"Show me, Jax," she breathes as she claws at the skin on my neck.

"You are fucking perfect," I groan as I grind against her clit, making her whimper. "Your pussy. Your ass. Your mouth. No one will ever fuck you or touch you ever again. Every single part of you belongs to me. You got that?"

"Yes," she groans.

My cock is rock-hard now and she's wet enough that I can slide all the way inside her. "Mine," I growl as I drive into her as far as I can go.

"Yours," she pants and I bury my head against her neck, sucking at her tender skin as I nail her to the bed.

She responds by wrapping her legs around my waist, pulling me closer to her. Her walls squeeze around me as I bring her close to the edge. I don't have the patience to draw this out for her and make her pleasure last longer. This is about showing her how much I need her. How much I love to fuck her. I shift my hips so I can hit her sweet spot and she hisses in my ear as I slam hard into her.

"Jax," she gasps as she comes for me.

"That's my good girl," I breathe in her ear as the waves of her climax wash over her and I bite down on her neck as I find my own release, marking her with my teeth and my seed so that everyone will know she belongs to me.

When we are both breathless and spent, I roll onto my side, pulling her against me so her back is flush against my chest, my arm around her and her perfect ass pressed against my cock. I breathe in the scent of her hair and she purrs contentedly.

"Is there anything else I need to know, Luce?" I ask.

"No, Jax. Promise," she whispers. "You know everything. You know me better than I know myself."

"Hmm. You'd better believe it," I say, nipping her ear and making her giggle. I love her laugh. It's completely infectious.

"What did you mean earlier?" she breathes.

"When, baby?" I frown.

"When we first got here and you made me pass out against my front door," she laughs again. "You said you knew exactly where that came from."

"Oh," I smile as I pull her closer to me. "You really don't know?"

She shakes her head. "No." she shakes her head.

"Whenever I call you a good girl? You don't feel that?"

"Oh," she breathes. "Well, yeah. It kind of does something to me, but I didn't realize it was so obvious."

"Anything that makes you wet is obvious to me, baby. Even more so if it's the thing that tips you over the edge when you're ready to come."

"Is that weird that I like that?" she whispers. "I mean I'm like a grown-ass woman who can take care of herself."

"It's no weirder than how hard it makes me to call you my good girl," I growl in her ear. "Because you are, aren't you?"

"Jax," her breath hitches in her throat. "Unless you're ready to go again, you need to stop right now."

I laugh as I pull her tighter. "I'm always ready to go with you, but you need some sleep."

"Are you telling me what to do now?" She feigns her indignation but her shallow breaths are telling me a different story.

"Oh I know you like that too," I chuckle. "But only in my bed, baby."

"Except that this is my bed," she reminds me.

I run my hand over her body and she shivers at my touch. When I reach her throat I squeeze gently. "That's where you're wrong, Lucia. Any bed that you are in is my bed. Do you understand me?"

"Yes, Sir," she purrs and the sound vibrates through my cock.

"Good. Now behave and go to sleep," I warn her with a final kiss on her temple.

CHAPTER 41

JAX

I unwrap Lucia's arms from around my waist and kiss her forehead.

"Please let me come with you, Jax?" she pleads, staring up at me with those huge brown eyes that will usually get me to agree to absolutely anything.

"No, Angel. This is between me and your father. I have to do this alone. Surely you understand that?"

She blinks at me. "But what if you start fighting again? What if you hurt him?" she blinks at me.

"I won't."

"What if he hurts you?"

"He won't. I'm not going to lie to you, he's going to hit me. And we'll probably fight, but we've fought plenty of times. I broke his trust, Luce. No matter the reason why, it doesn't change that fact."

"But, Jax..." I see the uncertainty in her eyes. That she still doubts my commitment to her stings, but I know it will take a long time to undo a lifetime of her feeling like she's not good enough.

"I don't regret a single second of any of it. Being with you is a decision I would make one thousand times over, Angel." I brush her hair back from her face.

"Just don't do anything stupid, okay?" She leans her head against my chest.

"Stupid? Me?" I kiss her head again. "I'll see you later."

I step out of the elevator and nod to the two armed guards who always stand outside this suite when Alejandro is here. I half-expect them to draw their guns and shoot me, but they greet me as they always do. I suppose he hasn't sent the memo that his most trusted employee and best buddy is no longer welcome.

I walk through the suite and his office door is open. He looks up at me when I step into the room. "I wondered when you'd finally have the balls to show up," he snarls.

"Well considering it's only 10 a.m. you didn't have to wait very long, did you?"

"What the fuck, Jax? She's my fucking daughter!" he bellows, standing up and planting his hands on his desk.

"I know. I'm sorry."

"You're sorry?" he growls. "Sorry is when you dent my car or break my fucking watch or something. It doesn't cut it when you are screwing my fucking daughter."

"It's all I have, amigo," I say, aware that my apology is futile, but I needed to say it anyway.

"When you were supposed to be working together these past few weeks, have you really been sneaking around? Laughing at me? Thinking I am some sort of *idiota*?"

"No!" I shout back at him. "Is that what this is really about? Your fucking ego?"

"Don't you fucking dare." He vaults the desk like an Olympic gymnast and punches me in the face. I stagger back and rub my chin. That stung like fucking hell, but I deserved it.

He comes at me again, but this time I defend myself, ducking to avoid his punch while landing a right hook on his jaw. Then we go at it again, like two brawlers in a street-fight, neither one of us prepared to back down, too matched in strength and agility for either of us to best the other. We have sparred together for over twenty years. We know each too well.

When my lungs are burning with effort and the sweat stings my eyes, I drop to my knees and hold my hands up in surrender.

"Alejandro," I shout. "I love her."

He staggers back as though I've just punched him in the gut. Surely he knew that? Surely he knows me well enough to know that I wouldn't put us through this if it wasn't for something real?

He glares at me. His tongue darts out of his mouth as he licks the blood from the cut on his lip. I stand now too. My head is pounding from where he has just landed me a right hook on my temple and my blood thunders in my ears as my heart races in my chest.

"When did it start?" he growls.

"A few weeks ago. Just before Dallas?"

"So that was why you took her there?" he rages at me. "Not to protect her, but so you could take advantage of her?"

"No," I shout.

"I would never have allowed you to take here there if I'd known you were fucking her."

"I wasn't fucking her," I run my hands through my hair. "Not then."

"You said before Dallas?"

"There was one night before Dallas, but then I realized how wrong it was and I put a stop to it—"

He scowls at me. "Because you're such a fucking stand up guy!"

"I tried to ignore how I felt, but I couldn't."

"You didn't try hard enough, Jax. Of all the women in LA, in the whole fucking world, you had to choose my daughter. It's fucked up."

"It's not like I watched her grow up—"

His entire face darkens further and he squares up to me again. "Are you suggesting because she's adopted that this is somehow okay?"

"Not even for a second," I snarl back at him. "All I mean is that she was almost seventeen and pregnant when I met her. It's not like I used to take her the park and push her on the fucking swings."

"So you've always looked at her like that?"

"Fuck, no. Not until—"

"Until when?"

I swallow hard as I recall that night I picked her up from some dive bar downtown. I walked in there and saw her dancing with some guy, wearing the shortest dress imaginable. It's not like I'd never seen her body before then. I'd spent plenty of time with her wearing nothing more than a bikini around Alejandro's pool, but there was something about seeing her dancing in there. Watching the way she moved. The way some jock was salivating over her. Suddenly, she wasn't a little kid anymore. Then I'd taken her home; she was drunk and she'd thrown her arms around my neck, kissed me and told me that she loved me. I'd driven home with a raging boner.

"It was last year some time. I picked her up from a club and drove her home. Nothing happened, I just saw her differently."

"My fucking daughter!" he snarls at me, his teeth bared like a rabid dog.

"I know," I reply. Does he think that I've forgotten this fact? "I wish that it wasn't her, Alejandro." I shake my head because saying that feels like I'm betraying her. But I do wish that the one woman I can't live without wasn't my best friend's daughter. But he is more than that to me. He is my brother. Since we were fourteen years old, we have stood by each other's sides. He has been with me through every high and low I have ever experienced, and I for him. I am godfather to his sons. He is the only true family I have.

"What if I asked you to choose?" he says, his eyes narrowed as he stares at me.

"You wouldn't!" I glare back at him.

"Oh, I would. Choose, Jackson. You can't be my brother if you are screwing my daughter. So which is it to be?"

My throat constricts as I try to swallow. Surely he's not asking this of me? I have been nothing but loyal to him for over twenty years. I have watched him become the man he is today, stood proudly at his side as he took his place as head of the Montoya family. I can't imagine a life without him in it.

"Then there is no choice," I say as I drop my head to my chest and in that moment, the only thing I can think about is all that I have lost.

CHAPTER 42

LUCIA

I can't get a hold of Jax. He left my apartment over two hours ago and I've been calling him for the past hour but his phone goes straight to voicemail. I am frantic with worry and my mind is in overdrive, thinking of all of the worst things that could have happened. What if my father couldn't forgive him? What if he shot him and is currently driving him out into the desert to bury him in an unmarked grave? I know that's crazy-talk but the thoughts won't stop running around my brain.

As I take the elevator to the top floor of my father's hotel another, more realistic, thought enters my head. What if my father made him leave and I never see him again?

A few moments later, I burst into my father's office to find him sitting at his desk. He holds a large glass of whisky in one hand, sighing as he sees me walk through the door. I can't help but notice the cut on his lip and hope that Jax is okay. Guilt washes over me like a wave. My father and Jax are like brothers. They have never fallen out before and now I have caused this huge rift between them.

"Papi," I say as I walk into the room.

"Lucia," he says and the flicker of a smile pulls at his lips as he takes a glass from his desk and pours me a Scotch. "Sit down, *mija.*"

"Did you and Jax fight?"

He brushes his lip with his fingertips but he doesn't answer me.

"What happened?" I ask as he passes me the glass of amber liquid.

"I told him he had to choose," he says matter-of-factly, as though he hasn't just plunged a knife straight into my chest.

"What?" I stammer. "How could you do that?" I slam my glass down onto his desk.

"I had to, Lucia. I did it for you."

"No," I snarl at him. "You did it for you. So that you could keep your best friend and your most loyal soldier. I suppose this works out well for Mom, too. Does she think that I'll stop working for you now?"

"This has nothing to do with your mama," he snaps at me and his eyes darken. "You think that I don't want to see you happy, Lucia? It breaks my heart to see you in pain."

"So why did you make Jax choose?" I sniff as a fat tear rolls down my cheek.

He sucks in a deep breath and looks down at the glass in his hand, swirling the dark liquid around the bottom for a few seconds before he answers me.

"Because I know Jax better than anyone, Lucia. I know the kind of man he is."

"I know him too, Papi. I love him."

"I know that you do," he nods. "And I also knew that he would make the right choice."

"No," I cry as the tears roll down my face. I have lost Jax. For good this time.

"Lucia," he says, pushing back his chair and walking around

the desk to me. He places an arm around my shoulder and I try to shrug him off but he is too determined. That is my father after all. Determined. Stubborn. Always getting what he wants no matter what the cost. "He chose you, *mija*."

"What?" I look up at him, wiping the tears from my face. "I don't understand..."

"You think that I would believe the right choice was me?" He frowns at me. "You think I would sacrifice your happiness for my own?"

I look into his dark brown eyes and remember that while he is all of those things I just thought of, he is also the greatest father anyone could ever ask for. To the few people who are blessed with his love, he is the kindest and most loyal man there is.

"He chose me?" I whisper.

"Of course he did."

"But what about you and him?" I stammer. "You need him, Papi. He needs you, too."

He sits on the desk and sighs, running a hand through over the stubble on his jaw. "Your mama tells me you are a grown woman and I need to find a way to get past this. You know I hate to admit it, but she's right."

"She always is," I remind him.

He laughs softly. "Yes. But it will take me time, *mija*. I will try, for you. If he is the one for you, then I guess I'm going to have to get used to this, right?"

"He is the one, Papi," I say as I look up at him.

He nods his understanding, but then he narrows his eyes at me. "But me and him—we can never be what we were before, Lucia," he says with a sigh.

"No." I shake my head. "You can't say that. You and he are still the same people you were."

"No we are not. He has betrayed my trust. No matter what the reason."

"But, Papi."

"Besides, how can I ask him to do things I do, to put his life in danger when I know that you would be waiting for him to come home to you?"

"You can't live life like that. You of all people know that."

He stares at me and I see the anguish written all over his face. I hate that I have put him in this position. "Come here," he holds out his arms and I stand and allow him to pull me into a hug. "I want you to be happy more than anything in this world. If you are happy with Jax, then I will accept this, but do not ask me to change who I am."

"I would never," I whisper.

"If he ever hurts you though…" he warns and he doesn't need to finish the sentence.

"I know, Papi."

I'm walking through the lobby of my father's hotel fifteen minutes later when I see Jax running toward me. "Lucia." He pulls me into a hug as I reach him.

"Jax, where the hell have you been? Why aren't you answering your damn cell?"

"It fell out of my pocket when I was with your father and he stood on it. It's broken," he shakes his head. "I went to your place but you weren't there. Then I went to your mom's work to see if you were there. She tried calling your cell but it went to voicemail."

"Oh damn! My battery got flat. Sorry."

"You and that damn battery, Luce."

"It was only flat because I called you like a trillion times."

"Fuck." he mumbles, pulling me closer to him and burying

his head in my hair. "Your mom and I thought you'd be here. Have you spoken to him? Are you okay?"

"Yes, and yes. Everything's going to be fine." I untangle myself from his arms and slide my hand around his waist. "Can we go home? We have three hours before we need to pick Matthias up." I look up and smile at him. "Then we can tell him as soon as he gets home."

"What the hell happened up there?" He flashes his eyebrows at me.

"My father and I have come to an understanding," I reply with a shrug. "But I'm sure you already suspected that we would."

"Well, he can disown me, but I knew he would never do the same to you." He wraps his arm around my shoulder and we head to the exit.

"He hasn't disowned you, Jax. He needs you and he knows that he does."

"We'll see," he says with a shrug as we step out of the doors into the glorious sunshine.

"And you need him, too. I won't allow the two of you to be complete jackasses and stop being best friends because of me." I give him a playful nudge in the ribs.

"You better watch that mouth, Angel," he growls, making my insides melt like chocolate in the sun. "You can't wrap me around your finger the way you can your father."

I laugh softly because I know that's not true, not that I would ever take advantage of that—at least not often. "Is that so? I know that he made you choose and you picked me," I purr.

"Hmm," he mumbles as he walks us to his car and opens the door for me. Before I climb inside, he dips his head low and whispers in my ear, "Three hours is plenty of time to make you beg for my cock, Angel."

CHAPTER 43

JAX

I turn off the truck's engine and take a deep breath. Lucia places her warm hand on my thigh and squeezes reassuringly. She doesn't seem nervous about this at all. I'm fidgety as hell though and I hate it. This isn't a feeling I'm used to and I don't plan on feeling it often.

"He's going to be thrilled," she whispers.

I look in the back seat at Matthias' smiling face. I mean I adore this kid, and I know he loves me, but that was when I was Uncle Jax, and not the guy dating his mom. And if he's not okay with this, then I don't know what the fuck I'm going to do—I can't give up Lucia, but her son is her number one priority and I have to respect that.

I unclip my seatbelt.

"Are you coming inside, Jax?" Matthias asks.

"Sure am, buddy."

"Cool. Can we play dinosaurs?"

"Yep."

Lucia climbs out of the car and unbuckles him from his seat. "Jax and I want to talk to you first though, munchkin."

"Am I in trouble?" he stares, wide-eyed.

"No," she laughs and shakes her head.

"Come on. Let's go. We might even go for ice cream after."

"Ice cream," he squeals. "This is the best day ever."

I can't help but smile at the kid. I sure hope he still thinks that in a few minutes' time.

W hen we get up to their apartment, the three of us sit at the small table in the kitchen. Matthias stares at us waiting for us to speak. I wonder what we're going to say to the kid but Lucia just comes right out with it.

"So, munchkin, we wanted to tell you that Jax is my boyfriend now."

"Boyfriend?" he frowns.

Fuck!

"Yeah. It means he'll be here a lot more. And he'll have sleepovers."

Oh thank fuck. He's frowning because he doesn't understand what a boyfriend is.

"Sleepovers?" he grins. "In my room?"

She laughs. "No, in my room."

"Aw," he pouts.

"But I can still play dinosaurs with you before bed," I add.

"Okay," he shrugs.

I look at Lucia. "Is that it?" I whisper.

"What did you think was going to happen?" she whispers back.

"I feel kind of underwhelmed." I grin at her and she laughs.

"Wait for it." She winks at me.

Matthias sits in silence for a few minutes and I obviously forgot how this kid's mind works.

"Are you going to kiss?" he suddenly asks.

"Lots," Lucia replies.

"Like Papa and Nana?"

"Yes."

He makes a slightly disgusted face which makes me laugh and then I sit back and watch as Matthias asks his mom one hundred and one questions about what she just told him.

"Can we get a puppy? Like Blue?"

"No."

"Will Jax take me to kindergarten?"

"Sometimes."

"Will we have sleepovers at Jax's house?"

"Yes."

"Can we go to the beach in Jax's truck?"

"Yes."

"Will Jax have his own toothbrush?"

"Yes."

The questions are endless and she answers each one with patience and a smile—I can't believe how much I love this woman. But then he directs his final question to me.

"Will you be my new daddy?"

I sense Lucia bristle beside me. I open my mouth but for a few seconds nothing comes out. How the hell do I answer that? I go with my gut and hope I'm saying the right thing.

"If you want me to be, buddy, it would be my honor."

He smiles at me but Lucia pushes back her chair and walks to the kitchen counter. I look over at her but she's facing away from me with her hands splayed on the worktop. I can tell from the rhythmic movements of her shoulders that she's crying.

Fuck! Have I blown this already?

"Why don't you go round up some dinosaurs in your room and we'll play before dinner?" I wink at Matthias.

"Sure." He jumps from his chair and runs off to his room.

I walk over to her and stand behind her, placing my hands

on her shoulders. "I'm sorry if I overstepped, Luce. I should have let you take that one, too."

She shakes her head and a loud sob escapes her throat. "Luce?" I plead. I pull her up and turn her to face me and she buries her head against my chest, wrapping her arms around my waist and squeezing me tightly.

So, I haven't fucked up? "What is it, Angel?" I press a kiss on the top of her head.

"This is too much, Jax," she breathes.

I sigh deeply. I shouldn't have rushed this but I want to spend the rest of my life with her and her amazing kid. How do I pretend that I don't? "You want to go slower?"

She looks up at me, wiping the tears from her cheeks. "No." She shakes her head. "I'm sorry. I'm not making sense."

"Then take a deep breath and tell me what's going on, Luce."

She nods, taking a few deep breaths before she speaks. "Have you ever wanted something so badly that you think about it all the time? Like you almost want to wish it into being? And then when it happens you're not sure if it's real because it's so perfect that it must be some kind of dream or a trick?"

"Maybe," I frown at her.

"This is it, Jax. I wanted you for so long and wondered what it would be like to have you tell me that you love me. But more than that, I used to watch you with Matthias and wish that you were his father instead of Blake. I had this fantasy about how we would all live in a house by the beach and you would bring me coffee in bed and read bedtime stories to our kids."

"Kids?" I arch an eyebrow at her. "As in more than one?"

"Yeah. Like six or seven," she laughs softly.

"No way." I shake my head. "Three. Tops."

She smiles. "Four."

I lean down and kiss her soft lips and she melts into me as I explore her mouth with my tongue. She tastes so sweet and I can't wait to explore the rest of her later. This right here is everything I ever wanted and didn't even know that I needed.

"Gross!" Matthias shouts and I pull back from her and smile.

"You really want three more of them?"

"Not yet." She smiles. "But yeah, one day."

"Hmm. I'll see what I can do." I wink at her and the smile she gives me makes me feel like the happiest man on the planet.

CHAPTER 44
JAX

I flick through emails on my laptop but all I can think about is waking up to Lucia sucking my cock this morning. I can't imagine there is a better start to a morning, expect maybe to have her riding my face, which I made her do straight after. I love waking up with her. I love waking her up in the middle of the night by sliding my cock into her wet pussy. Damn, my girl loves to be fucked.

My cell vibrates on the kitchen counter and I glance down at it, hoping that it might be Alejandro calling. Lucia has taken Matthias out for the day with her friend from college and I am at a complete loss as to what to do with my days now that I am no longer Alejandro's right hand. I don't even know if I still work for the Montoya Corporation at all or whether I need to be seeking some alternative employment. Not that I worry I'll be stuck for offers—I'm kind of good at what I do—but I've worked beside Alejandro for my entire adult life. He is as stubborn as a fucking mule, though.

Unsurprisingly, it's not his number I see flashing on the screen, but I am intrigued to see who it is calling. I wonder if he's heard I'm out of a job—not that he needs me when he has the best hacker I've ever known at his disposal.

I answer the call. "Hey, Shane."

"Hey, buddy. How are things?"

"Don't fucking ask," I reply with a sigh.

"That bad, huh?"

"I'll get over it. What can I do for you?"

There is a moment's pause that makes me frown. Shane Ryan is never lost for words. "Look, I know you said you took care of that problem you had…"

"Yeah?" The hairs on the back of my neck stand on end.

"Well, my girl is kind of like a dog with a bone when she gets a sniff of something and she says the guy she was looking into is still active."

"What?" My heart starts to race in my chest. I'd say he was mistaken, but Jessie Ryan is the best at what she does. "How does she know?"

"You might be better speaking to her—I'll pass you over."

I wait for a few seconds while he mumbles something to her.

"Hey, Jax," Jessie says into the phone.

"You think this guy is still active?" I ask, my brow furrowed in confusion and worry, because the guy who was trying to hurt Lucia is most definitely dead as far as I'm aware.

"Shane said you took care of the problem, but the guy you asked me to look into is still very much alive. He seems pretty obsessed with Lucia too. It's creepy, but it's definitely him. He's got some sophisticated firewalls but once I got through them I found everything. Same IP address. Same usernames and passwords. Same speech patterns too. He never shows his face and he uses some tech to disguise his voice, but it's him, Jax. He's been quiet for a week or so but he was online about an hour ago."

"Online?"

"Yeah, he's a gamer—has a huge following on social media."

"A gamer?" I rub my temples. This isn't making any sense. "So, who the fuck did me and Alejandro carve into pieces last week?"

"I don't know. An accomplice, maybe?" she suggests.

"Or maybe someone was just in the wrong place at the wrong time? Fuck!" The Montoyas have so many fucking enemies, I can't keep track of them, so maybe the guy that Alejandro caught last week wasn't specifically looking for Lucia. She was in Alejandro's car, with Alejandro's driver. Owen kept on babbling about how he never meant to hurt her. Maybe he was telling the truth and Alejandro was his intended target.

"This gamer, Jessie, what's his name?"

"Dolos," she replies and my heart starts beating so fast it almost bursts out of my ribcage. That cunt I looked into a few months ago. The one Lucia said had zero interest in her because he was too busy jacking off to his x-box. She's gone to meet a college buddy today, too. I squeeze my eyes shut as I remember our conversation earlier this morning. It wasn't him. It was Jordan, the mom of three. Some kind of play date. She took Matthias with her, too. Fuck!

"Thanks, Jessie," I say, aware she is still on the other end of the phone. "I appreciate this."

"No problem, Jax. Shane says to let him know if you need anything."

"Thank you both. I gotta go."

I end the call and dial Lucia's number. It goes straight to voicemail, and blood and adrenaline starts to thunder around my body. I suck in a lungful of air. She never charges her freaking phone. Her battery may be dead. Except that I know it isn't. She knew she was going out for the day, she charged it up before she left.

But where the hell did she say she was going? The beach? It was definitely the beach.

I grab my laptop from the counter and fire it up. If Dolos has her then her cell will be long gone, so the tracking app on her phone is useless. I hack into the college campus records instead and pull up Jordan's details. As soon as I find her cell number, I call her.

She answers after a few rings. "Hello?"

"Hi, Jordan. My name is Jax—"

Before I can finish my sentence she speaks. "Oh, Lucia's guy friend?" she says in that way women do when they know something you don't.

"Is she with you?" I ask, trying to keep my voice calm and steady so I don't freak this woman out and have her clam up on me.

"Yeah," she says and the relief washes over me.

"Can I speak with her?"

"Oh, she's not with me right now, sorry." She laughs softly. "We're at the beach and the kids wanted burgers. She and Dolos just drove to grab some. They should be back any minute. You want me to tell her to call you?"

"Dolos?" I ask as relief turns to nausea.

"Yeah. Wait, she has her cell. Did you try calling her?"

"Yes. It's off." My mind races as I try to think of my next step. "Is Matthias with you?"

"Yeah. He's playing with my youngest."

"Jordan, I need you to listen to me," I tell her and she draws in a deep breath when she hears the urgency in my voice. "Do you have a car?"

"Yes."

"Dolos is dangerous. I need you to take the kids and drive them all to the Montoya Hotel right now. Either me or Lucia's father will meet you there and take Matthias. Can you do that for me?"

"Yes. Is Lucia okay? What's going on?" she stammers.

"I'll explain as soon as I can. You just get yourself and the kids to safety, okay?"

"Yes. Of course," she replies calmly and I'm impressed by how well she seems to be keeping her shit together. But then she got her degree while juggling three kids and a part-time job—of course she can handle a little pressure.

"Did they take Lucia's car?" I ask her.

"No, they took Dolos'."

Of course they did. "What car does he drive?"

"Oh, God. I don't know. A Prius, maybe? I didn't pay much attention. It was silver."

"Anything else that I need to know right now?"

"No."

"Get to the hotel. Call me on this number if you see him or Lucia."

"Okay. I got it." I hear her shouting the kids to her just before she ends the call. I look at my cell and my fingers actually tremble as I scroll through my contacts for the next number I need. But I have no choice right now. Lucia is out there somewhere with some sick psycho and he deserves to know. He is also the one man who will want her back safely as much as I do.

CHAPTER 45

JAX

My truck comes to a screeching stop outside Alejandro's hotel and I jump out, tossing my keys to one of his security who stands waiting for me. Alejandro is there too, holding Matthias in his arms. A woman stands beside him and two kids play around her feet while a third kid, older than the others, stands staring at a cell phone. I jog over to them.

"Jax!" Matthias squeals with delight as I approach. The kid has a huge smile on his face and I am thankful that he seems to know nothing of what is going on.

"Hey, buddy." I ruffle his hair as I shoot Alejandro an anxious look.

"You must be Jordan," I say to the woman standing beside him.

"Yes." She smiles but her face is full of anxiety and concern.

"Thank you for bringing him here."

"Of course." She nods. It's difficult to talk with four kids around, when we have to maintain a sense of calm.

"Do you know anything?" she asks.

"Not yet. You remember anything else that might help?"

"No. I'm sorry." She shakes her head and her eyes brim with tears.

"Are you okay, Mommy?" the little boy at her feet asks as he clings to her leg.

"Yes, sugar," she wipes the tears from her eyes and smiles at him. "My allergies."

"I'll have one of my drivers escort you all home. Thank you again," Alejandro says to her.

"Please keep me updated, won't you?" she asks.

"Of course. We'll call you as soon as we can."

I watch her and her children being escorted to her car by one of Alejandro's security staff.

"Alana is on her way. She's going to stay in the suite with the boys," he says to me as soon as Jordan is out of sight. As though he has conjured her by speaking her name, Hugo's car pulls up and Alana jumps out of it. She runs to us, taking Matthias from her husband's arms and squeezing him tight.

"Nana," he giggles, still blissfully unaware that his mother is missing. A few seconds later, Hugo unstraps the twins from their seats and walks toward us with them.

"Take them all upstairs and we'll call you as soon as we can," Alejandro instructs Hugo, who is one of the few people he trusts with his family's safety. There is no danger to anyone else that we're aware of yet, but having them at the hotel is a precaution in case there's something bigger going on. He knows they're completely safe here so he can focus all of his energies on finding Lucia.

"How will you find her?" Alana whispers as she presses Matthias' face to her chest and covers his ear with her hand.

"I have my methods," he says cryptically. "I'll have her back to you before tomorrow morning. I promise you."

"You'd better," she says and rests her hand on his cheek.

"Go inside," he orders and she does so, along with Hugo and the three boys.

"I've got all of the information Jessie could dig up on this guy. His parents' address. Every relative—"

"We can track her," he interrupts as he walks to the curbside where one of his drivers pulls up in his armored SUV.

"We can't. She's not in her car and he'll have ditched her phone. This guy is tech-minded and he knows who she is. He won't do anything to leave a trace of where he's taking her."

His driver steps out of the SUV and tosses him the keys.

We climb inside and as soon as we're buckled up he passes me his phone and pulls away from the curbside.

"Click on the webpage," he says as he floors the accelerator. "The tracker should come straight up. I was just on it."

"I told you, she doesn't have her car or her cell—"

"No, but she has a tracker anyway," he says as keeps his eyes fixed on the road ahead. "When I checked a few minutes ago they were headed south."

"What?" I blink at him. "What do you mean she has a tracker?"

"Don't lose your shit," he frowns as he keeps staring at the road. "I paid the doctor who gave her that contraceptive implant to add a tracker too."

"What the fuck?"

"I know, Jax," he snaps.

"Does she know?"

He shakes his head. "Of course she doesn't."

"Fuck!"

"What was I supposed to do? She wanted her freedom and that was the only way I could let her have it while giving me some peace of mind."

"But, fuck, Alejandro—you had her implanted with a tracker without her knowledge."

"It's not like I've ever used it to keep tabs on her. It was only for emergencies like this."

I lean back in my seat and open up the internet on his phone, and sure enough there is the flashing red dot heading south. I feel a wave of relief wash over me. That's her. The speed they're moving tells me they're in a vehicle of some sort, but she's there, isn't she?

"It only works if her vital signs are stable," he says quietly as though he's reading my mind and my heart stops racing for the first time since I got off the phone to Jessie earlier.

"Why didn't you tell me? How did I not know about this? I'm your head of fucking security."

"I hoped I'd never have to use it, Jax," he says with a sigh. "I knew you'd think that she deserved to know and I didn't want you to have to lie to her."

"Does Alana know?"

"Fuck, no," he shakes his head.

"She'll kill you when she finds out. Both of them will."

"I know, but I can live with that. Like it or not, that tracker is going to save my daughter's life."

"You are an evil genius. I mean putting a tracker in your daughter along with her implant is all kinds of fucked up, amigo," I shake my head. "But I also kinda wanna kiss you right now."

He arches one eyebrow. "Yeah, well let's wait until we get her back and then you can do whatever you want to me."

Fuck, I've missed him.

"So who is this cunt who's taken my daughter?" he asks.

"He calls himself Dolos."

"Dole-what?"

"Dolos. He's the Greek god of deception."

"Fucking nerds," Alejandro spits. "How the fuck do you even know that?"

"I guess I'm a nerd."

He ignores my sarcasm. "Who is he really?"

"His real name is Richard Peterson. Comes from Alabama. His parents still live there. Had a full scholarship to UCLA and finished joint top in his class."

"Joint with Lucia?"

"Yep."

He's a massive gamer too. Got his own YouTube channel with over half a million subscribers."

He shakes his head and frowns at me. "I don't even know what that means."

"Beats me, amigo. People like to watch other people play video games for some reason," I shrug.

"Why has he taken her, Jax?"

"I've picked through the stuff Jessie sent me and the best I can figure is he's obsessed with her. Jessie tracked his activity and he checks her social feeds all the time, even though she barely uses any social media."

"She ever spoken to you about him before?"

"He was one of the guys she led you to believe she was dating, remember? She realized you had me checking up on her and she decided to have a little fun with us. I checked him out and there was nothing at the time. Lucia said he was a buddy of hers and had no interest in her that way, and vice versa. Seems she was wrong."

"If he's touched her—" he growls.

"I know, amigo," I agree because I feel exactly the same. The self-proclaimed god of deception is about to meet his fucking maker.

We carry on driving in silence for a while. I stare at the red dot on the screen, worried that if I look away it might disappear and we won't find her.

"You truly love her?" Alejandro's voice breaks through the silence.

"Yes. With every fiber of my being."

"Why her though, Jax?"

"You're seriously asking me that?" I frown at him. He, of all people knows how incredible she is.

"Yes. I know she is beautiful and smart and kind, and amazing. But you have dated hundreds of women. Why decide my twenty-one year-old daughter is the one for you?"

"I don't know why it's her, amigo," I tell him honestly. "It just is. I think about her every second of every day. When something good, or funny, or anything happens, she's the first person I want to tell. When I'm not with her all I can think about is getting back to her. The thought of never seeing her again makes me feel like I can't breathe. I would die for her happiness—I know you know what love like that feels like."

"I sure do," he sighs.

"I'm sorry that I betrayed your trust, amigo. You are my brother and I love you, but I can't imagine a life without her."

He shakes his head in exasperation but he doesn't say anything further and we get back to focusing on finding our girl.

CHAPTER 46
LUCIA

Ow! My temples throb. Why is it so dark in here? I lift my head and cry out when it smashes against something hard. I try to stretch my legs but I can barely move. My hands and feet are bound. Oh, God! Where the hell am I?

My heart races and there's a rushing sound in my ears that makes it hard to think. My mouth is so dry. I try to shout but my voice is little more than a croak.

Think, Lucia!

The last thing I remember was going for burgers with Dolos. We bought some, didn't we? And I got an iced coffee too. I was drinking it in his car and then...

That's it. I don't remember anything else. Damn! That asshole has drugged me. The rushing noise in my ears is the sound of a car moving at speed. I'm in his goddamn trunk. I kick out and scream but the car keeps on moving. My breathing gets faster as the blood thunders around my body. What if I don't have enough oxygen? What if I die in the trunk of this shitty car?

Matthias!

Jax!

My mom and dad!

What if I never see any of them ever again?

I close my eyes and suck in a deep lungful of air. Just breathe, Lucia. You got this. It's Dolos. He's your friend. You can talk your way out of whatever this is. I feel around for something I can use as a weapon, but the trunk is empty. Shit!

I lie in the trunk, listening for any signs that we are stopping or there is someone else in the car. All I hear aside from the engine is the muffled sound of the radio. I wonder how far we've traveled—how long since I was knocked out. At least Matthias is with Jordan. She'll keep him safe and then she'll alert people when I don't come back for him. Then my father and Jax will find me. Everything will be just fine.

I don't know how long I've been lying here but the car comes to a stop and the engine is switched off. My arms and shoulders ache from the pressure of having my wrists tied behind my back.

When the trunk opens a few moments later, I blink as the sunlight almost blinds me.

"Hello, chica," Dolos sneers as he reaches in and stuffs something into my mouth. It's some kind of rag and it tastes of greasy burgers. I retch and the bile burns my throat, making my eyes water.

He grabs the top of my arms and pulls me from the trunk. I stumble forward and he catches me. "Steady, chica," he chuckles. "Don't want you to hurt yourself now, do we?"

I look around frantically, desperate to see someone who might be able to help me, but we're in the deserted parking lot of a boarded up diner. He's parked his car beneath some trees so it won't be so visible from the road.

I try to scream but the sound is muffled by the rag.

"Oh, I love a screamer." He leers at me. "I'm gonna make you scream, chica, and no-one will hear you out here."

I close my eyes as tears sting them. How the hell is anyone going to find me here? I can't even try to reason with him because I can't speak.

Dolos drags me roughly to the door of the diner. My feet drag along the asphalt as I try to resist but he is surprisingly strong for someone who spends most of his time sitting on his ass watching a computer screen. I try to remember what Toni taught me. Fight dirty. Use anything at your disposal. But in this situation, my mouth is my best weapon and it is completely useless.

I mumble through the rag, hoping that he'll want to remove it to hear what I have to say but he simply laughs. "You can't talk your way out of this, chica."

He pulls a key from his pocket and unlocks the door, pushing me inside a dark room. I blink and stumble over some debris on the floor while he turns on a small electric lamp that floods the room with light.

As I look around I wish that he hadn't. One of the large tables from the diner is in the center of the room and it has been made into some kind of makeshift torture device. It looks like something from a dodgy BDSM porno. It has shackles at the top and bottom for hands and feet and large chains hang from the sides. On a small table beside it are an array of weapons and sex toys—knives, scalpels, dildos and something I can't quite make out. As he pushes me closer I see that it's a speculum, the kind that gynecologists use when you go for a pap smear.

Bile burns my throat again. I pull away from him, shaking my head and screaming through the makeshift gag in my mouth but the more I struggle and cry, the more he seems to enjoy himself.

"Don't worry, chica. We're going to have so much fun," he laughs.

He pushes me over to the table and I take my shot, throwing my head back and catching him on the nose, but it's not enough.

"Fucking bitch," he screams as blood drips from his nostrils. He slaps me hard across the face and pushes me onto the bed. I kick out but he chains me down and one by one he releases my ties and shackles me to the hard table. I stare at the broken ceiling fan directly above us, praying that it will fall down directly on top of him. The prospect of what he's about to do to me is too much to consider, so I think of anything else and close my eyes, pretending I'm not in this room with him.

"No point closing your eyes," he says. "You can pretend you're somewhere else, but once I get started there'll be no doubt about where you are and who you're with."

I hear the clink of metal, signaling he's picked up one of the nearby weapons. I realize it's the knife as he slowly and methodically starts to cut through my clothes. Firstly he starts with my tank top. The metal blade is cold on my stomach and I flinch.

"You thought it was funny to have that pumped up jackass come to my apartment and question me about whether I was fucking you?" he snarls in my ear and his spittle hits my cheek as he speaks. "You thought it was funny to have him picking over my life? Looking at me like I was some fucking freak?"

I shake my head.

"I had to sit there and live up to your little fantasy of me, chica—just some nerdy little gamer who couldn't fuck a girl unless she's on a screen. Because if he'd have found out what I really like to do to filthy little sluts like you, then I would have been in quite a whole heap of trouble, wouldn't I?"

So he's done this before? And he was worried that Jax almost found him out. Oh my God! How many other poor girls has he done this to?

"You're not even my type. I prefer my girls much younger and skinnier than you," he sneers. "But I'll still take great pleasure in fucking every hole you have until you bleed."

Then his knife slides up my inner thigh, cutting away my jean shorts, and I lie there motionless, praying for Jax and my father to hurry up and find me. The only other thing I have left is my stubborn refusal to let Dolos see me cry again.

CHAPTER 47

JAX

"They've stopped," I say to Alejandro as I watch the small red dot fixed on the screen. "They're about twenty miles up ahead."

He nods and floors the accelerator. We were already way over the speed limit but he pushes the SUV to the max. "Let's go get her."

When we pull into the parking lot of the boarded up diner, I see a silver Prius parked beneath the trees. We jump out of the car, looking around as we run to the door.

"You think he's alone?" Alejandro asks.

"There's only one car. If he's not, there can't be many of them in there."

He nods and tries the handle. When he's met with resistance, he pulls his handgun from the waistband of his pants and aims it at the lock. I grab his arm before he can pull the trigger.

"What the fuck?" I hiss.

"We need to get in there fast," he snarls.

"It'll take me less than two minutes to pick that, then we still have the element of surprise."

"You got two minutes before I shoot my way in there."

I take a small pick from my pocket and get to work on the lock. I feel him fidgeting beside me. He has seen me do this countless times but today the stakes are much higher than they usually are. I feel it, too. I can't let my mind start to drift and contemplate what we might find when we get inside this place. What state she might be in. What he might have done to her. But the thought that keeps on persisting is the one that she might not be in there at all—that he's found her tracker and managed to fool us somehow. This guy is good with tech. Who knows what he's capable of?

"Come on," Alejandro hisses and I tune him out, keeping all of my attention on getting through this door as quickly and as quietly as possible.

I breathe a sigh of relief as I feel the mechanism inside give against the pressure and after a soft click, the door is open.

I look at Alejandro as I curl my fingers around the handle. "Ready?" I whisper.

"I want this cunt alive," he growls.

I nod my understanding. A quick death would be far too easy. Neither he or I are known for being men of mercy and I know he feels the hatred and venom for the man who took Lucia from us as fiercely as I do.

I pull open the door and the sight that greets us makes my heart stop beating in my chest. I see everything as if in Technicolor and it is an image that will be burned into my brain for the rest of my days.

Lucia is shackled to the table, naked except for her bikini bottoms. Her body shivers uncontrollably. There are large droplets of fresh blood on the floor and a psychopath is running the tip of a knife up the inside of her thigh.

I raise my gun and Alejandro does the same as we edge into the room, but the electric light casts a shadow and the movement alerts Richard to our presence. He drops behind the table, peering over the top like a frightened meerkat as he holds the knife to Lucia's throat.

She turns toward us too. Her eyes meet mine and they are filled with relief and tears.

"You come another step closer and I will make her bleed out faster than you can possibly imagine," he sneers as he presses the tip of his blade against the main artery in her neck. "Just a quick slice and she's gone. I even gave her some blood thinner along with her roofie. I like it when they bleed." He cackles to himself and seems genuinely impressed with his own genius.

"He's fucking loco," Alejandro hisses.

I aim the gun at him and he ducks lower while pressing the blade against her skin until it pierces it. A trickle of blood runs down her throat.

"Can you make that shot?" Alejandro whispers.

"Which one?" I hiss.

"I know you can kill him," he mumbles. "Can you make the other one?"

He knows I can. I can take the stalk off a cherry from fifty yards away. But if I miss—well, it doesn't bear thinking about. Unfortunately for Richard Peterson, I never miss.

"Yes," I growl.

Alejandro doesn't need to speak again for me to know what he's thinking. Richard continues to peer over the table, taunting us. He is talking non-stop but I tune him out. There will be plenty of time to listen to him talk—and scream—once I get our girl to safety. I squeeze the trigger and the bullet explodes through the second knuckle on his right hand, throwing him backwards with the force. The knife clatters to the floor and Lucia lets out a muffled scream.

Alejandro moves before I do, running to Richard as he lies bleeding and shouting profanities before he's hoisted up by his collar. Alejandro snarls something in the sick fuck's ear but I'm too far away to hear. I can imagine it was some kind of threat that involves his cock. Then he takes Richard's injured hand and pushes two fingers into the gaping hole left by the bullet before twisting it behind his back. His screams of agony fill the room.

I run to Lucia while her father keeps Richard restrained. The first thing I do is remove the rag from her mouth.

"Matthias?" she croaks.

"He's fine, Angel. He's with your mom."

She nods and a single tear runs down her cheek.

"Come on. Let's get you out of here," I say, brushing her damp hair from her face.

She nods again as she pulls at her restraints.

As I free her arms, my eyes roam over her body, giving her a quick check over but she has no visible injuries apart from the blood on her face that seems to have come from her nose. As soon as she is able to, she pushes herself up into a sitting position and I wrap my arms around her, pulling her close to me.

"Jax," she sobs against my chest.

"I got you, baby. You're safe now," I soothe as I hold her tight while Alejandro holds onto Richard, one arm wrapped around his throat and one of his large hands clamped over his mouth.

Lucia pulls back from me, wiping her eyes before she reaches down to her legs to free them.

"Hey, I got you," I say, pulling off my t-shirt. "Put this on, first."

She nods and I help her, feeding her arms through the sleeves.

"Are you okay, *mija*?" Alejandro asks as I work on releasing her ankles.

"Yes. Thank you, Papi," she breathes.

Once her legs are free too, I pick up her sneakers from the floor and crouch down to slide them onto her feet. When I stand again, she is smiling faintly at me and I thank God that she is safe and unhurt—it seems that sick fuck didn't get to do any of the twisted shit he obviously had planned.

"Shall we allow Richard here to give us a practical demonstration of what some of these things do?" Alejandro asks, indicating his head to the table of tools and sex toys that I have done my best to avoid looking at.

"Sounds good to me." I lift Lucia from the table and set her on her feet.

"You okay?" I whisper, keeping my arms around her.

"Yes. I can stand," she says as she takes a step back from me. Then she turns to her father who still holds onto Richard. I wonder if she has the stomach for what we're about to do. I look at Alejandro too. We have worked together for so long that he knows what I'm thinking without me having to tell him. He nods his agreement. Lucia needs to stay for this.

"Let's get him on here then?" I say with a flash of my eyebrows.

Richard kicks and screams as Alejandro and I lift him onto the table and shackle his arms and legs the same way he'd restrained Lucia.

"No," he wails, shaking his head from side to side.

I grab hold of his face, holding his head still while I glare at him. "Seems you can give but you can't take it, Richard. Is that right?"

"I can get you money," he pleads.

Alejandro starts to laugh his ass off as he picks up one of the huge knives and begins cutting through Richard's clothes. "Even if I needed money, you sick *hijo de puta*, you think I would allow the piece of shit who took my daughter to buy his way out of facing up to his crimes?" he snarls as the knife in his hand slices a welt into the soft skin of Richard's thigh, making him howl in pain.

"We got plenty of toys here to try on you too," I add as I pick up a huge black dildo and he starts shaking and crying again.

Alejandro slaps him across the face. "Shut the fuck up!"

Richard mumbles as tears run down his face and blood runs down his thigh. Alejandro works quickly and our captive is soon completely naked as he lies shivering on the table. I pick up a strange metal object. It's shaped like a cock but has some kind of mechanical part to it.

"What the fuck is this?" I hold up the offending item.

"A speculum," Lucia replies.

"A what?"

"They use them in internal exams," Alejandro replies as he steps toward me and takes it from my hand. Twisting the screw at the base, the tip of the metal object starts to spread open. "They use it to open a woman's cervix so they can see inside. This is a pretty outdated one though. I believe they mostly use plastic ones now."

"How the fuck do you know that?" I frown at him.

"My wife had twelve months of fertility treatment, amigo." He arches an eyebrow at me. "I've seen things no man ever should." He arches an eyebrow at me.

"Papi," Lucia admonishes him.

"Sorry," he mumbles, but then he holds it up again so that Richard can see it.

"Just what exactly where you planning on doing to my daughter with this, you sick fuck?"

"Nothing," Richard shakes his head.

"Liar," Lucia hisses.

"The more pressing question is what can we do to him with it?" I say.

"Hmm?" Alejandro rubs a hand over his jaw. And then he runs the metal over Richard's cock and down to his asshole making him whimper and beg.

"Maybe later," Alejandro laughs. "How about we start with your mouth?"

Richard clamps his lips together and shakes his head making Alejandro sigh loudly. "You wanna?" he says to me as he lifts the speculum up again and presses it against Richard's lips while I grab hold of his cheeks and squeeze hard until his mouth opens slightly.

Alejandro takes the metal instrument in his grip and smashes it through Richard's teeth. I don't see how many he breaks but bits of tooth and blood and spit dribble down his chin as my best buddy pushes the speculum deep into Richard's mouth, only stopping when he hits the back of his throat, making his body convulse as he gags at the intrusion.

"You wanna see how this thing works?" Alejandro grins at me.

"Seems like I'm the only person in the room who doesn't know," I say with a shrug.

Alejandro begins to turn the screw on the base of the instrument again and it expands further, stretching Richard's mouth with it.

"That looks kind of uncomfortable." I wince and turn to Lucia. "They really use those things?"

"Yeah," she nods.

"What exactly do you think this twisted fuck was planning on doing with this?" Alejandro asks again.

I glare at Richard as he lies there trembling. Alejandro takes the opportunity to walk to Lucia and give her a brief hug. Then he steps back, running his hands over her arms. "You sure you're okay?" he asks her.

"Yes."

"You mean the world to me, *mija*," he says before he kisses her forehead.

The sound of water trickling makes us all look back to the table to see Richard pissing himself. "Seems Dolos can't hold his bladder," Lucia says with a laugh and she steps closer to the table and leans over him. "You're pathetic," she hisses. "Who's the filthy little slut now?"

Richard's mouth is held wide open now at a strangely unnatural angle by the speculum which is opened to its limit.

He closes his eyes as though this might stop what is about to happen.

"He called you that?" I ask her.

"Yeah," she nods.

I noticed some Clorox when we came in here and walk over and pick it up. "Seems Richard has something of a potty mouth," I laugh as I unscrew the cap and hand the bottle to Lucia. "You would be doing him a favor by helping him clean it out, Angel."

She takes the bottle from me, her hands trembling as she holds it over his mouth. The smell must hit his nostrils because his eyes fly open and he shakes his head wildly from side to side.

"For fuck's sake!" Alejandro hisses as he holds Richard's head still. "You can do this, *mija*," he says to his daughter with a reassuring smile.

"I'm not the only woman he's done this to," she sniffs as she tips the bottle and starts to pour the Clorox down his throat, as though that gives her the strength to go through with it. "He said there have been others too."

Richard chokes on the harsh liquid as it burns his esophagus. She keeps on pouring until I put a hand on her arm. "That's enough for now, Angel," I tell her. "He'll choke if you keep going and we haven't ever started on him yet."

"Nope," Alejandro agrees as he eyes the array of tools on the table. "We won't be leaving here until every single one of those objects he planned to use on you has been forced into his body. I don't care if we have to cut him open to do it."

Lucia nods her understanding. She has a lot to learn about the way we deal with our enemies, but this afternoon she is about to be schooled in the fine art of causing extreme pain.

CHAPTER 48

LUCIA

Jax's huge arms are wrapped around me as I sit on his lap in the back of my father's car. The smell of blood fills my nose, its coppery tang in my throat even after I guzzled an entire bottle of water as soon as we got out of the diner. I'm not sure I will ever get the stench from my nostrils. If my father had any lingering doubts about me joining the family business, I'm pretty sure I just laid them to rest. I didn't know that people could endure the levels of pain that Dolos—or Richard, as I now know him—just did. Even when they cut him wide open and pulled out his insides, I didn't flinch. The screams and the smell made me want to retch, but I didn't. This is what the two men I love most in the world do and it's what I do now, too.

My father called some of his men to dispose of Richard's mutilated body, dump the Prius and remove any evidence of us being there, and then we climbed into his SUV to head for home. I catch him glancing at Jax and me in the rearview mirror and I offer him a faint smile to let him know that I'm okay. He winks at me before his gaze drifts back to the road.

"You okay?" Jax asks as I shift on his lap.

"Yes," I murmur. "I can't wait to get home and showered."

"We'll be home soon, *mija*," my father answers. "Magda has your old room ready."

"No, Papi," I reply. "I'm not moving back home."

"You're not going back to your apartment," he snaps.

"She and Matthias will move in with me," Jax says and I look at him and frown.

"I'm not moving in with you," I whisper and Jax frowns right back at me.

"You're not going back to that apartment, so you come home with me or you stay with Jax until I find you somewhere more appropriate," my father adds.

"So you're happy for me to live with Jax?" I ask him leaning forward in seat so I can see his face when he replies.

"No," he snaps. "But his house is like a goddamn fortress. So..."

I look back to Jax. "It's not up for discussion, Angel. One of us will be taking you home with us tonight."

"Fine," I mumble. "I'll stay with you, but I'm not moving in."

"Why not?" he whispers.

I beckon him closer, until I can press my lips against his ear so my father won't hear me. "Because you have screwed half the women in California in that house."

"Oh," he chuckles softly, "then we'll look for somewhere new then."

I shake my head. I don't have the energy to argue with the pair of them about my living situation right now. Whatever drugs Richard gave me are still making me feel woozy—or maybe it's the lack of food and the fact I just watched a man tortured to death—or a combination of all three.

I close my eyes and lean against Jax's chest and he strokes my hair.

"You said you weren't the first girl he'd done that to, *mija*," my father breaks the silence in the car.

"Yes. He said that he usually liked skinny girls that were younger than me. That was why he was so angry with me, because when I made you think I was dating him and you had Jax look into him, he was pissed that he almost got found out."

"But then he took you, so he must have known we would come for him?" Jax says with a frown.

"Yeah," I agree. "But I think he honestly believed he was some sort of criminal mastermind."

"Hmm. Naming yourself after a Greek god does kind of scream over-inflated ego," Jax says.

"You think you could look into it a little more, Papi? See if there are any other girls he's maybe taken, or even killed?"

"He's dead now, *mija*. He can't hurt anyone else. No good will come from digging into his past."

"But those girls might have people worried about them, Papi. Parents or brothers, sisters, children?"

He takes a few seconds to answer. "Fine," he eventually sighs.

"Thank you. From the way he spoke I think he'd used that place before."

"Hmm. That would make sense," Jax says. "There wasn't much likelihood of people finding the place or sneaking around there."

"So how did you two find me there, anyway?" I ask and immediately feel the tension in Jax's arms.

"It doesn't matter," my father snaps. "All that matters is that we did."

"I know that," I say with a frown. "I was just wondering how you did. The place was kinda out of the way and all."

Silence!

"So how did you do it?" I ask again only to be met with more silence.

"Why won't either of your answer me?" I ask. What could they possibly be avoiding telling me?

"Alejandro," Jax eventually says.

"Jax," he snarls back.

"She deserves to know," Jax adds.

I look between him and my father.

"Deserve to know what?" I demand.

"We can discuss it tomorrow when you're rested and we can all have a rational discussion," my father says.

"Papi?"

"Just remember that this saved your life, *mija*," he says. "Who knows what that cabrón would have done to you if we hadn't got there when we did?"

"Okay," I say and I look to Jax who narrows his eyes at me.

"Promise you won't freak out," he says.

"I promise. Would you both please tell me what's going on?"

"You have a tracker in your arm," my father says, matter-of-factly.

"A tracker? In my arm?" I look between the two of them.

"Yes."

"But how?" I rub my hands over my arms, not knowing what I'm looking for, but surely I would know if someone stuck a tracker in me, right?

"When you went for your implant, I paid the doctor to implant a tracker too."

"You what?" I snap. "But that's like illegal!"

My father arches an eyebrow at me in the rearview mirror. Like he doesn't break at least a dozen different laws on a daily basis.

"It's unethical," I try instead. "I thought doctors were supposed to be above all that shit?"

"Stop cussing," my father and Jax say in unison.

I shake my head in disbelief. Yeah, cut a guy's cock off with a rusty hacksaw, Lucia, but don't curse.

"I will cuss all I want to. You had something put into my body without my knowledge, Papi—do you get how wrong that is?"

He stamps on the brake and the car comes to a screeching halt on the side of the highway. He turns to me, his face full of anger. "No I do not, *mija*, because you are the most stubborn person I know. That tracker is for your own protection. If I had suggested that you have it, you would have refused."

I open my mouth to reply but he glares at me and I close it again.

"Do not even for one second try to tell me that you would have agreed, because we all know that is not true."

I clamp my lips together. Damn! It is true.

"I love you, *mija*. If anything happened to you because of me and what I do, I would never forgive myself. So, you wanted your freedom. You wanted to go off to college and live in an apartment with no bodyguard and no protection, and the only way I could give you that was to know that there was a way I could find you if anything ever happened to you. So, no, I do not think it was wrong. I am not sorry. And I would do it again without hesitation."

I blink at him. I mean I'm all kinds of pissed at him, but I can't even argue with any of that right now so I lean back against Jax and my father turns back to the wheel and drives off again.

"Did you know about this?" I murmur to Jax.

"Not until today," he replies.

I nod and feel a wave of relief. Somehow, that would have felt like more of a betrayal.

"Does mom know?" I say this louder.

"No," he snaps.

"Does she have one of these things?"

"No!"

"She's gonna be so pissed at you when I tell her what you've done."

Jax laughs softly and the sound rumbles through his chest, comforting me.

"I know," my father snaps.

"Or I could get it taken out tomorrow and we won't tell her," I offer.

"Lucia," he warns.

"I want it out of me, Papi," I say and I see him ready to argue with me again. "But I do see how useful they are. Maybe we need to have a family meeting about us all having one? If I have one then it will be my decision. And I think it's only fair that you have one, too. And mom and the boys?"

"Hmm. We'll see," he replies.

Jax kisses the top of my head. "And you too, Decker," I murmur.

I watch the sun setting over the ocean as I sit on the sofa in Jax's huge open-plan living room, cradling a mug of his Aunt Molly's soothing tea. My parents left about an hour ago and Jax is settling Matthias for the night. I'm trying not to think about what might have happened if Jax and my father hadn't got to me when they did. One thing I do know for sure, is that as soon as I've been to the doctor's tomorrow to get this damn tracker removed, I'm heading straight to Toni's gym to beg her to teach me every single thing she knows. I never want to feel as defenseless again as I did today.

Jax walks back into the room and I smile at him.

"He's fast asleep," he says as he sits down on the sofa beside me.

I place my mug on the table and he pulls me onto his lap, brushing my hair from my face. "Are you okay, baby?"

"Yes, I told you like a million times. I'm good." He frowns at me and I lean my head against his chest. "I'm sorry," I whisper. "But I'll tell you if I'm not okay. I promise."

"Okay," he kisses my head. "You want to watch a movie?"

"Yes. Which one?"

"Your choice, Angel."

"Really? Anything I want?"

"Yes."

"I'm going to make you watch something really girly and romantic, you know that, right?"

"Anything you want."

"Hmm. I should get kidnapped more often," I giggle.

"Lucia!" he warns.

"Too soon?"

"Way too soon."

I must have fallen asleep watching the movie because I wake up in Jax's arms as he's carrying me to bed.

"Hey sleepy head," he smiles at me as my eyelids flutter open.

"Hey." I yawn. "Are you taking me to have your wicked way with me?"

"No." He kisses my nose. "I'm taking you to get a good night's sleep for a change."

"Spoilsport," I grin as my eyes roll closed again and the next thing I'm vaguely aware of is having the covers pulled over me as I lie on Jax's chest. Then his huge arms are around me and I snuggle against him feeling completely happy and safe.

CHAPTER 49

LUCIA

I knock on the huge brown door of Toni Moretti's private gym and wait for an answer. Jax is parking the car a few yards away because I wanted to do this first part on my own. I had suggested that I come here alone, but Jax is refusing to let me out of his sight—I suppose I can't blame him after yesterday. He accompanied me to the doctor's office this morning to have my tracker taken out, too. I meant what I said to my father yesterday, I do see the benefit of having one, but it's a choice I want to make for myself.

It was almost time for my implant to be changed anyway, but I decided not to have one put back in. I find the damn thing messes with my periods too much, so I'm going to give the pill a go and see how that suits me.

The door opens and Benji stands before me, his arms folded across his chest as he fills the doorway. "Miss Montoya."

"Hey, Benji. Is Toni in?"

"She sure is," he grins as he steps aside and lets me into the room. Jax jogs up behind me, and he and Benji greet each other fondly. I look at Jax and smile. He knows I want to do this alone.

"You got time to make me a coffee?" he asks Benji as he indicates his head to the small kitchenette at the back of the gym.

"Sure," Benji replies and the two of them leave me standing alone. Toni is working on one of the bags and I stand and wait for her to finish her set.

"Hello, princess," she grins at me.

"Hey, Toni," I smile.

"I missed you last week."

"I know, I'm sorry. I had to go out of town."

"It's cool." She flashes a smile, showing her perfect white teeth. "Your dad told me. What can I do for you today?"

I swallow hard. "I just wanted to apologize for being a bit of an ass the first time we met."

"Oh, honey," she laughs. "Don't give it a second thought. I'm an ass about eighty percent of the time."

I arch an eyebrow at her. "Well, yeah. I kinda got that," I say and she starts to laugh. "I know you're busy, but I just wanted to let you know that I'm totally up for learning everything you can teach me. Any time at all you can spare me, I'll be here and I promise to give it one hundred percent."

"Something happen?" She frowns at me, her eyes full of concern and I feel a rush of guilt for what a jackass I was to her the first time I met her.

"You could say that," I say with a shrug.

"Are you okay?"

"Yeah. But I hated feeling helpless, you know? And I don't want to have to rely on the guys around me to fight my battles for me."

"I completely get that," she says with a knowing smile. "So, you got your gym stuff in there?" she nods to the backpack on my shoulder.

"Yeah. Just in case."

"I could do with a sparring partner"—she flashes her eyebrows at me—"but I'll knock you on your ass, princess."

"Not if I knock you on yours first, bitch." I grin and she winks at me.

"I hope you're not flirting with my girl, Moretti," Jax says as he walks up behind us.

"Wouldn't be the first woman I've stolen from under your nose, Decker." She flutters her eyelashes at him.

"Ouch." He puts his hand on his chest over his heart. "But you didn't exactly steal them because they were never mine." He puts an arm around me possessively and I should hate it, but I don't. Not even a little.

"But this one?" Toni arches an eyebrow at him.

"Yep. This is one is all mine," he growls before kissing my forehead and wet heat surges between my thighs.

"Noted," she laughs softly.

I t's dark when I wake and for a heart freezing second I think I'm in the trunk of Dolos' car, but I'm wrapped in huge, warm arms and Jax's soft breathing is all that I can hear. I breathe deeply. I'm safe. Nothing can hurt me when I'm with him.

I wriggle, shifting my arm from under his.

"What's wrong, Angel?" he mumbles sleepily.

"Nothing," I whisper. I drape my leg over his groin, nudging his cock through his shorts. We usually sleep naked, except for last night and tonight. I left my t-shirt and panties on, kind of hoping that he would tell me to take them off, but he didn't and I was too tired to complain. The doctor told me that the drugs Dolos gave me won't be fully out of my system for a few days and one of the side effects is tiredness.

"Why are you wearing pants in my bed, cowboy?" I fake a growl.

His hand skims over my back. "Behave."

"What if I don't want to behave?" I purr.

"Then you'll be spanked and fucked, baby, just like you always are."

Just like you always are. Those words mean so much to me and they cause a rush of wet heat between my thighs. "I want to be spanked and fucked, Jax."

"You do?"

"Hmm," I murmur as my hand glides over his hard abs and over his even harder cock. "And it seems like you're kind of in the mood, too."

"I'm always in the mood, baby."

"Then why aren't I flat on my back already?" I purr.

A growl rumbles through his chest before he flips me over, pinning me to the mattress with the weight of him and I suck in a deep breath. I need him so bad.

He rocks his hips, grinding his cock against the damp patch on my panties. "This what you want?"

"Yes."

"You sure?"

"I already said yes. Why would you ask me that?" I narrow my eyes at him, challenging him to tell me that it's because of what happened yesterday. Of what he saw. Of what that psycho Dolos would have done to me if he and my father hadn't got there in time.

"Because you had your implant taken out," he reminds me, "and you haven't started your pill yet."

"Oh, yeah. I forgot." I bite on my lip. "You could pull out before you finish?" I purr, because I need to feel him inside me.

"That's not foolproof. And I may not be able to," he growls.

"Why?"

"Because the idea of putting a baby in you makes me feel kind of feral."

"Jax." I giggle but he's distracted taking off my t-shirt.

"I'm sure the implant stuff is still in my system. We'll be okay, won't we?"

He's already pulling off my panties, trailing kisses down my body. "I'm willing to risk it if you are."

"I want you inside me," I groan.

He moves back up the bed and settles between my thighs. "You know you only have to ask, baby," he growls before he pushes deep inside me and wet heat slicks his cock. "Fuck! Your pussy is a magnet to my cock, Luce."

I wrap my arms and legs around him and he seals his lips over mine as he fucks me perfectly—the way only he can.

CHAPTER 50

JAX

The armed guards outside Alejandro's hotel room allow me through without any hesitation at all, so I suppose he still doesn't have a hit out on me at least.

I walk through the room until I find him in his office. He's on his phone. He's smiling but it turns to a scowl when he looks up and sees me standing in his doorway.

"I got to go, princess. Jax is here."

He's talking to Alana.

"I won't."

She just made him promise not to kill me.

"Love you too. Bye, princess."

He ends the call and glares at me. "Something I can help you with?"

"Yes. I need to ask you something," I say as I step inside the room.

"I don't have any more daughters for you to corrupt," he snaps.

"Alejandro!"

He shakes his head in frustration. "How is my daughter? I barely see her these days."

It's been four days since we rescued her from that psychopath and although we worked together to get her back, we haven't spoken since. I think he's pissed at me because I told her about the tracker, but she had every right to know.

"She was at your house last night," I remind him. I picked her up and had to wait outside like an employee. In fact worse than an employee—they are allowed inside his house.

He changes the subject. "What do you want to ask me?"

"I'm not asking for your permission here, but I do want your blessing," I say.

He leans back in his chair and frowns at me. "To do what?"

"To marry Lucia."

He laughs out loud. "You? Getting married?"

"Yeah."

"Seriously?" He stops scowling now and regards me with curiosity.

"I told you I'm in love with her, amigo. I plan to spend the rest of my life with her."

"And if I say no?"

"Then I'll ask her anyway."

He frowns again. "Is she pregnant?"

"No. And you know up until a few days ago she had an implant."

"Hmm."

"But we will have kids one day and if you want to be part of their lives—"

"What, Jax?" he snarls.

"I'll be their fucking father, Alejandro." I snarl back.

He licks his lips and leans back in his chair. "Seems you got this all figured out anyway."

"You're a stubborn asshole, you know that?"

"Yep." He nods and I can't help but smile. "You're just a regular asshole though."

I nod too. "Yep."

"There was another problem at the club last night. I think we need a whole new team in there," he says and for a second I have no idea why he's telling me this.

I can only think of one and I hope that I'm right. "When do you want the new team in by?"

"Tonight, if possible. You think you can swing that?" he asks with a flash of his eyebrows.

"I'll see what I can do."

"Good."

I stand up and walk toward the door.

"When are you asking her?"

"Tonight. At dinner. We're going for pizza. Matthias chose the restaurant."

"You're roping in the kid too? Smart move."

"She's going to say yes, amigo."

"I know she will," he sighs.

I stand awkwardly in his doorway.

"Alana will want to know as soon as possible. So swing by and tell her in person if you can."

"Both of us or just Lucia?"

He nods. "Both of you."

"We will."

"You're going to be my son-in-law?" he shakes his head.

"Don't," I groan. "You'll be my fucking father-in-law."

"You start calling me Papi and I'll fucking end you."

"Noted," I smile at him and he smiles back.

"Good. Now get out of here. You got work to do."

CHAPTER 51

LUCIA

I look in the back seat and shake my head at my son who is fidgeting and squirming like I've never seen him before.

"He's super giggly and fidgety tonight. Have you been feeding him sugar before I got home?" I ask Jax as he drives us for pizza.

"Yeah." He winks at me. "Cubes of the stuff, straight from the bowl."

"He's definitely excited about something," I laugh.

"He loves pizza, don't you buddy?" Jax says.

"Yes," Matthias squeaks.

We've ordered our pizzas and the waitress brings our sodas and a juice box for Matthias. He takes it and giggles at Jax who fake-scowls at him.

"What's gotten into you two tonight?" I ask. There's definitely something going on here.

"I was going to wait until after dinner until you had a full stomach and couldn't run away," says Jax, "but my wingman here is about to burst so I kind of think this is my window."

"Window?" I frown at him but he pushes his chair out and drops to one knee.

My heart starts to hammer in my chest.

"I know this isn't the most romantic setting, Angel, but our little guy picked the venue." He looks across at Matthias who giggles uncontrollably.

Our little guy? Damn, that makes my heart melt.

This can't be happening, can it? He's about to tie his shoelaces or something. But then he reaches into the pocket of his jeans and pulls out a beautiful platinum diamond ring. The rock is huge but I don't even care. It could be a piece of aluminum and it would still have the same meaning.

"You make me happier than I ever thought any person could be. Please say you'll let me spend the rest of my life trying to do the same for you. Will you marry me, Angel?"

I blink at him, and then the ring, and then my son. My heart is racing in my chest and I'm sure that at any moment I'm going to wake up and this will all have been some incredible dream.

"Momma," Matthias giggles and I realize Jax is still on his knees and I haven't answered.

"You are the only man I'll ever love, Jax." I lean down and kiss him. "You already make me happy beyond my wildest dreams, but I'll still marry you anyway."

"Yes," Matthias shrieks while Jax slides the ring onto my finger before pulling me up from the chair and kissing me.

There's a chorus of cheers and clapping from the other diners and the restaurant staff, and when he puts me back down on my chair, I can't stop smiling.

I'm going to marry Jackson Decker!

. . .

I've been in a blissful daze of happiness throughout our meal and then during the drive home, so I don't even notice that we're not driving toward my apartment or Jax's house until we're in the hills.

"Jax, where are we going?"

"To give your mom and dad our news."

"I think giving it over the phone might be best."

"It's okay." He winks at me. "He knows we're coming."

"My father knows about this? How?"

"I went to see him today."

"You asked his permission?" I frown at him. What is this, the nineteen-fifties?

"No, but I did want his blessing."

"And he gave it?" I blink in surprise.

"Well, he didn't punch me in the face."

"Oh well then," I chuckle.

"And he told me to bring you by after so you could show you mom your rock." He flashes his eyebrows at me.

"Wow!"

"I know."

I hold out my hand and admire my rock. "It's beautiful. Thank you," I whisper.

He reaches out and takes my hand, lifting it to his lips and kissing my knuckles. "You're welcome."

"It's very big," I say as it sparkles on my finger.

"I know, and I know you're not usually into flashy stuff, so I bought it for me, not you. You can change it if you don't like it though?"

"I love it, Jax," I say with a contended sigh. "But what do you mean, you bought it for you?"

He turns to me with a wicked glint in his eye. "I wanted it to be unmissable on your hand. Like so big it could be seen from space," he laughs. "Then everyone will see it and know you're mine."

"Your possessiveness is so hot," I purr.

"You'd better get used to it, Angel."

As Jax, Matthias and I stand on my parents' doorstep, I feel so nervous I might throw up. Matthias yawns loudly and Jax picks him up.

The door is opened by Magda and she looks surprised when she sees us. "Why didn't you use your key?" she scolds me.

"I never use it after eight when the boys are in bed. You never know what you might walk into in this house," I say, recalling the time I caught my parents half-naked in the hallway.

"Ah, yes," Magda nods. She knows. I wonder how many times she's caught them in an uncompromising position.

"Lucia." My mom comes into the hallway as we step inside the house. "Jax."

"Hey, Mom," I smile as my father walks up behind her, his hands in his pockets.

I look at Jax and notice that my son has fallen asleep in his arms. God, I love this man so much.

"Is everything okay, sweetheart?" she asks and I hear the concern in her voice.

"Yes, Mom," I say as I walk toward her. I hold up my hand. "Jax asked me to marry him," I squeal the words like an excited teenager, as though I'm channeling my sixteen-year-old self, who first laid eyes on the hottest man on the planet in this very hallway.

My mom shrieks too and I love that excitement is her first reaction—not worrying about how my father will react, but genuine happiness for me.

"Oh, Lucia." She wraps her arms around me and I bury my

face in her sweet-smelling hair as my cheeks actually ache from all the smiling.

"I'm so happy for you, sweetheart," she whispers.

When I look up my father is standing right beside us. "I'm getting married, Papi."

He wraps his arms around my mom and me together. "Congratulations, *mija*," he says and I swear my heart feels like it's about to burst.

"Jax. Get over here," my mom says and he walks over, too. My mom hugs him and then she glares at my father until he shakes Jax's hand.

"Congratulations, amigo," he says.

"Thanks," Jax smiles at him and then he puts his arm around me while he holds onto Matthias with the other.

"Oh you three look so adorable together," my mom says as her eyes fill with tears. My father rolls his eyes but then he catches my eye and winks at me.

"We need some champagne to celebrate," my mom says.

As we start to walk down the hallway, Jax stops suddenly and we all look at him.

"Fuck!" he whispers.

"What is it?" I ask.

"Who's going to be my best man?" he frowns.

"Jax!" My mom gives him a nudge on the arm.

"What? This is a serious question, Alana. There are not many people that I like in this world. And my best buddy will be pulling father of the bride duties."

"I sure will." My father wraps an arm around my shoulder and we start to walk through the house. "You're on your own, amigo."

EPILOGUE
LUCIA

Six Months Later

I frown at Jax as I follow him inside my father's nightclub. We're getting married tomorrow and I'm supposed to be on my way to my parents' house for an afternoon and evening of pampering and champagne with my mom, her friend, Kelsey, Jax's aunt Molly, Jordan and Magda. Jax is spending the night at my father's hotel with him, Hugo and my friend Archer, who Jax has taken a liking to. Matthias and the twins will be there, too, but on his way to drop me off, Jax detoured here and told me he had a surprise for me.

"What are we doing here?" I smile at him. It's only mid-afternoon. The place doesn't open for hours and there is nobody here. "My mom will be waiting for me and you're due at the hotel."

"Everyone can wait," he assures me, and then he takes my hand and leads me toward the huge dance-floor, right beneath the booth where the DJ is usually situated. It's strangely eerie in here like this. Usually, it's so busy it's impossible to move through the crowd without pressing up against dozens of random strangers.

"Jax?" I ask again.

"Patience, Angel," he says with a wink as he takes a small remote control from his pocket. He presses a button and the lights above us start to flash. With the press of another button, the club is filled with music as the opening beats of *Señorita* start to play.

"I love this song," I say, still unsure what we are doing here.

"I know," he growls, putting the remote back into his pocket and sliding his arms around my waist. "And ever since I saw you dancing with that asshole frat boy in that awful fucking club, every single time I hear it, I think about you. Twice I've had to watch you dance to this song. Now it's my turn."

"It is, huh?" I whisper as I snake my arms around his neck.

"Hmm." He bends his head and trails soft kisses over my delicate skin as he speaks. "I think about it all the time. The way your hips move when you dance."

Kiss.

"How hot your ass looked in that tiny dress."

Kiss.

"The way those guys had their hands on you."

Kiss.

"And how many times I used to imagine that it was me instead."

"You did?"

"Yes," he groans. One of his hands slides to the back of my neck while the other goes to my ass.

"But Jackson Decker doesn't dance," I tease him as I press my body closer to his and our hips sway together in time to the music. He grinds his cock against my abdomen and warmth pools in my core.

"This isn't dancing," he growls and heat flushes over my

chest and cheeks. His hand squeezes my ass as he holds onto the nape of my neck possessively with the other while he kisses my throat.

Damn! He's right, this isn't dancing. This is sex with your clothes on. Our hearts beat fast against each other's chests, our breathing becoming more frantic as we move. I press my lips against his ear and sing the words to him and he groans in my ear, making me giggle. I gasp as he spins me around. He pulls my hair to one side so he can nuzzle my neck before his arms wrap around me again. He has one hand splayed across my stomach while the other travels south.

"Jax," I pant as I reach back, wrapping my arms around his neck.

"Lucia," he breathes against my ear as pleasure skitters along my spine and all the way down to my toes.

Then his hand is beneath my dress, sliding up between my thighs until he reaches my panties. I groan loudly and push my ass back against his hard cock. When he tugs my underwear to the side a rush of wet heat floods my pussy. His fingers glide easily through my wet folds until he slides one inside me.

"So fucking wet," he groans.

"Fuck!" I hiss as my walls clench around him and he lazily finger fucks me while we dance to the song as it plays on repeat.

When I'm close to the edge, he slides his fingers out of me and palms my pussy, making me groan loudly and grind my ass over his cock. "Please, Jax," I beg him. "I need you."

"I know, Angel," he whispers. Then he undoes his belt and zipper with one hand while he holds onto me with his other, and all I can do is wait and pant as my body pulses with need. When he presses me against the wall a few seconds later, my legs tremble as he slides his cock deep inside me.

"Luce," he groans. "Your pussy is my addiction. You know that?"

"I hope so," I purr, "because I never want you to stop doing this."

"I never will, Angel. Who do you belong to?"

"You, Jax," I breathe as he drives deeper inside me, fucking me on the dance-floor as the song goes on playing around us. "Only you."

Jax and Lucia got their happy ending, but if you'd like to read about the next chapter of their story, Fierce Obsession is available to preorder now

ALSO BY SADIE KINCAID

Want to know more about Alejandro and Alana. Their complete story is available on Amazon and FREE in Kindle Unlimited.

Fierce King

Fierce Queen

Want to know more about Jax's buddy, Shane Ryan and his hacker, Jessie? If you enjoy reverse-harem, why not try Sadie's New York Ruthless series. The Ryan brothers are Irish Mafia, and nothing comes between them. That is until the tornado that is Jessie comes crashing into their lives.

Ryan Rule

Ryan Redemption

Ryan Retribution

Ryan Reign

If you'd like to read about London's hottest couple. Gabriel and Samantha, then check out Sadie's London Ruthless series on Amazon. FREE in Kindle Unlimited.

Dark Angel

Fallen Angel

If you enjoy a spicy short story, Sadie also has a collection ion super steamy short stories available on Amazon. FREE in Kindle Unlimited.

Bound and Tamed

Bound and Shared

Bound and Dominated

ABOUT THE AUTHOR

Sadie Kincaid is a dark romance author who loves to read and write about hot alpha males and strong, feisty females.

Sadie loves to connect with readers so why not get in touch via social media?

Join Sadie's reader group for the latest news, book recommendations and plenty of fun. Sadie's ladies and Sizzling Alphas

Printed in Great Britain
by Amazon